It's a dark place,

not haunted house dark, but so dim, objects are not easily defined; they have no form, no weight, no purpose, as if my mind is trying to recall what it needs in order to survive. A huge, empty void will not do.

I can't even begin to understand what happened to me. One minute, I'm eating a sugary glazed treat in The Mystic's chambers, and the next I'm here (wherever here is), face down on the ground.

I feel the area around me, trying to establish some bearings. A bumpy surface like cobblestones, uneven and rough, meets my touch. What I think is the leg of a chair gives me something to hold onto. I grip the leg with one hand, and use it to help me stand, then ease back and sit down before I fall. My head pounds, and I'm dizzy. It doesn't help having nothing to focus on. I'm lost in this vacant shadow world.

"Dixie." The word runs away from me in the form of an echo. Despite the constant throbbing in my head, I say her name again and again.

I thought I was alone, but a voice shouts back, spreading shivers over my skin. "It's no use. I'm so fucked, no one is coming to save me, are they? I thought you were here to rescue me…ha. It sounds like you can't even help yourself. Why are you yelling for Dixie? Do you mean Dixie Mulholland? You do, don't you?"

Sin City Mystic

by

Rick Newberry

Sin City Mystic

Cover Art by *Debbie Taylor*

The Wild Rose Press, Inc.
PO Box 708
Adams Basin, NY 14410-0708
Visit us at www.thewildrosepress.com

Publishing History
First Black Rose Edition, 2017
Print ISBN 978-1-5092-1599-7
Digital ISBN 978-1-5092-1600-0

Published in the United States of America

Dedication

For Richard and Nethella

Chapter One

Keeping secrets from the woman I love makes my stomach gurgle. What's worse, Dixie Mulholland is more than a woman, she's a Daemon, capable of rummaging through my thoughts whenever she wants. With her abilities, it's a wonder she hasn't discovered what I'm doing. Either she isn't looking in the right corners of my mind, or I've gotten better at hiding things. In any case, she doesn't let on if she knows my plan, so I keep quiet…and keep doing it.

When she's sleeping—dead to the world and fully engaged in dreams—the telepathic connection we share severs, giving me time to pursue a dream of my own.

I sneak out of bed, being careful not to jiggle the mattress. One last glance at Dixie's serene face tells me the timing's right, so I rush down the hallway to the back door.

That door tends to squeak. I nudge it open nice and slow, then ease it shut from the other side. Although I possess incredible night vision, it's so blindfold-dark outside, I have to pause to let my eyes adjust. I've negotiated the shaky wooden steps leading down to the backyard a thousand times, but now I take them with extra care, just in case.

After darting across the yard, I turn back and glance over my shoulder. The neon glow of the Las Vegas Strip silhouettes the home I share with Dixie.

Silence rules the night.

When I think it's safe, I scratch at my fur sending sheets of skin to the ground. I've become an expert at quick transformations, and in just a few moments, my canine form lies in a pile in the dirt. Once again, like a ninja, I stand on two feet, unseen by a single soul.

"Adam Steel!"

Shit. I spin around, catching a glimpse of the accuser as my heart nearly explodes. After several deep breaths, I say, "You scared the hell out of me."

"Good," Charlie Nguyen says, "maybe that'll leave room in your noggin for a little intelligence."

"What's that supposed to mean?"

"How do you think Dixie will feel when she finds out you've been sneaking away from her so you can play at being human?"

"Play? You don't know anything about me…or her, for that matter. Were you able to get my note to Marco?" She only raises her eyebrows at the question, so I turn to leave.

"She trusts you, you know. She wants to live the rest of her life with you. Doesn't that mean anything?"

More than this Daemon can imagine. She and Dixie have become fast friends, and although the three of us share the house at Claremont Estates; it's not a harmonious existence, particularly between Nguyen and myself. She knows why I'm here, and she knows what I'm trying to do. "Is it in your nature to be so ill-mannered, or is it just you?" That shuts her yap.

"Do not toy with Charlie Nguyen." She sidles next to me and whispers, "The only reason I haven't told Dixie what you're up to is because I don't want to hurt her. But I think a little hurt now is better than a big hurt later."

I don't know what to say so I shut *my* yap, turn, and jog down the hill. Claremont Road winds around tall palm trees and thick pines. I catch a full panoramic view of The Strip, its lights twinkling in the distance. The colors are dazzling—colors Dixie will never be able to see if she remains a canine.

The house at 7011 Claremont is a dilapidated ranch, much like mine. Situated halfway down the hill, it has breathtaking views of The Strip, as do all the abandoned properties on Claremont. However, I'm not here for sightseeing.

I walk inside, throw on the clothes I stashed away, and hurry to the kitchen. Sketches I made of Dixie stare at me from the walls. I enjoy drawing, something I can't do as a canine, and I pinned my best ones of her on the kitchen walls. Seeing her face always inspires my creative juices. After opening a bottle of water, I ease into a rickety chair and grab the notebook I stowed in a cupboard.

It's time to put the finishing touches on the handwritten story I've been working on every night these past few weeks. It's the story of how I met Dixie Mulholland three years ago. I originally called it *The Las Vegas Disaster*, but I think the new title has better punch: *Sin City Wolfhound*.

People need to know the truth about Dixie, about me, and the battle between good and evil on the streets of Las Vegas before it's too late; before Dixie and I are dead.

Death: my chief motivator, the main reason I find myself here tonight. Life is short enough without—

"Adam."

I look up and smile. It's been weeks since I've seen Deputy Chief Marco Ramirez. Charlie Nguyen may be the world's biggest pain, but at least she gave him my message.

"I'm so glad you came." His handshake is warm and friendly. I wrap an arm over his shoulder, pulling him in for a hug.

"How could I refuse?" Ramirez gives me a broad smile. "Your note sounded desperate. Is Dixie okay?"

I nod. "She's sleeping. She doesn't know I'm seeing you, and I'd like to keep it that way."

We sit down at the table and I begin, "Like I said in the note, the longer Dixie stays in canine form, the faster her life races by—seven times faster to be exact."

Ramirez grimaces. "Same goes for you."

"I don't care about me. I'm six years old in canine years. According to 'the experts,' Giant Irish Wolfhounds only live six to eight years. I'm about at the end of my run."

"Nonsense. Despite a few gray hairs and crow's feet, you're in amazing shape."

That makes me laugh. "Save it. Listen, every time I transform, my inner clock slows down and I age at the same rate as you. In other words, by changing form, I lengthen or shorten my life span. I have that luxury. Dixie doesn't—she has no choice. She's aging at canine speed every single day. She says she's okay with the way things turned out, but I'm not."

"Sorry." He motions to a bottle of water on the counter behind me. "Do you mind?"

"It's warm." I hand him the bottle and wait 'til he spins the top off and takes a sip. "Warm water, no electricity which means no a/c in this heat—all of it

4

takes its toll on her. I have to get her off this hill. If we don't do something quick, I'm afraid she…" I can't finish the thought. I'm certain Marco feels my desperation, I see it in his face. "Will you help me?"

"What about Charlie Nguyen?"

"She says the curse is irreversible."

"Can she contact Major Ransom? Maybe that'll give us a different perspective."

I shake my head. "She hasn't been able to talk to the other side for months. No Ransom, Aunt Rose, not even Gorgeous—nothing."

His words come without hope. "I don't know what you expect me to do."

I hand him my notebook. "This is the story of what happened in Las Vegas three years ago. I thought someone should write it down. I want you to have it."

He reads the title and smiles, then offers it back to me. "No. You keep it, it's your story."

"It's our story. And I don't want it to end here like this. I have to find help for Dixie, and that means I have to leave. I want you to keep the story safe."

"Where will you go? Where will you even start?"

"There's a place in The Lakes. I can start there. Can you take me?"

"Of course," he says at once. "What about Dixie?"

"Nguyen agreed to keep her busy tomorrow. She'll tell Dixie you and I went into Vegas for supplies."

Marco takes the notebook and holds out his hand. "I'm at your service; anything you need. Let's get started."

****

I step out of Marco's car, taking a moment to stare at the Daemon house.

The last time I came here, in a section of Las Vegas known as The Lakes, was about a year ago. Dixie and I were sent here so she could experience, what Daemons call, The Sufferings: a sort of speed camp for supernatural knowledge. Young Daemons learn all about their history, powers, and limitations. Aunt Rose made a point of having me accompany Dixie to this house. I now wonder if Aunt Rose had a premonition that one day I'd have to revisit this very home to save Dixie's life.

The outside of the stucco home looks much the same as it did the first time I saw it. Cacti cover the front yard, leaving no room for a path to the door. I scamper around aloe, Joshua, and beavertail cactus. Two huge saguaro cacti stand guard, like sentinels, on either side of the entrance to the front porch. I hurry between them and gather my nerve before knocking on the door. I have no idea what to expect.

As soon as my fist touches the brick-red paint of the front door, it opens. A young girl's voice comes from the darkness beyond the threshold. "Who are you?"

I lower my hand and take a step back. "Adam Steel."

"What do you want?"

I have trouble answering that question. What I want seems to be a miracle. "I want to talk to the owner."

Giggles greet my request. Finally, after a few moments, an older voice asks, "What do you want?"

"I'm here to save Dixie Mulholland's life."

The door opens wide. "Please, come in, Adam. Would you care for refreshment?"

The sudden hospitality makes me uneasy. A year ago, I did everything I could think of to gain access to this fortress. It's a virtual stronghold; impenetrable. Now, the simple mention of Dixie's name and I'm treated like royalty. I don't get it.

"She is The Treasure. We know what you want."

I smile. "You can read my mind." Giggles all around. "Why Treasure?"

"Chosen; favored; beloved; cherished—"

"All right, I get it."

"Follow me."

"I can't even see you." Then I notice a pinpoint of light ahead.

"This way," the voice says.

I follow the small dot of light for what seems like a hundred yards. This house is not that big on the outside. It must be an illusion, like one of the magic shows on The Strip; either that, or I'm under some sort of spell.

Giggles again. "Sit down."

"Where?" A bright flash of light brings an overstuffed recliner into view. I settle in, and the room fades to black again. "I don't know how you're making this house bigger than it really is, or why you decided to let me in, but I need your help. Please."

"*You* need our help?"

"Okay, Dixie Mulholland needs your help. She's aging at the speed of—"

"Shhh. Close your eyes and relax."

My eyelids feel like they're made of stone. I shut them tight. In a few seconds, my eyes refuse to open. In a few more, I pass out.

Chapter Two

Somehow, in some magical way, the Daemons enter my mind (not that I try to keep them out—if I hope to find a solution that will break the curse on Dixie, I must cooperate with them). But even though I'm relaxed and allow them access to my most inner thoughts, it's soon apparent I have little choice in the matter. This is forced entry. Still, it doesn't frighten me. In fact, in a strange way, having them inside is almost comforting.

There are hundreds of them in my mind, scouring my brain, rummaging through my thoughts, my ideas, and dreams. I feel them banging around in my skull like it's a china shop, and they're the uninvited bulls. It doesn't hurt—not physically—but their presence makes me light-headed.

I feel the weight of the Daemons as they wander, scanning my mind; a sensation so difficult to describe, it may be impossible—but I'll try.

They're not exactly stealing my memories, more like lifting them up and examining them as if seashells on a beach; brushing the sand off, turning them over, and seeing what's inside. When they finish with one, they move on to the next in a methodical procession. As they crawl through the tunnels of my memories, I have flashbacks to the particular event they're investigating: meeting Dixie for the first time; being attacked by my brother Mikael; taken to prison by Colonel Jon Dayton. The memories are examined, analyzed, and carefully placed back where they were found. The visions continue; scenes of what the Daemons explore come to life in my mind's eye, like a slideshow of my life.

The Daemons learn all about me: the endless sketches of Dixie Mulholland I carefully drew and saved; a young Humphrey Bogart delivering his now famous line, "Here's looking at you, kid," from my favorite black and white movie, *Casablanca*; a scruffy young pup (me) howling at the moon and feeling invincible.

I feel naked under their relentless scrutiny. There's no use trying to hide anything. All my most intimate secrets are on display. Everything I am, have been, or hope to be is absorbed and processed by their supernatural force.

The most frustrating part of the entire process is the contact is a one-way street. It's not an exchange of information—I don't learn anything about them. Whatever they want from me, they take. They're in charge; all I can do is lie still and let them have their way. They split up and march through the corridors of my mind as if hunting for information in packs, each pack roaming around like little Roombas vacuuming up my thoughts.

They're almost insect-like in their attention to detail—ants tending a nest. They don't stop until they've examined every single thought I've ever had. For good measure, they go round again and make one final sweep. When the process is complete, my eyes pop open. It takes a few moments to realize where I am. Once I regain my faculties, my thoughts immediately turn to Dixie and the reason for being here. I'm certain they've gotten what they want (whatever that may be), and now it's my turn.

Even before I can ask what they can do to help Dixie, a girl's voice whispers, "We are unable to do anything for her. You will leave now." The voice is flat, unemotional. After scouring my thoughts, the Daemons must know how desperate I am to help Dixie, yet they exhibit no empathy whatsoever.

"What? After all that?" I'm suspicious of their findings. "You spent a lot of time in my mind. You know everything there is to know about me. Now it's your turn to tell me what to do. There must be a way to undo the curse on Dixie."

No answer. The room is cold, the air stale. The girl's voice shouts, "You will leave now."

"Not until I get what I came for. If there's one thing I know about Daemons, you never do anything without a reason. There's a reason you let me in this house. There's a reason you entered my mind. If you won't help Dixie, what was the point? I trusted you."

"Trust is conceptual—intangible."

I struggle to my feet and demand to see the Daemon in charge. My ultimatum garners laughter, hundreds of tiny voices giggling and cackling.

They give their order again, this time in a brash command, "You will leave now."

The voice grates at me. A shrill whistle echoes through the chamber. It grows louder, making me slap the palms of my hands over my ears. That does little good as the whistle graduates to a shriek, then a screech. My head vibrates to the wavelengths of the sound. I have to get out of this place before my brain explodes. I take a few steps away from the recliner and feel my way down the pitch-black hallway. The whistle softens. I continue my trek down the hallway to the front door, grateful to escape that god-awful sound.

The door swings open and sunlight flashes across the entryway. Again, the girl's voice fills my ears, "Do not come back."

I open my mouth, but the whistle sound grows again, making me race outside. When the door slams, I know I'm never getting in again. The Daemons are finished with me.

I have no choice but to return to Claremont.

As my eyes adjust to the sunlight, a car horn breaks the afternoon silence. I shield my eyes from the sun and squint toward the vehicle. Marco Ramirez waves at me to get in.

****

My first instinct is to ask him if I can use his service revolver to take a few random shots at the Daemon house—I'm that angry, but it wouldn't solve the problem so I take a few deep breaths to calm down the way Dixie does. When I feel reasonably composed, I say, "Thank you for coming back. I didn't know it would take so long."

"Come back?" Marco's face tells me it's a ridiculous statement. "Get in and I'll fill you in on the latest."

I slide into the passenger's seat and close the door as he starts the engine, pulling away from the curb.

"Were you able to get any information out of them?" Marco asks, "Or did it go the way you thought it would?"

"What a big waste of time. I've hated that place for

over a year, now I hate it even more." I keep staring at the house as we drive away. It blends in with the other homes on the block: single story, light tan stucco, water-smart front yard. Nothing special about it stands out, not from the outside, anyway. But inside, it's like no other home in the world.

Marco concentrates on the road as he speaks, "Sorry to hear it was a waste of time."

More than a waste of time, disappointment gnawed at me. I felt the Daemons did something—meddled with my inner self somehow. I came for information, but I leave with much more. I can't pinpoint the exact sensation (completeness, unity), I decide to let it be, for now.

"Speaking of time, how long *have* you been waiting for me?"

"Just a few minutes."

"A few minutes?" That wasn't possible. The Daemons had me in some kind of a spell while they rummaged around in my mind for what seemed like days.

"Yup, I never came back, because I never left. Plus, as soon as you went inside, I got a call. You'll never guess from who."

I wasn't in a guessing mood, so I just shook my head.

"Tina. She said she may have an idea of how to help Dixie."

My mood lightened. I turned in my seat to face Marco. "Tell me."

"She works at The Sterling International Resort. That should give you some clue."

Once again, I refuse to participate in a guessing

game. "No clue."

"The Sterling is home of The Mystic. Tina said she can get you in to see him…sort of."

"I'm still not following."

"The Mystic: surely you've heard of him. He can fix anything—so they say."

"So, I've heard. How's Tina able to arrange a one-on-one meeting with him?"

Marco grinned. "I got her a job last year at the Crystal Palace Casino—working in the promotions department. Turns out she's a real go-getter; attention to detail, good communication skills—everything employers want. Well, she worked her way from the casino floor to the front office. A couple months ago, The Sterling recruited her to work on The Mystic's promotions staff. She's now in charge of his schedule—can you believe that?"

"Still, a one-on-one meeting with The Mystic is a little—"

"Whoa," Marco says as he hurries through a yellow light on Hualapai Avenue, "I never said one on one. I said she can get you in to see him…sort of."

"What does that mean exactly?"

"Apparently, The Mystic is having a small get together for his staff—a sort of thank-you-for-all-your-hard-work kind of party. She's been invited, and her invitation says plus one."

"I don't know what plus one means. I've never gotten an invitation to a party."

He gives me a sideways glance and a chuckle. "Plus one means she can bring a friend. Guess who she's bringing?"

This time I guess. "Me?"

"Right. She figures if you get close enough to The Mystic and turn on the charm, there's a chance he may suggest a solution to our problem."

It sounds like a long shot. "I know the city's been going gaga over The Mystic since he started telling fortunes, but if I'm not missing my guess, he's just human, isn't he?"

Even though I can tell Marco's pressing the accelerator hard to beat the next yellow light, he has to hit the brakes as a Toyota Prius stops short ahead of us. Marco uses the opportunity to ask, "Is he human?"

"What do you mean by that?"

"With everything that's happened in Vegas over the past three years, I'm not betting on anyone being who or what they say they are. There are so many supernatural creatures in this town—who's to say he's not one of them?"

"Is that what you think of me? A supernatural creature?"

He doesn't answer; he doesn't have to. I'm living proof of his point. I apologize.

"Besides," he says, waving away my apology, "Tina seemed pretty confident The Mystic can help, or at least point us in the right direction. In any case, it's worth a shot, isn't it?"

I nod.

"Good. Let's meet up with Tina, what do you say?"

With a smile, I nod again. Anything is worth a try, even seeing a fortuneteller who performs nightly on The Strip at The Sterling International Resort; a skyscraper built just after The Las Vegas Disaster.

Chapter Three

Marco Ramirez pressed his foot hard on the accelerator, leaving Las Vegas, and zipped into the adjoining city of Henderson, Nevada, at ninety-five miles per hour over County Road 215. He jumped onto Green Valley Parkway, joining the rush hour traffic heading south to Horizon Ridge Parkway.

He and Adam arrived at The Paradise Luxury Development twenty minutes after leaving the Daemon house. Marco entered a code at the call box, and the gates of the community swung open. He drove across the gate track and turned right. Lush grassland hugged the road, and mini-mansions dotted the distant landscape in a parklike setting.

"Tina's doing pretty well," Adam said.

Marco smiled. "I'm proud of her. She's one of the few wolfhounds able to live free, with no further help from me or Charlie Nguyen."

"Or me."

Marco glanced at Adam. "Of course, I didn't mean to leave you out."

"That's okay. I know you and Nguyen have done most of the heavy lifting, and I know my concentration's pretty much been on Dixie."

"Nothing to apologize for. We all want to help her. I only wish we could do more." Adam gave him a warm smile. He knew Adam wanted each one of the wolfhound survivors to succeed in the human world as much as he did. But with Adam, Dixie always came first. "Here we are." Marco pulled into the circular driveway.

The not-so-modest two-story brick and stone home stood silent watch over the empty street, like a sentinel guarding hallowed ground. Marco noted the absolute quiet surrounding them: no children hurrying by on bicycles or skateboards, no dogs barking, nobody washing cars or mowing lawns. The only touch of playful humanity were two uncarved pumpkins placed on either side of the home's entrance.

"She's doing pretty well, indeed." Adam glanced at the surroundings.

Marco joined him and grinned. "Better than me, that's for sure."

The front door swung open, and Tina waved from the threshold. She wore jeans, a loose-fitting t-shirt, and a broad smile. "C'mon in, guys." She beckoned them into the house, hugging each of them in turn.

"Wow, The Mystic must pay pretty well," Adam said.

Tina laughed, a warm and inviting sound. "Same old Adam."

"What do you mean by that?"

Tina frowned. "Practical. Honest. That's all; just being frank." She shut the door and ushered them into the great room.

"Frank?" Adam said, "I don't understand."

"Adam," Marco said, "she didn't mean anything by it. Relax."

Adam let out a long breath and faced Tina. "I'm so sorry. It's just that Dixie's in trouble, and she doesn't even know it; at least she doesn't admit it."

"Well, The Mystic may just be the one to help." She motioned to the couch facing the fireplace while she sat in a recliner. "Marco told me what's going on. Listen, I'm invited to a little get together tonight, and I can bring a guest."

"Plus one," Adam said.

"Good," Marco said, "then it's settled."

Adam rubbed his eyes. "Sorry, I've been up all night. I'm probably a little cranky due to lack of sleep." He yawned.

"We have a couple of hours before we have to leave," Tina said. "Why don't I show you to the guest room? I'll wake you up when it's time to go. I hope you don't mind, but I took the liberty of buying you a suit for the occasion."

Marco chuckled. "Good job, Tina. I didn't even think about that."

She grinned. "Men. Follow me."

Marco waited on the couch while Tina got Adam settled. She returned in a few minutes with two glasses of water.

"It's important to stay hydrated."

He stood, accepted the glass, and took a sip. "You've got it all down."

"Got what all down?"

"The job, the house...even hydration. It's a compliment, I envy you. I wish all the wolfhounds were as...what's the word? Independent, as you."

Tina wrinkled her brow. "Funny, I don't even think of myself as a wolfhound anymore." She eased back into the recliner. "I've been so occupied with just living day to day, I've almost forgotten what it was like before—on Claremont. Sorry."

"No, no, nothing to apologize for. You're exactly what Aunt Rose intended from the beginning. All the wolfhounds blending in with humans, living productive, meaningful lives. I'm very proud of you."

Tina smiled. "That means a lot coming from—"

"An old policeman?" He wanted to stop her from saying "human." He wanted to stop her from apologizing. "You're the best and the brightest, Tina. You've done well, but this is only the beginning. You have your whole life ahead of you."

Her eyes glistened.

"What's wrong?"

"I miss Cutty so much. All this," she said, gesturing toward the house, "means little without him. Sometimes I don't know why I bother with the house, the job; without someone to share it with…what's the point? It's like I'm just pretending at life."

Her words struck him hard. Hadn't he been pretending for the past three years, buried in work, trying to forget his own losses?

But wasn't it worth it? Seeing Tina succeed like this? Knowing there are other success stories in Vegas thanks to you? The words entered his mind.

He bolted off the couch. "Who's there?" Who had the balls to invade his thoughts?

Up here. Look up, to your right.

He peered at the balcony running the length of the great room. Adam stood in a relaxed pose, hands on the railing, smile on his face. "I heard you, Marco, in my head. I came out of the bedroom and 'talked' to you with my mind. Isn't that cool?"

"How…uh, is that even possible? When did

you—"

"I don't know how. I mean, when I communicate with Dixie, she's the one with the telepathy; at least I think she's the only one. I mean, she's the Daemon, right? I heard you like you were standing right next to me, but you weren't. So, I just 'thought' what I wanted to say back to you, and bam, you got it. It's like a super power or something."

Marco glanced at his watch. "Okay, super-human, you should get some sleep."

Adam smiled and turned away.

"And Adam. Stay out of my head."

****

The guests wear, what I think is called, casual-formal: suits and ties, evening gowns and high heels. Nothing over the top, but definitely not relaxed. I blend in well with the clothes Tina bought for me—she has excellent taste. Everyone seems in a jovial mood. The suite atop the Sterling International Resort affords spectacular views of the Las Vegas Valley. I glance to the south and see Claremont in the distance. I can't help but wonder what Dixie's doing.

The Mystic has not yet made an appearance, and the anticipation of his arrival is palpable. I hear guests, huddled together in groups of twos and threes, whisper about what *he'll* wear, his first words will be or if he'll levitate.

Tina, wearing a spectacular blue evening gown, puts her arm in mine and leads me to the buffet table. "Grab a plate and help yourself."

"I'm not here to eat. I'm here to talk to your boss."

"But he's not here, so in the meantime, grab a plate and help yourself. You look so wound up; you're even making me a little jumpy. His security people won't let you within ten feet of him if you don't loosen up. Calm down, eat."

"You're right," I say, letting out a long sigh. I pick up a plate and slow-march down the line, allowing servers to dish up chicken, ham, potato salad, bread, and butter. Tina follows, asking for extra helpings of prime rib, ham, and chicken.

We find two seats at a small table and settle in. Tina pushes the salad around her plate, concentrating mainly on the meat. Her eyebrows rise. "I love meat, can't get enough," she whispers.

"Are you having a problem with control?" I ask, just as hushed. I've always liked Tina, and despite the story of success Marco tells, I'm worried about her. I can't put my finger on anything concrete, but she doesn't look balanced. Nothing "crazy" but still…

She shakes her head. "No, absolutely not. I'm in complete control of the change. I just crave the taste of meat sometimes. Red and raw. Don't you?"

"Sometimes."

"And the blood."

I say nothing. I don't miss the blood—call me a snob—I don't miss it at all.

"Is there something wrong?" The voice is soft, easy on my ears. We both turn and look up. The Mystic stands behind us surrounded by a small army of hangers-on. "You can order anything you want, you know," he says, "anything at all. It's one of the perks of being me." He laughs; a small, self-effacing giggle. Everyone smiles and laughs with him.

Tina and I spring to our feet.

"I'm so glad you came, my dear," The Mystic says,

taking her hand and putting his lips to her knuckles. He straightens up. "And who is this? A boyfriend?"

She blushes. "No, sir. Just a friend."

"Ah, it is good to have friends. How do you do?" He holds out a hand to me. "I am The Mystic. Welcome to my small get together."

I swallow a mouthful of bread, manage to force it down without choking, and shake The Mystic's soft, feminine hand. "Good to meet you." If this is what he considers a small get together, I'd hate to attend one of his celebrated galas.

He wrinkles his brow. "Yes? And?"

Tina and I exchange a quick, nervous glance.

"There is more," The Mystic says, "you are here for something. You need something from me."

"Sir," a burly security man says, approaching The Mystic. "You're wanted at—"

The Mystic holds his hand up, and the room calms. All the superfluous noise ceases as if he controls a secret volume button. But that's not all; the movement in the room seems to slow down as well. All actions are more deliberate, measured and precise. People remain in motion, but their movements are so gradual they could be measured by a calendar.

I glance around the room to gauge the crowd's mood. Every one of them is smiling. Those still sitting at the dinner tables are eating—or are they? Some are in mid-bite, forks hovering near their mouths. A chill washes over me. "What's wrong with everyone?"

"Nothing," The Mystic says, offering a quick smile. "They're perfectly fine. I simply thought you and I needed a chance to discuss your problem without being interrupted."

As The Mystic speaks, people's actions slow even further to the speed of mannequins. All sound, except for what The Mystic and I say, ceases.

I shake my head. "This is incredible; it's like being inside a dream."

The Mystic grins. "Well said. I applaud your insight. Actually, we are inside a kind of dream world—my dream, my world. Nothing to be alarmed about, I do it all the time. Now then, tell me your concerns and I will certainly do my best to help, provided it is within my power to do so."

I glance around the room again. The sight of so many people posing like statues, the eerie silence, and the attention I get from The Mystic, all combine to buckle my knees.

"Whoa," he says, sliding a chair under me as I waver. I plop into the padded chair, and he takes the seat next to me. Tina stands by my side, her gaze still aimed at the spot where I stood only moments before.

The Mystic chuckles. "Despite the many people I entertain, very few mortals have ever been privileged enough to witness this particular realm."

I stare at him for a moment. "You're calling me mortal? Excuse me, but you do realize what I am, don't you?"

"Of course. I use the term mortal to mean an earthly entity—nothing more, nothing less. But, please, it's clear you need a minute to compose your thoughts. Take your time."

"Time…that's why I'm here." My thoughts seem guided, following a path The Mystic has laid out in advance.

"Tell me more about your problem with time."

I'm sure he'll know what I'm talking about if I just open up and speak honestly. After all, if he has the power to slow the world down to a near stop, and knows I'm a canine, I'm sure he'll understand what I'm trying to say. "My friend, Dixie Mulholland, is running out of time. She's locked in a canine curse, even though her true form is…is…"

"She's a Daemon," he deadpans,

I nod, straight-faced myself. "Her life is flying by. Even though she's supposed to live forever—"

"Almost forever."

He understands all right. Dixie once explained to me she's not immortal—more or less. "That's right," I say, "almost forever. Instead, her time on earth is racing by."

"And you think I can do something about this problem?"

I nod.

"Why is this Daemon so important to you?"

The words come easy, "I love her."

"And?"

"And? What do you mean?"

"There's something more important about her than just love."

It's as if he sees right through me, to the truth I promised to keep.

Chapter Four

Dixie scampered off the bed and dashed outside, racing across the expansive backyard. Adam who greeted her each and every morning was gone. In fact, his scent had all but vanished; he was nowhere on this hill.

Charlie. She let the name rise from her thoughts. *Charlie, I can't find Adam.*

"Did you forget?" Charlie answered, her voice ringing out nearby, "he's gone to Vegas with Marco."

Dixie relaxed. She did forget. As a matter of fact, morning was gone. The remains of the sun speckled the wrong side of the hill, almost evening. She must have taken a nap and lost track of time. Adam had reminded her Marco was coming over and they planned to check on some of the survivors, get supplies, and be back before nightfall.

But the panic remained. She relied on Adam for nearly everything now.

"So, it's just us girls," Charlie Nguyen called out.

Dixie zeroed in on Charlie waving her over at the far edge of the backyard facing the Las Vegas Valley. *What would you like to do then, girlfriend?*

She trotted over to Charlie, sat down, and felt the Daemon's hand brush across the nape of her neck. Not a "petting" motion per se (no condescending "good girl…who's a good girl" banter offered to canines in

24

search of returned affection). More the touch of friendship—the kind of touch two equals exchange, although as a canine, Dixie would be hard pressed to return Nguyen's touch of approbation short of a lick on the face, and she wasn't about to venture into that territory.

"Why don't we go for a walk?" Charlie said.

Ha, you get the leash, and I'll jump up and down.

Charlie gave Dixie a sideways glance. "Humor?"

More like reality. It's getting dark.

"So's your humor."

Sorry, it's just Adam should have been home by now. Dixie watched the lights of The Strip twinkle in the distance as the sun dipped behind the Spring Mountains. *I'm worried.*

"That boy can take care of himself. It's you we're worried about."

We?

"All of us: me, Adam, Marco, Tina—"

Wait a minute is this an intervention?

Charlie Nguyen chuckled. "You might call it that. C'mon, walk with me and we'll talk."

Dixie followed Charlie across the gravel street and down the hill. They passed the abandoned houses once teeming with wolfhound packs. Her gaze ran over the old battlefields of Claremont where canines, humans, and Daemons fought for their lives almost a year ago. She thought of Aunt Rose, and missed her for the tenth time that day.

Where are we going?

"Just a little farther," Charlie Nguyen said. She led Dixie up the steps of a ranch-style house. Once inside, Nguyen lit a candle. A soft glow illuminated the room.

"Do you know this house?"

No. Where are we? She ventured farther into the dilapidated structure, loose floorboards creaking under her paws. Nguyen followed behind, lighting candles as they went. Dixie spied empty cups and glasses on tables in the living room; a pair of slippers near a recliner. *It looks as if someone lives here.*

"Adam spends time here."

Dixie edged forward and sniffed the slippers. The reality hit her all at once: Adam spent time here as a human. She turned and glared up at Charlie Nguyen. *What's happening? Why is he doing this?*

"Calm down. He's doing this for you."

At the touch of Nguyen's hand on her neck, Dixie growled and backed away.

Nguyen straightened. "Oh, so that's how it's going to be?"

I'm sorry, I just don't know what's going on.

"He's worried about you, has been for a while. Your life span is…well. Let's just say it's not as robust as it used to be. He wants you to be around for a while. Look, he has every right. He's trying to help you, and he's worried sick about your well-being. Adam's been coming here on and off for the past few months."

Dixie sat down and considered what Nguyen said. This should have been the happiest time of her life; she'd always wanted children. But this situation was unique, to say the least, she'd been a Daemon now forced to live as a canine. Adam was part canine, part human, and from what she learned from Aunt Rose, part Daemon as well. What did that mean for her child? *What's he been doing here?*

"Thinking. And worrying. And writing."

Writing? What do you mean? Writing what?

"Some kind of a journal. He never lets me see it. He gave it to Marco for safekeeping."

How do you know so much and I know so little?

"He didn't want you to be upset…like you are right now. I'm kind of sorry I let you in on his secret plans."

Well, don't be. He shouldn't keep secrets from me in the first place. That shows a definite lack of trust.

"But he's doing this for you."

Dixie detected something in Nguyen's voice she'd never heard before: empathy? *Why are you telling me this?*

Charlie Nguyen hesitated. "Adam thinks the world of you. I'm afraid he might do something foolish to try to help you."

Foolish? What do you mean?

"Something he won't be able to take back."

Again, *what's that supposed to mean?*

"He's the kind of guy who might just trade one problem for another. He might—"

Don't say it. Dixie turned away and hurried down the hallway to the back door. *I don't want to hear it.*

But too late. Charlie Nguyen yelled, "He might do something stupid, like trade his life for yours; you know how he is."

****

For what seems like time without end, all I can concentrate on are The Mystic's eyes, even though now, I scarcely recall their color. In one moment, I'm sure they're gray, in the next, purple. Teal?

Regardless of the color, they grabbed my attention. The dining room, and its occupants, swirled away into nothingness leaving The Mystic and I alone. We're standing in a sort of emptiness, neither real nor imagined. If there is a limbo—a station between this world and the next—this must be it.

I've always prided myself on possessing a heightened sense of canine awareness, although, being caught in The Mystic's microscopic scrutiny, I feel as exposed and naïve as a babe. The surroundings melt into a smoky haze; air pulses in and out of my lungs in a slow and steady rhythm but it's only afterward, when I think about it, I'm aware of breathing. I feel as though I'm floating through a fishbowl under the watchful gaze of an unseen observer. No, that's wrong. The observer is visible. He's the only other person in the room with me: The Mystic.

I finally break free of his steady, laser-like gaze. "Where's Tina?"

He ignores my question. "You know, I've always wondered what it would be like to shed my outer appearance and walk the earth as someone— something—else. Do you know what a fortunate individual you are, trading human nature for animal instinct?"

I back away from him. He's hypnotized me and I can't seem to shake the man's control over my thoughts. I've gotten used to Dixie combing through my mind, but she's always welcome; this man is trespassing.

"You're not being hypnotized," he says. "*You* are the visitor entering *my* world. I often come here when I want to be alone. But now, we're alone, together." He smiles and waves at a couple of chairs, which seem to have just materialized. "Please, have a seat."

"Is this what they call the other side?"

"Ha. No, my boy. You're not dead. Please, relax," he says, motioning again to the chair, "and I'll explain exactly what I want from you."

I sit down (no, that's not entirely correct—I fall back into the chair as my knees buckle and I collapse). Did he say *he* wanted something from *me*?

"That's right, I did. I hope there's no problem with that."

After a long, cleansing breath (more to calm my heart rate and give me a chance to compose my thoughts than anything else), I say, "Listen, I don't know how you're doing any of this: making everyone disappear, making objects materialize, or reading my thoughts, but I think it's time we be honest with each other—"

"Honesty is the best policy, isn't that what the humans say? Or are they lying?"

I let the tired cliché echo through my mind as I fight the urge to transform. I don't know what, if anything, would be solved by giving The Mystic a few good clean bites, but it might make me feel a heck of a lot better. "Like I said, Dixie is aging too fast. The spell she's under, the one that keeps her in canine form, has to be broken. I came here tonight to ask you if you would help us."

"Is that all?"

My heart bangs in my chest. He's as calm as ice, acting as though everything—anything—is within his power; as if he controls the very spin of the earth. I try to match his attitude, and calm my voice, but I'm sure he sees right through me. "Yes…that's all."

"Consider it done."

Did I hear him right? Months of worrying, racking

my brain for a solution, of telling myself everything will work out fine even though I knew it couldn't, has come down to three simple words: consider it done. My emotions are mixed. On one hand, I want to holler and race around in joy. On the other, I feel as though I'm being tricked; this is the answer I want to hear, but is it the answer he has the power to deliver?

"You're skeptical," he says. "You have every right not to trust me. In fact, I find most people are born skeptics. After all, trust is conceptual—intangible."

How could this man know the exact words I heard at the Daemon house earlier in the day? What kind of a trick is this? Am I imagining everything, letting my mind make up the images? Is all this real?

The Mystic reaches forward and pinches me. I yelp. "There, you see," he says with a grin, "this is real. Now then, I want both of you to visit me tomorrow— you and Dixie. There's something we must discuss."

My emotions flat line. "The cost?"

His brow furrows. "The cost? I'm sure I don't understand."

"If there's one thing I know about Vegas—about the human world—there's a cost for everything. What if we're not able to pay?"

His smile grows. "A meeting, that's all. Surely, that isn't considered a *cost*. I wish to meet with Dixie and have a chat."

"And what if she declines?"

The smile he wore only a moment ago is now a distant memory. Chills scamper through my body. "I wish to see her within twenty-four hours; otherwise our agreement is null and void."

"And the cost?"

"The cost will be paid, Mr. Steel. If not in this world, in the next."

Did he just threaten me? I cock my head at his choice of words, but know in the end it doesn't really matter. I don't care what it costs. If he wants to meet with Dixie, he'll get a meeting with her. Having Dixie back in human form for the sake of her health, the sake of the baby, is all I want. I nod at The Mystic.

The dining room comes back into focus and voices crawl into my ears. Tina has a hand on my shoulder. "Adam. Adam, are you all right?"

It takes a moment to realize where I am. I smile at her. "Yes."

"Good. The Mystic is here." She takes my hand and moves me away from the table. "Let me introduce you."

Guests are drawn to the small figure of The Mystic like bugs to a campfire. Well-wishers, acquaintances, and inquisitive guests surround him. His security men politely, but firmly, push back those who let their curiosity get the better of them.

I hold fast to Tina's hand and stand my ground. "No. Let's get out of here."

"But what about The Mystic? The whole reason for being here is to meet with him. What about Dixie?"

"It's all taken care of. Let's leave. I'll tell you about it later."

And I do, although the story is too fantastic even for me to believe. Tina and Marco listen, wide-eyed, as I relate my journey into The Mystic's realm. I tell them everything, ending with the thinly veiled threat: the cost will be paid—if not in this world, in the next.

Chapter Five

The change began all at once, without warning: a spasm, a sudden jolt. Dixie pawed at Charlie Nguyen's hand, yelping as she lost her balance and fell to the ground, rolling up into a tight ball, and shivering in pain. A natural instinct, deep inside, told her what was happening. It didn't matter, whether she knew what was taking place, however, the pain was real, and would not be intellectually brushed aside.

Nguyen crouched down, stroking Dixie's fur. "What's the matter?"

Dixie stared up, helpless, pleading. *The transformation...it's coming.* The confusion on Nguyen's face told her she'd botched the explanation. Daemons were fully capable of changing shapes, without pain, in an instant. The agony brought on by a tedious physical transformation would be unknown to Nguyen—unknown to Dixie. Until now. *I'm changing...the way Adam changes—*

The pain kicked up a notch, somewhere between agonizing and intolerable. She scampered away from Charlie Nguyen, an attempt to seek privacy. The canine need for solitude as she suffered; a deep-rooted instinct from the dawn of wolves.

She found a clearing surrounded by pine trees and lay on the coarse bed of needles. The full moon climbed high overhead, big and yellow, languishing above The

Strip. She panted in a cadenced rhythm, blood trickling from her throat and nose, it's metallic taste filling her mouth. She gagged.

"Dixie." Nguyen called out, her voice sounding above the breeze rustling through Claremont. "Dixie, where are you?"

Dixie checked her rough breathing and pressed down harder into the pine needles. No canine wanted their moment of weakness seen, unable to protect itself, unable to attack. Her skin burned, bones cracked, and fur flaked off her body. She dug her claws deep into her flesh, scratching through the heavy pelt. Her frantic clawing didn't even begin to relieve the pain, but no choice. She *had* to escape the suffocating cocoon.

"Dixie," Nguyen called, her voice louder.

The first glimmer of hope revealed itself as a smooth patch of tender skin under her fully formed hand. Dixie's human body emerged from the mounds of scraggily wolfhound fur. She probed the inside of her mouth with her tongue. Her canine teeth were gone, small smooth pearls took their place. The level of pain eased.

"Dixie, where are you?"

"Over here, on the ground."

Nguyen appeared almost at once, standing in front of Dixie, blocking her view of the now pale moon. "Oh my God. Your voice." She crouched down and put a hand on Dixie's shoulder. "You're human."

Nguyen helped her up. Dixie shivered in the wind, a slick paste of blood and viscera covering her newborn body. "I need a shower."

Charlie Nguyen laughed. "You sure do. How did this happen?"

"I don't know."

"You had nothing to do with it?"

Dixie shook her head and turned for the gravel road. "I definitely need a shower. And something to eat. And something to wear."

Nguyen wrapped her arms around her friend. With a long, tight hug, she said, "Welcome back, sweetie. I'll get you fixed up. C'mon, lean on me."

Together, they ascended Claremont and entered the house at the top of the hill.

"Jump in the shower and I'll fix us something to eat."

Dixie nodded and headed for the master bathroom. Marco Ramirez used a connection he had in the Las Vegas Valley Water District to keep a few pounds of pressure delivering a sometimes unreliable source of water running up the pipes—and off the books. Dixie stood under the cold drizzle. Waves of dizziness hung over her, but retreated in a few moments. It had been over a year since she stood on two feet, and the sensation, at first, unnerved her.

A knock came at the door. "Dixie," Nguyen shouted above the sound of the shower, "are you going to save some water for the rest of the valley?" She cracked the door open a smidge. "I made some finger food. You know I'm not very good at chefing, but it's better than nothing." She tossed some jeans and a black Las Vegas Wrangler's hockey jersey onto the vanity. "Come out when you're ready."

"Won't be long. I think the pump's broken again…no more water. Sorry."

"Good, I have a thousand questions."

So do I. She shut off the tap and smoothed a towel

over her body. After stepping from the shower, she wiped and gazed in the mirror, surveying her reflection. She remembered the last time she glanced in a mirror: taut skin, smooth and glowing; straight blonde hair and tiny crow's feet at the sides of her eyes, the kind that accompany a good sense of humor. The person she stared at now had aged almost two decades. The crow's feet had deepened and joined by little wrinkles around her mouth. Her blonde hair mixed with streaks of gray. Her skin, however, still looked lean and taut, outlined by well-defined muscles, especially in her legs and arms. She turned to view her profile, and frowned.

The small bulge of her abdomen could not be disregarded; then there were her breasts. Larger, rounder, and quite tender. She knew she was pregnant as a Wolfhound after just a few weeks. The typical full term for canines was two months. As she glanced in the mirror, she did the math; four week's pregnancy as a canine seemed about four months in human form.

Dixie slipped into the jeans, threw the pullover on, and revisited the mirror. "It is what it is." She ran fingers through her hair and joined Nguyen in the kitchen. A single candle lit the room with a soft, flickering glow.

Charlie Nguyen's lips broke into a grin. "I've missed you, girl. Hearing your thoughts is okay, but listening to you talk is, I don't know, a different animal altogether."

"You did not just say that." Dixie sat down and picked up a slice of bread, sprinkled bits of shredded mozzarella cheese on top and folded it burrito-like. "Do we have any mayonnaise?"

Nguyen shook her head. "Nope."

"Oh well, down the hatch." Dixie shrugged her shoulders and took three bites to finish off her makeshift sandwich. She grimaced. "That was garbage."

"Would you prefer…" Nguyen motioned to a bag of kibble near the fridge.

"Ugh. I didn't even like that when I had a tail. We got any pizza?"

The sound of tires biting into the gravel outside, and the sweep of lights across the kitchen ceiling interrupted their late-night conversation.

****

I can't wait to see Dixie. For some reason, Marco takes the 215 like a student driver. He seems nervous, quiet, almost ashamed. Despite my eagerness to get home, I have to ask him what's wrong.

"I understand your enthusiasm," he says, "The Mystic told you everything you wanted to hear. I haven't seen you this happy since our reunion last year at Aunt Rose's."

"But…"

He sighs. "I did some checking on our friend, The Mystic, while you were at the party. I understand if you don't want to hear what I found."

I didn't. "Tell me what you found."

After, what I've heard called, an awkward silence, Marco said, "That's just the thing, there's nothing to tell, and that's what bothers me." He hit the turn signal for the I-15 off-ramp and concentrated on merging with the traffic headed south. A majority of vehicles headed to California, some to Primm and Searchlight, but I guessed only we were bound for the Claremont exit. Marco continued, "I've been looking into his work history starting with The Sterling."

"And?"

He chuckled, a sarcastic laugh accompanied by a shake of his head. "The file is useless. Oh, there's a record of him being employed by the resort, but that's about it. I even called in a few favors to get more background, but it's a dead end."

"What does that mean?"

"Look, Adam, I've been a cop a long time. Bottom line is there are two types of people: those who leave no trail and have nothing to hide, and those who leave no trail because they have everything to hide."

I furrow my brow, trying to understand his words. Marco wasn't with me when The Mystic somehow changed reality. He didn't experience the power and control I felt while under The Mystic's influence. "You're looking at this entirely wrong."

"What's the *right* way to look at it?"

"You said there are two types of people in this world. What if he's not of this world?"

"I thought you didn't believe in the afterlife."

"With all that's happened, how can I not?"

Marco is silent. He presses down on the accelerator, finally making the miles race by. After taking the Claremont exit, we soon climb the winding gravel road that leads to the top of the hill. The full moon obscured by clouds; darkness covers everything like a veil. In a few moments, the house where I was born looms ahead. My eyes are wide in anticipation of seeing Dixie.

The tires crunch onto loose gravel as Marco stops and parks the sedan. He leaves the headlights on, cutting a bright swath through the night. "Whatever it is that happened between you and The Mystic, I hope it's what you wanted."

"You'll be the first to know. Thanks for everything." I wink at him. "Talk to you tomorrow."

He reaches out his hand. I push it aside and give him a hug before hopping out of the car. Marco waves and puts the car in reverse, turns, and drives away. I face the house, noticing a light flickering in the kitchen window, so I decide to go in the back door.

The light from the single candle is dim, but my eyes adjust quickly. Charlie Nguyen blocks my view of the kitchen.

"What are you doing here?" she says.

I think about rushing past her, but resist the urge. "I live here, remember?"

"Are you sure you want to—"

A hand lands on Nguyen's shoulder and a voice says, "Oh, for God's sake, move out of the way." It takes me a few moments to realize it's Dixie's voice, a voice I haven't heard in over a year.

My heart throbs when I see her in human form. She pushes past Charlie Nguyen and rushes in to my arms. It feels as though it's been forever since I wrapped my arms around her. No matter how close we were as canines, nothing can ever match a human hug.

She pulls back, her hands still hanging onto my waist, and stares at me. I gaze at her face, taking in her green eyes, smooth complexion, and full lips. I breathe her in and hug her close again, moving my mouth over hers.

In one quick motion, she steps back, pulls away, and pushes her hands against my chest sending me a few steps backward. "What the hell did you do?"

"What do you—"

"Where the hell did you go, and what the hell happened to me?"

"I thought, um…I mean—"

She mimics me, "Um, uh, I thought, um…what the hell are you trying to say?"

I raise my hand and imitate Aunt Rose's well-known admonition: "Language, my dear." The wrong thing to say. Dixie moves toward me and scowls. I back away and catch Charlie Nguyen smirking at me.

"I went to see The Mystic."

Dixie stops in her tracks. She scrunches her eyebrows together. "You saw who?"

I don't know if she's ready to hear the whole story. "I saw The Mystic."

Her voice is soft, almost childlike. "Why?"

"For you."

Dixie turns and plods back to the kitchen table. She sits down, props her head in her hands, and says, "Why?"

I step past Nguyen, joining Dixie at the table. "I did it for you; for both of us. Our lives were racing by as canines. I had to do something to slow down the clock."

Her glare pierces right through me. "And did you ever think about asking me what I wanted? What I might have thought was best?"

"I don't understand why you're so angry. I did it for the baby, too."

"You're pregnant?" Charlie Nguyen says. She sits down across from Dixie. "Why didn't you tell me?"

Dixie glances from me to Nguyen and back again; her eyes filling with tears. She stands quickly, knocking

39

her chair to the floor. "Oh, go to hell, the both of you." With that, she races out of the kitchen and down the hall.

I want to go after her, but a hand on my arm stops me. Charlie Nguyen shakes her head. "Let her calm down. She needs time to think."

"Since when did you become so considerate?" It's the wrong thing to say.

"Fuck you." Nguyen disappears in a cloud of yellow smoke.

I sit alone at the kitchen table, Dixie crying in the bedroom, and her best friend gone in a flash. This is not how I imagined my triumphant return. All the scenarios of how I could have handled the situation differently race through my mind. I could have been open with Nguyen; I should have been honest with Dixie.

The Mystic's words from earlier tonight rip through me: *Honesty is the best policy, isn't that what people say? Or are they just lying?*

Chapter Six

Her voice was calm, soothing. "Come and sit down next to me. Why don't you want to talk about it? You know it only makes you feel better when we talk."

The Mystic clasped his hands behind his back and continued his slow march, head bowed, as if being led away from a protest demonstration in shackles. He kept his head down as he acknowledged Ayala's presence in monosyllabic grunts of "um" and "oh." He halted his trek in front of the fireplace, gazing at the flames, and pushing his hands forward for warmth. Although the temperature outside registered triple digits, the penthouse was always a chilly seventy degrees, The Mystic's preference.

Ayala swiveled to face him. "Did you hear me? You'll feel better if you talk about it—you always do."

"Um."

"This whole business about the Gateway troubles you."

Her words grabbed his full attention. He turned, catching her in a slow and thorough scan, holding her in his sight for one quick moment before releasing her just as fast. With a sudden shake of his head in surrender, he said, "You're right, sweet child."

The Mystic strolled across the room to where his private assistant sat. He commandeered the leather chair facing her. "Very well, let's talk." He smiled, an inviting notion, almost challenging her to begin the verbal joust, the word games they engaged in often and late into the night. He enjoyed the banter with Ayala. She managed to draw him out, to make him look at himself as if she were his muse, his conscience, and his judge. He enjoyed it, until he didn't.

"You said you met with her lover. Why did this meeting upset you so?"

"It wasn't the meeting with him, per se. He's a nice enough fellow...for a canine. He's intelligent, rather good looking, and extremely down to earth. No, it wasn't him at all, it was the meeting itself. What's gotten me so upset is the fact I must rely upon such a meeting to accomplish my task."

"I don't understand"

The Mystic scoffed. "Nor do I expect you to. You see, I'm not one to delay my wants; to defer my desires, so to speak. What I want, I want now, consequences be damned. I've made promises to certain people— promises that can't be revoked."

"You mean the Fiend?"

"Hush, child. The less you concern yourself with the likes of him, the better off you are." He stood and paraded around the penthouse once again. "The Gateway has been a monumental task entrusted to me. Years of planning, delicate negotiations, and it finally comes down to this: relying on a canine to arrange a meeting between the Treasure and myself. Without her, the Gateway will never materialize."

"I'm sorry, sir, but getting back to Dixie Mulholland; at this time, you have her support?"

"No." The Mystic turned to face her. "I've done a favor for the canine in order to secure a meeting with her. It's just another step in the journey toward the goal." He smiled. "Always another step, then another. The wolfhounds, the Convergence, and, well, here we are, at the threshold."

"Of what, exactly?"

He turned and stared into her eyes. "Think about it. A covert doorway to Hell. Its existence kept secret, even from the council—no one will know."

She smiled. "A secret gateway."

"Just so. And every step I've made has been orchestrated toward this very goal."

"I understand all that. It's just…" She bowed her head, avoiding his glance.

"What, Ayala? What is it, my dear?"

"Why does there have to be a secret doorway at all? I mean it seems to me everything runs just fine the way it is."

"Ah, but that's just it, my love. It isn't." The Mystic returned to the chair facing her and sat down, crossing his legs in his lap, yoga style. "The Gates of Hell are closely monitored. Every coming and going scrutinized and discussed. I'm told He wants a chance to get out once in a while, stretch his legs, and look around without everyone knowing about it. To tell you the truth, I can't blame Him. Look at how many times I've left this penthouse in order to think; to be alone for just a moment. And I've only been here three years. He's been stuck down there for all of eternity."

"Well," Ayala said with a shrug of her shoulders, "if you put it that way—"

"There's no other way to put it."

"But what happens when he has this backdoor—this secret Gateway?"

"I'm sure I don't know what you mean."

"What happens to you? To me? What happens when it's over?"

The Mystic rubbed his chin and closed his eyes. "What indeed." The sound of water running down a glass wall echoed through the room. The Mystic stood and traipsed to the sound, running his finger through the water and along the wall. "He's made certain promises upon completion—promises that should leave us quite well off."

"What about the Treasure and her friend, the canine?"

"Let's not get ahead of ourselves, shall we? As was said this evening, there is a cost for everything in this city."

"And that's what concerns me. I've heard rumors."

The Mystic engaged her eyes again, holding them in a cruel grip. He blinked, slowly releasing the supernatural grasp. "Rumors?"

"They say you look tired lately, as if you haven't been sleeping well."

He chortled. "I haven't been sleeping at all."

She jumped up from the chair. "But, sir—"

He raised a hand, waving her off. "Sleep is overrated. Besides, we'll soon have more than enough time for sleep. I believe the humans call death The Big Sleep."

"We're going to die?"

"Everything dies. Speaking of which; there's a certain palm tree, down there that needs some attention." He strolled to the window and pointed down to the Welcome to Fabulous Las Vegas sign. Ayala stood by his side and glanced down. "That palm tree, just there—see it?"

She nodded. "What kind of attention is required?"

The Mystic chuckled. "It must be burned. Can you arrange it?"

"But I don't understand why—"

"You need not understand," The Mystic shouted. In a moment, he stroked her hair and his tone softened, "I'm sorry, my child. It's just another step in the journey. That palm tree needs to burn to the ground. The whys and wherefores are not important—not to me, they shouldn't be to you. Can you, just please, arrange it?"

She nodded.

"Good. Have it blamed on vagrants, vandals; I don't care, just so it happens." He smiled and kissed her cheek. "Thank you, Ayala. I don't know what I'd do without you."

****

"I wish you wouldn't say that."

"Then what else should I say?" Dixie says. "You go off and meet with The Mystic, and arrange for him to put a whammy on me or something (which, by the way, I thought was way out of his wheelhouse), and now I'm supposed to go see him to return the favor. Is that pretty much it?"

I don't know what a wheelhouse is. "In a word, yes. But look at it from my point of view before you crucify me."

She sits down at the kitchen table, folds her arms, and glares at me. I take that as my signal to keep talking. Talking? It feels like I'm treading water. "I don't know why, but canines have short lives, that's just the way it is. Biological madness if you ask me." I take a seat at the table across from her. "Anyway, I know I've extended my lifespan while in human form. If I gave up on myself and remained a canine…" I let the words hang in the air; the wrong words as far as her expression is concerned. "In any case, with you being pregnant, I want us both to be around for a long, long time. I'm not just thinking about us; I'm thinking about our child. Does that make sense?"

Her glare hardens. "How do you know what my transformation did to the baby?"

"How do you know it did anything?"

"I don't," she said, her fist pounding the table, "and that's my point. You acted on your own without any input from me."

"I did what I thought best."

"For who? The baby? Me? You?"

My heart falls. "For all of us." Her argument is nonsense. If I hadn't found a way to alter her physical form, she would have died in just one or two more years. Now, we could both enjoy our lives for years to come—and we could be there for our child. What was she not getting? I want to say that to her, I want to make her understand my motives. Maybe she'll be more receptive later; right now, she's in no mood for logic.

I try humor to lighten the mood. "You know, most parents wonder what sex their child will be. We don't even know what species it'll be."

Dixie stands up, glares again, and holds open the door to the backyard. Humor was a big mistake, at least my dark sarcastic humor was. Without looking back (she's probably all glared out) she whispers, "When am I supposed to meet The Mystic?"

"I'll make the arrangements and let you know."

She steps outside without saying a word. The backdoor swings shut behind her. I decide, this time, to heed Charlie Nguyen's advice and give her time to calm down. I make my way down the hall to the front door, step outside, and sit on the porch.

Maybe because we'll soon bring a child into the world, or maybe because these feelings have always been there, I stare back through the screen door into the living room and think about my childhood. It wasn't too long ago, in that very room, my brothers and sisters played as puppies. We scampered through the woods surrounding our house. Then, when we were very young, the transformations began. Some of us enjoyed walking the earth on two legs; some despised it. A caretaker and an Alpha, hardly a replacement for a mother and father, raised us. Not only that, we were mistreated, abused, and taught to kill.

I turn my back to the living room with its fractured memories and sordid past. It has no place in my life anymore. I want Dixie and I to get as far away from Claremont as we can; maybe a new city; a new state. My eyes grow heavy as I contemplate starting over.

The sun pounds on the back of my neck as I wake up. The porch makes a terrible bed. I see the high-rise hotels on The Strip. It's a clear day and the valley stretches out like a crazy quilt from Sunrise Mountain to Mt. Charleston. I really do like Las Vegas and know I'll miss it (I've always enjoyed the blazing summer heat with its surprise monsoons, and the oh-so-short, sometimes snowy winters). I know first-hand Colorado is nice, and I've heard California has amazing beaches. I've never seen the ocean. What a sight that would be.

"Daydreaming?"

I spin around and face Charlie Nguyen. "You scared the hell outta me."

She laughs. "You're getting lazy in your old age. You had no idea I was here."

She's right, an unforgiveable sin for a canine, but I'm not a canine anymore.

"Did Dixie get it out of her system?"

I snap back, "Did you?"

"Don't start with me. I took off so you two could work things out." She turns toward the backyard, then faces me. "Looks like you didn't."

"We did...it's just, she's got a little more working out to do than me. Don't worry, she'll come around."

With a huff, Nguyen says, "What choice does she have, right?"

"Look, I'm tired of arguing. I did what I did and that's it. I don't have to explain my motivation to you, and I know Dixie will understand in time. In any case, what's done is done."

"Ah, the famous human saying: it is what it is."

I nod. "That's right. In any case, I have to set up a meeting between Dixie and The Mystic. He's given me one day to make that happen. Can you get word to Marco?"

"Anything else, my lord?"

"Yeah. Lose the attitude."

She laughs. "My middle name is attitude." Nguyen dissipates in a yellow haze.

I turn my attention back to the Las Vegas Valley. In a few minutes, the soft rustling of pine needles sound from the side of the house. Without turning, I know it's Dixie, her sweet jasmine scent fills the air as her arms fold around me. I hold her close and kiss the top of her head. We sit in silence, together on the porch. The weight of her caress, the feel of her warm body against mine, tells me all is, if not forgotten, at least forgiven.

Chapter Seven

Marco Ramirez' eyes flew open. In all the years of living in Summerlin, he'd never suffered the indignity of a break-in. The sleepy, suburban neighborhoods to the west of the Las Vegas Strip, nestled against the Spring Mountains, were relatively free of crime, so much so, he never bothered to install an alarm system (although Metro routinely suggested the practice as a deterrent to home robberies). Too late.

The sound of glass shattering on ceramic tile in the living room was unmistakable. An intruder had broken in. Marco eased open the nightstand drawer and pulled out his Glock, confident the encounter with the uninvited visitor would not end well for the burglar. The digital numbers on the bedside clock read 2:22 a.m. Wind played with the chimes in the backyard.

He took a deep breath and slid out of bed, his pulse kicking up a few notches in anticipation of the impending confrontation. Metro protocol dictated he announce his presence and the fact he was armed to the suspect. He might have done so had he been on the clock, and had this not been his house. As it stood, he did not intend to avoid a conflict. On the contrary, he would do his best to stop this thief cold.

Even though he took no pleasure in shooting someone first and asking questions later, this was his home, his castle, and he would defend it.

His feet moved silently across the smooth tiled squares of the hallway floor. In contrast, the sound of glass crunching underfoot, sudden thuds and thumps against furniture, and constant heavy breathing came from the living room. His intruder was either a brazen sort, indifferent to the clatter he created, or never attempted a break-in before. In either case, time to illuminate the situation. Marco slid his hand along the wall, feeling for the light switch.

The cloudy sky seemed in league with the stillness of the night. The wind gave up the ghost and went silent. All the sounds of the street, the block, the city seemed to have stepped aside, as if in anticipation of the coming confrontation in Marco Ramirez' living room.

With one quick flick of his wrist, he pushed on the light switch. Darkness still prevailed. He knew he'd made noise by hitting the switch, but it seemed to have gone unnoticed by the intruder. The circuit breaker must have tripped—or been tripped.

He listened to the racket as he continued his slow and steady approach. In two more feet, he would risk a quick glance into the black abyss of the living room in hopes of spotting his target. With pistol pointed toward the ceiling, he edged forward and took a deep breath.

The din came to an abrupt halt. "Don't come any closer, I implore you." The voice, a tenor, light and airy, belonged to a male as far as Ramirez could tell.

Ramirez' heart sank. He'd obviously been spotted, and that made this the defining moment: shoot or be shot. He sprang from the hallway, leveling his weapon at anything that moved. He may as well have been on the dark side of the moon. Not one single object, not even those he knew to exist by daily use appeared. Not the television, the couch, the recliner, the coffee table; not even the outlines of those things, let alone the shape of a burglar stereotypically dressed in black.

He knew it was a stupid thing to say even before it left his lips. "Show yourself."

"You first." Did the voice come from behind him? From the right, the left?

Ramirez' eyes were wide, trigger finger poised, ready to fire. He kept a silent vigil, breathing in a steady even rhythm, waiting for the slightest sound he could zero in on. For the time being, he felt a certain amount of security under the shroud of darkness, probably how the intruder felt as well. But eyes tend to adjust to the dark. His only hope of survival rested in keeping his wits about him.

"You have to the count of three to come forward, otherwise I start shooting." The confidence in his voice had taken years to perfect. "One." He racked a round in the chamber.

"Okay, okay, you win. Don't shoot."

The *tick-tock* of the kitchen clock cut through the silence. Holding his ground at the threshold of the living room, Ramirez waited for the intruder to come forward. He kept his weapon aimed straight ahead in a two-handed grip. His arms experienced minute spasms; the gun felt heavier with each passing tick of the clock. "Come out. Follow my voice."

"How can I read your lips, I can't even see your face."

"I didn't say read my lips, I said follow my voice."

With a childlike quality, the burglar said, "What's the difference?"

Ramirez felt a drop of sweat roll down his nose, pick up speed, and fall to the tile. He removed his finger from the trigger, placing it alongside the guard, and relaxed his stance. He lightened the tone of his voice. "Don't be afraid. I won't hurt you. We can straighten this whole thing out." Moments ago, he was prepared to use deadly force against a burglar. But the intruder's awkward question and carefree behavior suggested the prowler was either a child, mentally impaired, inebriated, or suffering from some other form of confusion.

"You think I'm confused? Oh, contraire."

Ramirez lowered his gun and whispered, "How do you know what I'm thinking? Who are you?"

A shadowy figure, hands in the air, stepped forward. Smiling blue eyes, wide grin, and mahogany skin. "Allow me to introduce myself."

"That would help."

"Good evening, sir." He bowed at the waist, made a flourishing gesture with his arms, and rose to attention. With the tip of a finger to his forehead as, what Marco took to be a salute, he announced, "My name is Adrian Gray, at your service. I'm a Miscreant."

****

As a law enforcement officer in a major metropolitan city, Marco Ramirez routinely found himself face to face with the scum of the earth: con artists who victimized young and old alike, rapists, sexual predators, and a macabre assortment of murderers, gang members, and thugs who held no regard for human life. But, as a police officer in *this* metropolitan city, he'd also faced his share of shape-shifters, Daemons, and now a Miscreant—whatever that was.

"Keep your butt glued to the couch and I'll go check the breaker panel."

"Don't bother," Adrian Gray said, a broad grin snaking across his lean face, "I made the lights go out. Watch." He snapped his fingers and the soft glow of recessed ceiling lights bathed the living room. "After all, I didn't want you to get a clear shot at me." A curious sound followed the statement; a sort of high-pitched laugh mixed with a low-toned grunt, forming an almost inhuman bellow that echoed off the walls.

Marco grimaced. "What was that?"

"What? Oh, you mean this?" He reproduced the sound. "It relaxes me when I'm anxious. I hope you don't mind." He smiled, closed his eyes, and repeated the unusual sound.

Marco plopped down in a recliner opposite the intruder. "As a matter of fact, I do mind. Does that mean you're anxious right now?"

"Oh, I've been anxious for a long time tonight, ever since I was sent here." Adrian glanced down toward Ramirez' hands. "I'd feel a lot less anxious if you'd put that gun away." He bellowed the nervous sound again.

"All right, all right, I'll put it away, but only if you stop making that annoying noise."

With another grin, "That's a deal, isn't it? Ha! Humans call it a deal. You've got yourself a deal."

Marco traipsed to the kitchen, tucking the pistol away in the silverware drawer. The Miscreant seemed harmless enough, like a big kid caught in some kind of otherworldly adventure. The kind of adventure Marco knew he needed to identify and put a stop to before it got out of hand. Las Vegas had been nearly destroyed by supernatural creatures before, and even though this Miscreant creature appeared above suspicion (in fact, downright friendly), Marco wasn't about to ignore any hint of a clear and present danger.

"There," Marco said, returning from the kitchen and settling back into the recliner. He held his hands out, palms up like a blackjack dealer, proof the gun was gone. He leaned forward, staring into the young man's eyes. "Now, suppose you tell me why you're here."

With an attitude generally reserved for a human teenager, he said, "And what if I don't?"

Marco deadpanned for effect. "Well, if you don't, I'll have to go back to the kitchen, get my gun, and shoot you." Adrian straightened. "After that, if nothing else, at least I could crawl back into bed and get a good night's sleep."

The bellowing noise cut through the living room.

"Relax, I'm only half-joking. In any case, I insist you tell me why you're here. Who sent you?"

With a huff, the Miscreant said, "That would be a bit difficult to explain. Let me just say: there's trouble afoot." He squinted, making a big show of glancing from left to right, and whispered, "Really, really big trouble."

Marco grunted. "In other words, you have no idea what's going on."

Adrian hung his head. "True." He stared back at Ramirez. Were there tears in his eyes?

"Look, relax and maybe we can figure it out together."

The Miscreant brightened. "Together." He said the word in a satisfied fashion, as if he'd just discovered the way through a maze. "We can figure it out together, like a team."

"That's it. Like a team." Marco decided to play on his visitor's sudden interest. "But first, why don't you tell me exactly what a Miscreant is."

The young man scrunched his eyebrows and cocked his head. "What an odd question; kind of like me asking you to explain what a human is. What would you say to that, huh? That you're normal? You have no special powers? That you enjoy being His favorite—"

"Wait, slow down—whose favorite?"

Adrian raised his eyes to the ceiling and said, "You know, the big guy."

"Is that right? Well then, as one of His favorites, may I respectfully request you explain to me what you're doing here? And remember," Marco said as he pointed upward, "the big guy's listening."

The stranger stood, causing Marco to do the same. "Don't worry, Detective, I'm just stretching my legs."

"It's been a long time since anyone called me a detective," Marco said. "If you want to be accurate, it's Deputy Chief Ramirez. However, in your case, I think I'd prefer a simple 'sir.'"

"My, my, my, my, my, quite the ego we've got there. I can certainly respect that. All right then, Deputy Chief it is, if it makes you feel better."

Ramirez plopped back into the recliner. He'd had a tough day and his eyes started to glaze over. This Miscreant creature wore on his nerves; he had half a mind to call a patrol car and have the little guy thrown in jail for the night—if it weren't for the ton of paperwork that created. He rubbed at the dull pain throbbing just under his temples and shut his eyes. He determined earlier, about the time he stowed the pistol in the kitchen, that this sentient creature posed no real threat to his well-being. After all, he'd faced angry Daemons and hungry wolfhounds—what harm could a diminutive, other-worldly fellow like this little guy do?

Arson investigators later claimed a short circuit in the gas dryer caused the inferno—a fluke accident, one in a million. In due course, however, Marco learned the truth about why his home in Summerlin burned to the ground that night. It had nothing to do with a short circuit, and everything to do with a pintsized Miscreant named Adrian Gray.

Chapter Eight

Dixie snaked her arms around Adam as he slept, making her feel warm and safe, a reliable port in an unsteady sea. She understood his motives for doing what he did, but only wished he had included her in the process. Then again, after making it clear to him she accepted her destiny to live as a canine, maybe he felt compelled to act alone. Her surrender to a fate that could harm their child must have hurt him deeply. For that, she was sorry.

A slow, wry smile crawled across her face. It had been well over a year since they shared a bed as humans, but he hadn't missed a beat. Even though their love making tonight was frenzied, she felt tenderness just below the surface of his eager touch.

For her part, Dixie had to admit the sensation of human skin on skin exceeded the feeling of coarse wiry canine fur, paws down. Not that there was anything wrong with cavorting as canines, but it just wasn't the same. The act wasn't as passionate, the stimulation not as heightened, and the final moment somewhat anticlimactic. Perhaps, one of the reasons Adam sought to free her from the canine curse, but she doubted it. That would have been completely selfish, not his style at all.

No, she had to take him at his word: he did it for the baby. He wanted their child to grow up knowing a mother; knowing a father for that matter—something Adam never had. The accelerated lifecycle of the Wolfhound would not have afforded them the luxury of raising offspring. She closed her eyes, satisfied in the knowledge of Adam's good intentions. Putting aside her concerns about what The Mystic wanted from such a covenant, her breathing soon fell in line with his and she drifted off, joining Adam in blissful sleep.

The sound of tires crunching on the gravel driveway, and the flash of headlights piercing the thin bedroom curtains jolted her out of deep slumber. Adam sat up in bed, his muscles taut, his breathing rough. He vaulted out of bed and raced to the window.

"Who is it?" Dixie said. She saw Adam's naked body visibly relax as he peered through the glass.

"Marco Ramirez. What time is it?"

She fumbled with the wind-up alarm on the nightstand. "Three."

"Stay in bed. There's someone with him I don't recognize. I'll go and—"

I'll throw a robe on. Dixie sent her thoughts to him. "Here." She tossed him a robe and they both hurried down the hallway to the front door.

Adam took hold of the knob, pulling the door open in one swift motion. Ramirez' eyes widened. The man beside him stepped back a pace.

"What's wrong?" Dixie said, "Who's this?"

"Dixie?" Marco said, a smile growing across his face. "Oh my God, is that really you? I haven't seen you in almost a year."

"Sure you have, silly. You saw me just last week."

"As a wolfhound. I haven't seen you—the real you—for so long. I'd almost forgotten how beautiful you are." He stepped forward and gave her a long embrace. "Welcome back, sweetie."

"Whoa," Dixie said, surprised by the power of Marco's hug.

"So," Ramirez said with hands on his hips, "The Mystic is a man of his word."

"Apparently," Adam said. "Who's that?" Adam stepped aside, allowing both men enough room to enter.

The wind howled through the trees across the street. Marco took a step forward, stopped, and reached back, grabbing the slender young man behind him by the collar. "C'mon you. Inside." When they crossed the threshold, Ramirez said, "May I introduce Adrian Gray. He's a Miscreant."

The stranger made a show of bowing. "Happy to make your—"

Marco pulled the slight man forward and into the living room. "He's the one who just burned my house to the ground."

Dixie felt a rush of dread ice her blood. She shook her head, giving a false chortle. "What do you mean?"

Adam ushered them down the hall to the kitchen. He lit a candle and placed bottles of water on the table. "Sit down. Tell us what happened."

Ramirez spun the cap off a bottle and plopped into a kitchen chair. He gazed straight ahead as he answered Adam's query. "Well, as I said, this little guy's something called a Miscreant. Do you know what that is?"

Adam closed his eyes. "A creature of the dusk, neither noble nor crass, content when left to busk, messengers of the ruling class."

Dixie furrowed her brow, diving straight into

Adam's mind. *How could you possibly know that, unless...You experienced the Sufferings, didn't you? What made you seek the knowledge?*

"What are you talking about? Marco gave me a ride to that crazy house in The Lakes to try to find out how to get your canine hex reversed."

"Thanks for throwing me under the bus," Marco said.

She turned away from them both, trying to hide her blush. "Of course."

Adam's thoughts were quick to materialize. *What do you mean* of course?

He invaded her mind as fast as she'd entered his. She felt him rummaging through the recesses of her inner most thoughts, looking for answers, prying secrets from her, willing or not. She couldn't hide the truth any longer. *Aunt Rose once told me you are part Daemon. She said since you were created by a Daemon curse—*

His eyes lit up; he understood at once, repeating the credo of the beginning of life: *The creator's touch instilled in all; likeness and spirit, e'er to befall.*

Ramirez stood up. "What's going on? My house just got torched, I came to you for help, and you give me the silent treatment?"

Dixie stood and reached across the table, putting her hand on Ramirez' arm. "I'm so sorry, Marco. We'll straighten it out later," she said, giving Adam a sideways glance. "Tell us what happened, please."

Ramirez sat back down and took a long pull at the water bottle.

The Miscreant cleared his throat. "I can explain what happened if—"

"No." Ramirez thumped the bottle on the table.

61

"Adrian here said he *had* to burn down my house. He told me Shadow Daemons were on their way to kill me."

Dixie peered into Adrian's eyes. "And you couldn't just warn him?"

"He wouldn't have listened," Adrian answered, "you know how hard headed he is. I needed him to leave the house immediately."

Ramirez slammed his fist on the table. "So you burned it down?"

"We've been over that, Marco. I did it to—"

"Tell me about the Shadow Daemons," Adam said, "how did you know they were on their way to do Marco harm?"

"The Mystic told me."

Dixie blew out a long breath. "So, The Mystic wanted you to warn Marco about the Shadow Daemons."

The Miscreant shook his head in a slow and steady cadence from side to side. "No. The Mystic *sent* the Shadow Daemons."

****

I listen to every word Adrian says while at the same time considering what Dixie said earlier: I'm a Daemon. And, of course, she's right—she has to be. How else would I know what a Miscreant is? The knowledge is there, in my head, just waiting for recall, along with countless other facts, pieces of trivia, and remembrances of a history I should know nothing about, but do. The Daemons tucked the wisdom of a thousand lifetimes in the corners of my mind. That's why I also know what a Shadow Daemon is: not quite as deadly as the True Blood Daemon (*Sangre di Real*), but nothing to ignore. Both are lethal in their own way.

No matter how much knowledge I've been given, however, nothing prepares me for what the Miscreant says next.

"The Mystic sent the Shadow Daemons to kill Marco Ramirez. I was sent to warn him about the attack, with instructions to get him out of his house by any means necessary."

Marco's voice raises a few decibels. "So, you thought it would be a good idea to burn my house down?"

"It worked, didn't it?" Adrian grins. "You're still alive, aren't you?"

Marco sets his jaw. "That is the most illogical—"

"Marco," Dixie says, "calm down. Your house can be replaced. You can't. Shadow Daemons are nothing to take lightly. They can be deadly given enough motivation."

I watch Dixie, Marco, and Adrian argue about cause and effect, blame and accountability. I follow their reasoning in the abstract, but on a personal level, none of it makes any sense. When I met with The Mystic, he seemed far from an evil assassin type, if there even is such a type. I don't know too much about him, but still, I'm pretty good at reading people when I first meet them. His vibe was soothing, trusting; not to mention he removed Dixie's canine curse.

I stand up in an effort to grab their attention. Silence soon fills the nooks and crannies of the kitchen as their gazes rest on me. "I think the main question we should ask Adrian is who sent him to your house. If The Mystic sent the Shadow Daemons, who knew about that? Who wanted to spare your life?"

"Excellent," Marco says. "It's wise to determine motive. Good thinking."

I consider the compliment high praise coming from one of Las Vegas' top cops, not to mention my best friend in all the world. I've tried hard to fit in with the human world, and this show of support is more than I ever expected to receive. I acknowledge his words with a quick grin. "Now then, I think I can make an educated guess as to why The Mystic wanted to harm you."

"And why is that, Sherlock?" The words come from Charlie Nguyen, and they're full of snark. She brings my short-lived ego dance to a crashing halt. She steps out of a cloud of golden smoke swirling in the air with her arrival. "You seem quite the sleuth. Go on, tell us." She glances at Adrian. "Well, well, well, who do we have here?"

The Miscreant stands and offers a quick bow. "Adrian Gray, at your service, my lady."

"My lady? I like this one."

The way they stare at each other is nauseating. Dixie is the first to comment on their open show of passion. "He's a Miscreant, Charlie. A Miscreant."

"No need being rude," Nguyen says. "And what do you know of my bucket list?"

"Anyway…" Marco says, turning back to me.

"Thanks," I say. "You told me you were looking into The Mystic's past. Could it be, like you said, he has something to hide? Enough to want to harm you."

"Could be," Marco says.

"What about the unknown person who sent you on a rescue mission?" Dixie asks the Miscreant. "I think that's the key to unraveling this mystery. And since you can't remember who it was, there's only one way to find out." Dixie stood up, walked around the table and peered into Adrian's eyes.

"Nope." He shook his head. "You're not welcome in my mind."

"Why not?"

"You're a powerful Daemon. I'd be mad to let you snoop around inside my head."

"Can he do that?" I said. "Can he keep you out of his thoughts?"

Dixie nodded. "You know the rules; you learned during the Sufferings. Miscreants are a very guarded lot. If he won't let me in, I don't get in."

Adrian stares at me. "I'll let *you* in."

"What about me?" Charlie Nguyen swipes a finger under his chin. "I'd love to know what you're thinking."

"Maybe later, my lady."

She winks at him. "You got yourself a deal."

The Miscreant laughs. "Two deals in one day…hot damn."

"Enough." Marco bolts away from the table. "Would you two stop with the goo-goo eyes? We need to find out what's going on. My house is toast. I don't want that to happen to anyone else."

"You're right," Adrian says. He points a finger at me. "You have permission to enter my mind. Hurry now, before I decide against it."

Thanks to the Sufferings, I know exactly what to do. I enter his mind at once, and just as fast, I wish I hadn't. Images of Charlie Nguyen dance through his newly created thoughts. The fantasies repulse me at first, but I convince myself his infatuation with Nguyen is none of my business, and so I rush past the lustful creations of The Miscreant's imagination. With my eyes closed, I speak to him, trying to focus his thoughts, "Concentrate on what brought you to Deputy Chief Ramirez' house last night."

He sends forth strong visions of The Mystic, in one moment commanding Shadow Daemons to find Ramirez, in the next, summoning the Miscreant to his chambers. The Mystic ordered him to do everything possible to save Ramirez' life.

I open my eyes and tell everyone what I discovered. "The Mystic ordered the Shadow Daemons to kill Marco; he also sent the Miscreant to warn him."

Dixie wrinkles her brow, rubbing at her temples. Marco, leaning back in his chair, shakes his head. They both seem confused by what I discovered. Nguyen, on the other hand, takes a seat as close to Adrian Gray as she can, putting her arm over his shoulder. I don't need words to guess what each person around the table is thinking. Even though it's as silent as a casino with no slots, I hear all the wheels spinning.

Chapter Nine

Marco Ramirez went back to Las Vegas, insisting on staying at the Bellagio for the night. And why not live in luxury for at least a short while? His house has been destroyed; he's earned it. Besides, the Shadow Daemons will have no idea where to find him; he should be safe blending in with all the tourists on The Strip. And, as he said to me before leaving, "I don't fully trust that Miscreant character. The farther away I get from him, the better I'll feel."

He also lists the practical excuses for leaving Claremont: he has to call his insurance company, arrange time off work—all the things that make sense in a normal, earthly world. He also wants to check in with Tina for any word from The Mystic.

As I walk him to the front door, I ask about the copy of my handwritten book, *Sin City Wolfhound.* He shakes his head and says he's sorry.

"Watch your back, Marco." I give him a hug.

"Someone needs to keep an eye on that Miscreant," Marco says.

I agree, and say goodnight, watching as he drives away, then close the door and return to the kitchen. I tell Nguyen what Marco said as the Miscreant is in the restroom.

She brightens, jumping at the chance to keep her eyes on Adrian Gray—as well as anything else she can lay on him. I agree as long as he's not left on his own. After all, Nguyen's a big girl, she can take care of herself. What she sees in him, I'll never understand, but there's a human saying that seems to cover this situation: no accounting for taste.

Dixie warns her to stay alert. "After all, we don't know him very well."

"Miscreants are goofs," Charlie says with a grin, "kinky goofs."

And so, the night, what's left of it, anyway, moves by like an homage to the old black and white movies I love, filled with muted shadows and stark images. The sun is staged behind Sunrise Mountain, waiting to fill the desert with its power and heat. But the night isn't finished wrapping the earth in its safe and nurturing cocoon—not yet. This tug of war between what's to come, and what's past, results in a safe harbor, a suspension of time and an excuse to drift over deep waters without care. I pull Dixie close as she sleeps, and enjoy the moment, truly hoping this peace and quiet will last, but knowing it won't.

Dixie stirs, yawns, and nuzzles my arm with her cheek. She glances up at me and enters my mind. *I feel the same way.* She chuckles. *The calm before the storm.*

"I'm tired of it always being this way," I whisper. After so many months of talking via telepathy, I don't want to use my thoughts to communicate anymore. It feels good, using long dormant verbal skills—like stretching muscles that haven't been worked in a while. "You know what I mean? Always on the lookout, always on guard. I wish…"

Her voice tries hard to revive my fading thoughts. "Tell me what you wish."

I pause for a moment before responding, curious if she'll jump into my mind for the answer. I'm glad she doesn't. "I love being human. The things that make me *different* get too heavy to carry sometimes. I wish we were like everyone else; that we could just live in the human world, you know: you and me, a house by a lake, a bar-b-que in the backyard; one point five kids, normal jobs, regular problems like a/c repairs and car payments—"

"Sounds like you've given this a lot of thought." She extricates herself from my embrace, propping up on her elbows.

"I have. Why, does it sound too sappy?"

"Sappy? I don't know about that. I'm not so sure about the one point five kid thing. How can you have half a kid?"

"I don't know, maybe it means one kid and a dog."

"A dog? Are you serious?"

"Sure, why not? Most dogs out there in the world are just dogs, you know. They don't transform. I like that; I like them, and they like me. They make me happy."

To my surprise, she leans into me and kisses my cheek. She picks up my arm, placing it over her shoulder, where it rested before she tunneled out. "I think it sounds just elegant. A house, a kid, a job, even the bills…" Now it's her turn for her voice to grow soft, timid and unsure. "You know a life like that is impossible for people like us."

I cock my head. "People like us?"

"Immortals."

"Almost immortal," I correct. "Besides, Aunt Rose seemed to have it all figured out. She had a house, a life, and she had you."

"True, but Aunt Rose was a whole lot smarter than me." She squeezes her eyes shut and purses her lips.

"What's wrong?"

"I miss Aunt Rose so much. I feel like I never finished grieving, like I never will. She was my whole world until…until you."

I kiss the top of her head. Noises from the bedroom next door resonate through the wall. Charlie Nguyen and the Miscreant bunked down together in the adjoining room. Judging by the muffled sounds, however, bunking isn't the only thing going on. Dixie and I exchange a quick glance and short chuckle as their carnal sounds grow louder. Every once in a while, a strange animal noise, like the braying of a mule, grabs my attention.

I turn away from the wall and gaze at Dixie. "I feel like a peeping tom."

"Oh really?" She squirms out of my hug and kneels on the bed facing me. "I'll give you something to peep at, Mr. Steel." With a sly smile, she slips out of her white t-shirt. Her smooth skin and intoxicating scent invites my touch. Our lovemaking earlier tonight was hurried, almost aggressive, as we reconnected in human form for the first time in months.

Now, after having experienced the rushed emotions and physical senses of a human reunion, I want to re-discover Dixie in a more leisurely approach. I long to take my time.

My hands wander across her body, unhurried, enjoying the soft and silky texture of her skin. I continue my journey at a casual pace in all directions. She catches onto my mood, her lips and tongue exploring my body in a deliberate and delicious tempo.

The sounds of our passion rise, mingling with those from next door. My mind stumbles across Adrian and Charlie Nguyen eavesdropping on us, as we had on them, but I don't care. The notion vanishes as soon as I enter Dixie, leaving only the two of us in my thoughts.

Dixie and I are in perfect rhythm, holding onto one another as our desires grow. Several times, I force myself to relax, slow down, and lie still, doing my best to prolong the sensation. I hold back as long as I can, barely moving, riding a wave of pleasure. All at once, the logical side of me gives way to a frenzied drive for satisfaction. I can't delay my basic needs anymore. We come together in a rigid embrace, before collapsing in the final surrender.

I lie limp in her arms, my skin slick with sweat. She kisses me. Her breathing heavy, uncontrolled and wild, just like mine.

Moans and groans from next door drift into our room again. Dixie and I hug tight, wrap the sheet around ourselves, and snicker.

"A normal life with you sounds good," Dixie says. She snuggles close and yawns before her breathing settles into a relaxed and even pattern.

A normal life does sound good; maybe too good to be true.

****

"Hello…is anybody here? Are you awake, yet?"

Marco Ramirez' voice cuts through my late morning dreams. I raise an eyebrow, then an eyelid, and take stock of where I am. This is the first time in months I've been able to wake up next to Dixie in human form. The sheets are bunched down around her waist, leaving her silky flesh exposed.

"Is everybody okay?" Marco tromps around in the kitchen.

As I massage Dixie's skin, human nature tries to talk me into another round of lovemaking. It's a persuasive argument, but I have to postpone the need.

"Dixie," I whisper as I nuzzle her earlobe, "we gotta get up. Marco's here." The scent of her skin is intoxicating, forcing me to pull away.

She opens her eyes and smiles. "I had the best dream last night," she says, closing her eyes again, as if trying to hold onto the moment a bit longer.

"Me, too," I say, as I roll out of bed and jump into some shorts, "but it wasn't a dream." I wink at her. "I'll be in the kitchen with Marco; catch up to us whenever you want." It takes real will power to close the door behind me, but I need to speak to Marco and find out what he discovered from Tina about The Mystic.

"Hey, there you are. Good morning, sleepy head," Marco says.

We shake hands. "Morning. Did you enjoy your room at the Bellagio last night?"

"Room?" Marco beamed. "Try Fountain View Suite and it *was* sweet. I slept like a baby; got up early this morning and had a fantastic breakfast. Out of the blue, I decided to put a twenty in a machine and won five hundred bucks, just like that. You know, it's amazing what a good night's sleep can do to lift your spirits. Sorry, I don't mean to make you jealous."

Dixie enters the kitchen wearing a long white t-shirt and sleepy smile. Her blonde, windswept hair falls in tousled wisps onto her shoulders as she aims her bedroom eyes at Marco.

"So much for making *you* jealous," Marco says with a grin. He offers us coffee from a cardboard carrier he placed on the kitchen table. "Where's Nguyen and Adrian?"

Dixie shrugs her shoulders and air toasts Marco before taking a sip of coffee. "I'll go and try to get their attention." She takes another drink.

"They're at it again?" I ask.

"What do you mean by that?" Marco says.

Dixie grins, wiggles her eyebrows, and disappears down the hallway.

I tear my gaze off her and turn back to Marco. After a taste of coffee, I ask, "Were you able to contact Tina?"

He nods. "The Mystic wants to see you and Dixie today."

"Sounds good to me. Where and when?"

"Now just a minute. Don't you think you should postpone meeting with him?"

"Why? I don't follow."

"Well, for one, he tried to kill me last night."

"He also saved your life."

"That's another reason not to see him. The man has issues. He obviously—"

"I don't think he's a man at all—not a human man, anyway."

"And that's probably the best reason for steering clear of him. We don't know what we're up against. I mean, who is he...*what* is he?"

Dixie enters the kitchen followed by Charlie Nguyen and Adrian. "Here they are," she says, "I had to pry them apart."

"What's that all over your throat?" Marco steps

forward to examine Charlie Nguyen's neck. "Don't tell me they're hickeys. Are you two seventeen?"

"Please," Adrian says, "they're called love bites, and no, we're not seventeen, we are simply—"

"Don't bother explaining to this one," Charlie Nguyen says to Adrian with a wave at Marco, "he wouldn't understand. He's only human, after all. Besides, it's none of his business."

"Fine, fine," Marco says as he raises his hands in the air and backs away. "I brought some coffee if you like."

I put my arm around Dixie's waist. "Marco told me The Mystic wants to see us."

"When and where?"

"Whoa, whoa, whoa," Marco says, "I've also been explaining to our hard-headed friend here all of the reasons why you *shouldn't* go see him, but he won't listen. Maybe you'll have better luck." Marco sits down at the kitchen table. "Go on, Dixie, tell him to forget it."

"Are you serious?" she says. "The Mystic had the power to remove my canine curse. He has the power to summon Shadow Daemons. Do you really want to piss this guy off?"

Obviously, Marco knows she's right. "We're all in a tough spot right now, and it could get worse no matter what we do." I'm taken aback when he turns to Adrian. "What do you think we should do?" Marco seems to feel my surprise. He addresses me. "The Miscreant, besides saving my life, was the last one of us to see The Mystic. I want his input."

Adrian takes a seat at the table across from Marco. Nguyen wastes no time in sitting on his lap. "Well," he says, "on the one hand, The Mystic did remove the canine curse as promised. On the other hand, he summoned Shadow Daemons to kill you. Then again, on this hand, he saved your life. And on that hand, he obviously needs something from Dixie. And then on the that hand—"

"That's *five* hands," I say. "You'd better stop while you're ahead."

"Five hands?" Nguyen wraps her arms around him. "I like the sound of that."

He produces a devious smile. "That settles it. Adam and Dixie will go see The Mystic."

I'm taken aback. "Whoa, now I'm not so sure we should consider—"

"Adam," Dixie says, waiting for my full attention. "Marco's right. Adrian was the last one to see The Mystic. We should listen to him. Go on."

"Thank you. Where was I...oh yes, Marco, you should go back to your hotel room and keep a low profile. It seems like the most reasonable course of action at this point. Why? Since The Mystic wants something from Dixie, he would never harm her. So you obviously don't fit into The Mystic's plans one way or the other. Just keep your head down and you should be fine."

"Should be?" Marco says.

Adrian lowers his head and makes a god-awful braying sound that fills the kitchen.

"What the hell is that?" I say.

Charlie Nguyen laughs so hard she snorts. "Isn't it cute?"

"Anyway," Marco says, "what about you two?"

Adrian smiles. "Well, I can't go see The Mystic for obvious reasons. He would crawl into my mind and understand everything, all our doubts and fears, in no time at all. Besides, I have more pressing details to attend to right here." He locks lips with Nguyen.

"Despite his selfish motives," Dixie says, "I think he's right. Are you going to be okay, Charlie?"

Charlie Nguyen dismisses us with a wave of her hand as her lips fuse with Adrian's like two sticks of gum.

Chapter Ten

Marco warns us to keep our eyes open as he pulls over and lets us out in front of The Sterling International Resort.

Even this early in the morning, hundreds of tourists trek by, their cameras aimed in all directions, seeking out the wonders of The Strip. Most glance up at the tallest obelisk in the world, standing like a sentinel near the entrance of The Sterling. It proclaims the hotel as Home of The Mystic. Some sightseers journey across the street to the median in the middle of the boulevard, and the Welcome to Fabulous Las Vegas sign. A line of people wait to have their picture taken in front of the world-famous landmark. The Mandalay Bay Hotel and Casino a few blocks up the street gets its fair share of selfie shots as well.

"I can have a dozen patrol cars here in a few seconds," Marco says.

"No, you should stay in the background," Dixie says to him through the open window of the sedan. "You'd just expose your involvement. For your own sake, go back to The Bellagio and we'll meet you there when we can. I think it's best for everyone."

He shakes his head. "It just doesn't seem right to leave you—"

An urgent honk blares behind Marco's vehicle. Apparently, he's been stopped along the curb three minutes too long for one motorist. He glares into the rear view at the driver of the convertible behind him. "Here," he says, focusing his attention back on us, "at least take this."

I grab the cellphone he holds out and stick it in my pocket. "We'll be fine; we're doing the right thing." At least, I hope it's the right thing.

"Just be careful," Marco says, "and use that phone if you need it."

"Yes sir, will do." Dixie offers him a faux salute.

"I mean it," he admonishes, "I want you to use—" A few more horns, along with some choice words, urge him to move along.

I tug at Dixie's elbow and we both back away from the car. Parking on Las Vegas Boulevard is not only against the law it's also causing a scene we don't need. He nods at us, hits the gas, and disappears down the road.

Despite a crush of tourists milling about the property with their cellphones and video cameras, it takes us only a few short minutes to journey from the sweltering heat of the sidewalk, to the chilly confines of the Sterling's casino floor. We find our way through the deliberate maze of slot machines and table games to the escalators.

A flurry of movement claims the third-floor administrative offices of The Sterling Resort. Countless employees dart from desk to desk, office to office, performing the myriad of tasks needed to keep this massive resort functioning. I think of all the casinos dotting The Strip and downtown area. I'm overwhelmed as I realize each of these properties employ thousands of hard-working, dedicated people keeping all the moving parts in motion; from the gambling personnel to the hotel staff, the food service employees, to the building and maintenance engineers, from the security teams to the people Dixie and I came to see, the entertainment crew.

Each night, Las Vegas visitors are afforded the finest in live entertainment, from the latest musical acts to the best in variety performances be it comedy, drama, or magic. These typically short-lived acts run one or two years. One act, however, has played to standing room only audiences night after night for the past three years: The Mystic.

The Mystic combines elements of magic, psychic readings, and a musical light show all geared for full audience participation. His performance defies categorization. The Mystic makes believers of skeptics and fans of believers. I've heard it said, no two performances are ever the same; one reason his shows are a constant delight to young and old alike.

You know, you sound a lot like a travelogue? Dixie fills my mind with her special brand of sarcasm.

"All I'm saying is it takes an army of professionals to keep Las Vegas afloat."

Afloat? That's funny—it's a city in the middle of a desert.

"Just a metaphor, sweetie." I ignore Dixie's cynicism and step up to a desk labelled information. "Excuse me, but we have an appointment with The Mystic."

The clerk, seated at the mahogany desk, glances at us and swallows a chuckle. "The Mystic does not see hotel guests. But I must admit, you get an A for effort. What's your room number? I'll try to arrange tickets for tonight's performance."

"We don't want to go to tonight's show," Dixie says, her voice direct and firm. "The Mystic asked to see us. Check his schedule. We'll wait."

The chuckle is not hidden this time. "The Mystic keeps no schedule. He simply—"

"Sammy," a female voice, light and airy, cuts him off. The owner of the voice offers her hand to Dixie. "I'm so sorry, but Sammy's right. Except in this case when he's wrong. My name is Ayala, The Mystic's personal assistant. He's been looking forward to meeting with you. Please, follow me."

This is it, Adam. Dixie enters my mind with words of caution. *Keep your wits about you. It could be a trap.*

"I assure you, this is no trap," Ayala says. "Please stay close."

Dixie steps in front of Ayala, making the woman stop in her tracks. "How is it possible you can read my thoughts?"

Ayala smiles, bows her head, and moves around Dixie. "Patience. All will be revealed."

Dixie gives me a quick glance, then traipses after Ayala. I follow behind them both and can't help but wonder, in shrouded thoughts so as to keep my fears from Ayala, is anyone following us?

"You're not being followed," she says, glancing back at me with a smile.

Now it's my turn to wonder what type of creature Ayala is. For the past few months, I successfully kept certain thoughts from Dixie, and now this complete stranger enters my mind with ease.

Don't be afraid, her thoughts fill my head, *The Mystic wishes you no harm.*

I touch the cellphone in my pocket. It gives me a small sense of security.

You must surrender all electronic devices before entering The Mystic's chambers. Not to worry, it's standard procedure to prevent clandestine recording.

My small sense of security vanishes. I decide to give it, what I've heard called, the old college try. "I don't have a cellphone."

Right front pocket. She takes the phone away as I bring it out. *Follow me, please.*

When the door opens to The Mystic's private chambers, my nose twitches. I close my eyes and breathe in lunch.

****

"These sandwiches are excellent," Adam said.

The Mystic studied him with cold, gray eyes. "They should be. They've been prepared by the finest chefs in all the world." He turned his attention to Dixie Mulholland. "How's your tea, my dear?"

"I'm more of a coffee girl." She returned the paper-thin china cup to the silver tray and placed her hands on her hips. "Extra black, extra hot; double shot. Now if you can handle that, maybe we can talk."

Adam took another bite of his sandwich. "Yum. Bacon and lettuce." He wrinkled his brow and took another bite. With a full mouth, he said, "And tomatoes. This is great."

"It's called a BLT, sweetie," Dixie said. "Someday, now that we can finally go shopping ourselves, I'll be sure to make you one." She gazed across the cavernous suite and zeroed in on The Mystic. "Do you always keep your chambers so chilly? The a/c bill for this place must be murder."

The Mystic snickered as he shook his head. "We manage." The door swung open, grabbing his attention. A lithe figure stepped inside holding a large white cup. "Ah, Ayala, thank you. This is for you, Miss Mulholland. I hope you enjoy it; double shot as requested." He grinned and waved Ayala out of the room.

Dixie took a sip. "Not bad." She placed the sturdy cup down next to the china teacup and eased into her chair. "Now then, let's get down to business. What is it you want?"

Adam finished his sandwich, wiped a hand across his mouth, and took a seat next to Dixie. They both stared at The Mystic, awaiting his reply.

"I want nothing."

Dixie chortled. "I find that hard to believe. You mentioned something to Adam about there being a cost for everything. Why'd you help us if you wanted nothing in return?"

"Ah, I want nothing for myself, that is. I have an associate—a very powerful man—what I ask is at his request; for his sake, not mine." The sound of water trickling down the side of a glass wall echoed over the awkward silence. With a grin, he said, "This associate requires a small sacrifice. That's where you come in."

"Let me guess." This from Adam, gazes turning to him. "A human sacrifice, at midnight." He held a straight face for a few seconds, then burst into laughter.

The Mystic chuckled. "Amusing thought, Mr. Steel."

"A resurrection then?" Adam continued. "Bringing someone back from the dead?"

The Mystic spoke in a calm, measured tone. "Why

don't I simply tell you what it is he wants? No doubt, that would save time, agreed?" He smiled and sipped his own cup of tea. "Very well then, I'll take your silence as acquiescence. Perhaps it would be best to tell you a story first."

"The world today is very different from when it was originally created," The Mystic said with a smile as he shifted in his chair. "Can we at least agree on creation? Creation, not evolution? I'm not a big fan of the Big Bang...you?"

"Is this relevant?" Dixie said, sipping her coffee.

"Relevant? Why, my dear girl, it's absolutely essential. You see, evolution insists all this," he motioned about the room, "everything—including us— is just an accident. I don't think we're accidents, do you? Coincidence cannot create life." He chortled. "At least not my life."

"Is this story going to take long?" Dixie asked. "I gotta get back to—"

"To what, Miss Mulholland?" The Mystic raised his voice. "To a life alone on a hill, living day to day, eating scraps, enduring the company of fools—"

"Hey," Adam said, "we don't have to put up with your insults."

"I'm afraid you do, Mr. Steel."

Dixie stood up. "Adam's right. We came here in good faith."

"Good, faith has everything to do with it." The Mystic raised his hand and Dixie sat down.

She intended to storm out, but her legs buckled and she plopped back into the chair.

"Faith is a fickle mistress," The Mystic continued, "called upon in times of trouble, and shunned when times are good. Perhaps, if anyone truly *did* do anything in good faith, the world would be a much different place. Ah, but alas, we have no time for digressions; back to our story.

"No doubt, you've heard of the Gateway; both an entrance and exit to the nefarious world beneath this one. Only one Gateway has existed since creation and therein lies the problem. My associate has worked very hard, day and night, to rectify the shortfall. And, indeed, he's made progress, amazing strides toward that very goal."

"Wait a minute," Dixie said, her brow wrinkling, "you're saying another Gateway exists? Your associate actually found a way to—"

"No, Miss Mulholland. My associate has not found a way…he constructed a way—a new Gateway, and this new site must be consecrated, venerated, and cleansed as the old ways require. That, of course, involves a sacrifice; not just any sacrifice, no. The second Gateway requires a special ransom steeped in tradition. That's where you come in…Treasure."

Dixie closed her thoughts to The Mystic, masking them from the man as he went on with his story. She had no intention of being blackmailed by this bizarre little man, so it made sense to shield her mind from him; the less he knew her thoughts, the better for the safety of all concerned—namely her and Adam.

While pretending to listen to his story, she focused on all the creatures of the supernatural world. The knowledge resided in her—placed there during The Sufferings. She realized if she were able to identify The Mystic on the list of beings, the better to counter any malevolence he might suggest.

She started at the top of the list, working her way down, remembering the axiom she'd been taught: nine above—nine below (meaning, nine main classifications of beings above human, and nine below). The beings grouped as "likes" into an organized structure. In other words, the main classification of Daemon included Sangre Di Real as well as Shadow Daemons, even though, in truth, the three were as different from one another as humans were from plants and insects.

Since the list held no major classification for Mystic, per se, and he seemed a darker force than, say, a Visionary, she doubted if she'd find his likes toward the top of the list. Still, the seriousness of the moment required a thorough examination of *all* sentient beings.

She kept her eyes on him, nodding when she felt necessary. He continued his story, but the words no longer held her interest as she focused on the list:

The God
Angels
Spirits
Visionaries
Sprites
Muses
Empaths
Nymphs
Miscreants
Humans
Shapeshifters
Banshees
Witches
Daemons
Imps
Ghouls

Sorcerers
Fiends
The Devil

That was the lot, as prescribed by The Sufferings, and unless some new form of other worldly being came into existence, the list was complete. Of course, the list left gaps, as it should, for the inclusion of various minor beings: Leviathans, Zombies, Reapers, Fairies—*that* list was endless. No, nine above and nine below stood the test of time, and she did not intend to manipulate it to suit her needs.

Now then, where would The Mystic fall on such a list? She ruled him out of the nine beings above humans for obvious reasons. His dark aura became apparent at once upon meeting him. Being on the bottom half of the list herself, she enjoyed the ability of being aware of the presence of others like herself.

"You'll be hard pressed to find my name on that, or any other list."

The Mystic's words sent ice racing through her blood. He'd strolled through her thoughts all along even as he continued his story, even as she ignored him.

He gave her a gentle smile accompanied by a shrug. "You can no more stop me from entering your mind as an insect can stop me from squashing it."

The analogy chilled her even more. Her lower lip trembled as she scanned the room. Her voice cracked, "Where's Adam?"

"Not to worry, my Treasure. Your only concern is your decision. Will you help me?"

Chapter Eleven

Marco Ramirez' eyes had just closed when a gentle whooshing sound rustled through his suite at the Bellagio. He jerked his head off the pillow, scanning the room. Golden mist swirled at the edge of the bed. As it dissipated, Charlie Nguyen appeared.

"What are you doing here?" he asked, slipping out of bed. "What's wrong?"

"I got here as fast as I could. The Miscreant just told me," Nguyen said.

"Told you what?"

A knock sounded at the door. Marco kept his eyes trained on Nguyen as he strode across the room and grabbed the knob. He took a quick glimpse through the spyhole. "Dixie?" He yanked the door open, nodding her inside.

Dixie took a moment to catch her breath, sweat rolling down her brow. "Marco, he has Adam."

He glanced at Nguyen to Dixie and back again. "Take a breath, Dixie. Who has Adam?"

Charlie Nguyen turned to Dixie. "Is that sweat on your skin? Oh my dear girl, did you walk here? I mean did you actually walk? Why didn't you tele transport?"

Dixie spoke through heavy irregular breaths. "The Mystic held some powers back from me when he lifted the canine curse—transporting was one of them."

"Whoa," Marco said, "slow down, both of you.

Tell me what the hell's going on." He pointed at Nguyen. "You first."

"Adrian," Nguyen said, "who, by the way, might be the single most exciting person I've ever had the pleasure of—"

"Stay on message," Marco said, "please."

Charlie Nguyen huffed. She crossed the room and settled in a recliner in the sitting room. "He told me about The Mystic—in between…well. He said he wanted something from Dixie and he'd stop at nothing to get it."

"And what is it he wants?"

"Who the hell knows? Adrian said something about torture and blood pacts, that's when I took off and tried to enter The Mystic's chambers at the Sterling, but I couldn't. A charm sealed it against superior beings such as myself. I tried everything: every spell, curse, oath, whammy—zero, nothing, zilch. That's never happened to me before—ever. So, I decided to come here."

Marco turned to Dixie. "Your turn; where's Adam?"

Dixie sat down, chewed on a nail, and whispered, "The Mystic's powers are greater than I anticipated. He certainly formed a protective spell around his nest. That's why you couldn't get in."

"Nest?" Marco flinched. "What are you talking about? Tell me where Adam is."

Dixie peered up at him with a sideways glance. She spoke in a slow, even tone, "The Mystic took him." Her shoulders trembled as she buried her head in her hands. "The Mystic is holding Adam hostage."

Marco placed his hands on her shoulders. He waited for her to make eye contact before speaking.

"I'll make a call. We'll get him back."

"No," she whispered, "like Charlie said, The Mystic's chambers are sealed. There's no way into his nest."

"Why do you keep saying nest? What is he, a desert scorpion?"

Charlie Nguyen chuckled. "A scorpion would be a piece of cake." She turned to Dixie. "So, you found out what he is."

Dixie nodded. "I went down the list—nine above, nine below."

"What the hell are you talking about?" Marco said.

Nguyen glared at him. "This is not your conversation." She turned to Dixie. "Go on, sweetie. Take your time and don't leave anything out."

Dixie stood up and moved to the window. "He entered my mind, even though I masked my thoughts from him. He told me he'd held back some of my powers when he removed the canine curse, like teleportation and certain spells—"

"Let me guess," Nguyen said. "*Imobili* and *exteritus?*"

"You got it. *Exteritus* is gone from my repertoire for sure; don't know about *imobili.* Anyway, I'd already figured out what he was before he told me, but that didn't stop him from bragging about it."

"A Sorcerer," Charlie Nguyen said.

Dixie turned around, furrowing her brow. "Very good. How did you know?"

"Simple. He can enter a masked mind; he not only removed curses from you, he held back some of your powers. And he encased his chambers in a protective shield. That, and the fact you called his chambers a nest—what else can he be?"

"Excellent," Dixie said with a smile.

"Okay, okay, so he's a Sorcerer," Marco said. "What does that even mean, and how do we get Adam back?"

Nguyen jerked a thumb toward Marco. "He doesn't understand."

Marco tightened his lips. "Forgive my lack of knowledge about such things; I am after all, as you keep reminding me, just a simple human."

"A Sorcerer, my dear human," Nguyen said as she marched toward him, her voice gaining momentum with each word, "is just two steps away from The Devil himself; virtually limitless powers; absolute dominion over his realm, and almost impossible to defeat."

Dixie drew close to them and put her arms around their shoulders in a small huddle. A smile widened across her face. "Exactly right."

"Why the smile?" Marco said.

"He's *almost* impossible to defeat. He kept calling me the Treasure, as if I were some kind of gem or precious metal."

Marco spoke slowly, deliberately, "So, The Mystic wants you to do something. Tell me what it is."

"From what I could understand, he wants me to perform some kind of a sacrifice."

"What?" It came out more of a moan than a word. Marco shook his head. "Do you mean…a real human sacrifice?"

"More or less," she said. "Oh, and he said he's not the one who wants me to perform the sacrifice. He said his *associate* does."

In more of a whisper than a moan, Marco asked,

"Who's his associate?"

"Could be The Devil himself for all I know."

Another soft word, not even a whisper. "What?"

"Why does The Devil want a sacrifice?" Nguyen asked.

Dixie spoke in rapid fire. "Some nonsense about doing things the old way, like in the days of old, you know, tradition, blah, blah, blah. I think the more pertinent question is why he needs *me* to perform the sacrifice. Oh well, we don't have to worry about that right now, but if he thinks I'm some kind of royalty, that's good. We can use that."

"I'm not following," Marco said.

"Leverage, my dear Deputy Chief. If he wants me to do something that, apparently, something only I can do, then he'd damn well better let Adam go."

"That's *his* leverage, not ours."

Dixie's smile faded. "Didn't think of it that way." The smile reappeared. "But, we've got Charlie Nguyen on our side. Not to mention Tina and the wolfhound packs. That's a whole lot of us against him."

"If he's as powerful as you two say," Marco said, "that may not be enough."

Dixie scrunched her brow. "So, he gets what he wants."

"Not necessarily. Did he give you a time frame?"

She shook her head. "Nope."

"Good, because we've got one more card up our sleeve; someone who can help push the odds in our favor."

"Who?"

"Who do you think?" Charlie Nguyen said, "Colonel Jon Dayton."

Marco picked up the room telephone and held it toward Dixie. "Here, explain to the good colonel what we're up against. Convince him to get out here. In the meantime, let's get some shut eye—I have a feeling we'll need it."

****

Colonel Jon Dayton knew what was coming next.

"In all fairness, colonel, I think some time off would do you good." Admiral Reginald T. Garrison of The United Nations Paranormal Activities Division stared into Dayton's maple brown eyes. "After all, you nearly lost your life in Kenya—damned African Imps."

"Sir, I don't need time off. I've been hunting for the past six months and, quite honestly, every time I go out, I come back with a new piece of the puzzle. I feel we're getting closer to some kind of grand plan."

The admiral placed his teacup on a coaster. "What type of plan? What exactly do you think we're dealing with?"

"It's difficult to explain, sir, but I'll do my best. There seems to be a pattern emerging. For example, a while back, in Iran, I came up against a pack of Ghouls hoarding a supply of anthrax. To us a deadly biological weapon; to them a drug—their version of cocaine."

"I remember the incident; job well done, by the way."

"But do you remember where the cache of anthrax originated? I traced it back to Russia—a nest of Vampires had manufactured it and sold it to the Ghouls. That's unheard of: Vampires consorting with Ghouls. As you know, Admiral, anthrax is used as payment for certain otherworldly services. Take the incident in Peru last summer. The Patasola supposedly working alongside a tribe of Ghosts in the rain forest to eliminate thousands of indigenous tribe members—their hearts were never found. Human hearts are the staple food of the Jinn, the inhabitants of an unseen world below our own."

"Make your point, Colonel."

"My point is I believe otherworldly beings, normally at each other's throats, are now working together for a common purpose."

"What purpose?"

Dayton hesitated. "That, sir, is still not clear to me. But given enough time—"

Admiral Garrison tapped his pipe against the crystal ashtray. The clinking noise muted in the soundproof office. He swiveled in his chair, hands folded, as if in prayer, under his chin. "Something I've long suspected. That business in Las Vegas three years ago—what did you call it? The Convergence. That was most definitely an example of your pattern. Thank God you thwarted the plan."

"Exactly, sir," Dayton said. "It wasn't just Daemons." He let his thoughts end there. The importance of explaining to the admiral the supernatural forces amassing against humanity, without naming the wolfhounds he'd helped save along the way, was paramount. It was difficult enough to justify the unheard-of signing bonus he'd arranged last year. Most of the money went to the Wolfhounds who survived the Convergence—a fact no one in UNPAD knew anything about, least of all the admiral, the man entrusted with explaining to the council every pound his unit spent.

"No, not just Daemons, Colonel, I see your point.

The shapeshifter we captured confirmed that. Do you suspect Daemons assisted in his escape?"

"More likely a darker form of Daemon, closer to a Devil."

The admiral jerked forward. "The Devil you say?"

"No, sir. Not The Devil himself, but a lesser form; a second-class devil. I believe there are various categories of sentient creatures roaming the earth, some evil, some good. The wolfhound that escaped, Adam Steel, may have been one of the good ones."

"But wolfhounds killed humans. You captured this Steel animal yourself; threw him in prison personally."

I also helped him escape. "I know it sounds absurd, Admiral, but just as humans can be good and bad, otherworldly creatures can be good and bad as well. Take Angels for example—"

Dayton's cell phone rang, interrupting their conversation.

"Ignore it, Colonel."

Dayton slipped the phone out of his pocket, intending to follow the admiral's instruction to cancel the call, until he glanced at the caller ID: Dixie Mulholland. "Sir, this is urgent, would you mind terribly?"

The admiral waved his hand in dismissal and picked up a file folder marked in bold red letters: Case 2211, Top Secret—Kenya.

"Dixie," Dayton said in a hushed tone as he stepped toward the bookshelf opposite the admiral's desk. "My God it's good to hear your voice. When did you transform back into," he glanced back at the admiral and whispered, "human form?"

"It's a long story, and we don't have a lot of time."

Her voice sounded hurried, scared.

Dayton put the phone to his breast and turned to the admiral. "Sir, I'll be right back. I need something from my office; won't be more than a moment."

The admiral nodded as he lit a new bowl of tobacco. "Hurry back."

Dayton stepped out of the admiral's office, raised the phone to his ear, and dashed down the hall to his office. "We? Whom do you mean?"

"Marco Ramirez, Charlie Nguyen, and me. Jon, Adam's been taken."

"Taken? What's going on?"

"Do you remember The Mystic? Adam went to him for help to remove my canine curse. Well, the curse has been removed, but in exchange for something…" Her voice quivered. "As I said, it's a long story, but the bottom line is we sure could use your help."

Dayton took one second to answer. "I'm on my way. I'll call you just before I land at McCarran." He ended the call, slipped the phone back into his pocket, and returned to the admiral's office. "Sir, I may have been a bit hasty in my original decision. I could really use some time away. Is it too late to change my mind?"

"The phone call?"

Dayton nodded. "Personal business, I'm afraid."

"Nothing serious, I hope. Right, take as much time as you need. We'll pick up our conversation when you return. The idea of a global supernatural force working together against humanity is fascinating and will top the agenda when we resume. Dismissed, Colonel."

Dayton saluted the admiral and returned to his office, plucking his well-worn passport from the roll top desk. He strode to the private washroom adjacent to his office, and splashed cold water on his face. With towel in hand, he paced the office, examining the photographs on the fireplace mantel: Dixie Mulholland with an arm around her aunt Rose, Marco Ramirez shaking hands with Paul Cuthbert (Cutty), and Major Jean Ransom. He stroked the wooden frame of the major's photograph with an index finger. A smile crossed his lips.

With a raincoat draped across his arm, he locked the office door, hurrying down a tiled hallway toward the exit. Clouds hung low outside, pregnant with the promise of an early evening rain, typical for a late October London night.

Although millions of travelers flew to Las Vegas as a respite from troubled lives and gloomy weather, Dayton held the uneasy feeling his flight would be a one-way journey straight to trouble, to a destination he would forever call: Sin City.

Chapter Twelve

"The proverbial ball," The Mystic said in his quiet, gentle tone, "as the humans say, is in her court now." He smiled at the analogy. "And to think, I don't care for sports at all, not one bit."

"I don't understand; what does that even mean?" Ayala asked, her voice trembling.

"So right, my sweet girl, I see your dilemma. Sporting terms are far too vulgar for someone as enlightened as me: saved by the bell; swing and a miss—bah. In future, I'll use more civilized references; how about the game of chess? Yes, that will do nicely."

She filled two small cups from a decorative silver teapot. Steam swirled over the tops, saturating the chamber with a sweet, honeyed aroma. After placing the teapot down, she offered a cup to The Mystic. He nodded, taking a sip of the dark brown liquid. A smile curled Ayala's mouth as she spoke again, "Sports or chess, I still haven't a clue as to what you're saying."

"What that means, my dear lady, is the next move in our little game is up to Dixie Mulholland. I've made it abundantly clear what's required of her: a sacrifice, plain and simple. You were witness to it all. She knows what's expected of her, and still, to my credit, I let her walk out of here with only a warning—check, not checkmate mind you, merely check—with the stipulation she must eventually comply with demands."

Ayala did not respond. The Mystic cocked his head. "Was I wrong to let her go? Had I hoped she would view my action as a sign of strength? Perhaps. Maybe she misunderstood my show of authority; maybe she thinks I'm weak? What say you?"

"It's not for me to say. Your wisdom is, and always will be, greater than mine," Ayala said with a slight bow of her head.

The Mystic strode forward, put the teacup down, and caressed the sides of her face in his hands. He waited until her eyes met his. Then he waited a few beats more for effect. He knew she held something back. "That's no answer—no answer at all. You know, I've always relied on your honesty, and now we're so close to completing the task entrusted to us, don't revert to assuming the role of the lowly pawn. You have an opinion; an opinion I value. Tell me what you're thinking."

Ayala stepped back, lowered her head, and spoke in a compelling tone. "The sacrifices she must make…they are too great. You—especially you—in your infinite wisdom, must realize this. If I were given the choice, I would rather die than submit."

"Ah, and so you believe Dixie Mulholland, the Treasure, is too weak to forfeit the lives of the trinity? Her mother married into the royal line. She has powers other Daemons do not possess, chief among those, the power to kill another Daemon. This trait alone makes her worthy of the sacrifice, yet you disagree. Perhaps I overestimated you; maybe you truly do see events through the eyes of a mere pawn."

"When it comes to this particular trinity, yes, maybe I am, as you say, just a pawn."

The Mystic turned, clasping his hands in front of him as he paced across the chamber away from her. He spoke in a voice just audible over the ever-present echo of trickling water, "You know me, Ayala. You know who I am, and what I am; you know my values, my views. Believe me, if there were any other way…but you know whom I'm dealing with. He doesn't care about the sacrificial trinity. He doesn't care about ties or bonds. He wants results, and that's exactly what he'll get."

"Surely, my lord, even he would be willing to change the rules if you explained—"

"There's no bargaining with him. Period."

"But even you must understand that—"

"Enough." The Mystic lowered his voice and continued in a softer tone, "Listen, my sweet, since it's of such concern to you, let's examine the sacrificial trinity, shall we? First, we have Adam Steel, now *that* is a non-negotiable requirement; she must end the life of someone she loves. Next, she must terminate a human familiar to her—I've chosen someone even she disdains, Peter Hudson, so that particular sacrifice shouldn't be a problem. Of course, another human can replace him at any time, but why bother? I loathe him as much as she does, so we'll both be glad to see him ended. And, finally, as I made abundantly clear to her, a relative must die. So, where's the problem?"

"Where's the problem? Are you mad?"

The Mystic turned and faced her with cold gray eyes.

A knock at the door broke the awkward silence. "One hour 'til call time, sir," a muffled voice wafted through the room. "One hour."

"Understood," The Mystic said. He turned to Ayala and lowered his voice, "Perhaps we can continue our discussion after my performance. Would that be acceptable?"

"Forgive me, my king," Ayala accompanied her words with a slight nod, "but I must insist we continue it now."

"But, child, I've never been late to a performance, and—"

"You ask too much." Her voice soared through the chamber, "You can't expect her to slay her unborn child."

He tossed up a dismissive hand. "Oh please, there's nothing new in that; even Abraham was forced to sacrifice his child."

"Yes," Ayala's voice rose, "but that order was rescinded."

"So, it is said, at the last minute."

"Even at the last *hour*, you can't expect a mother to—"

"The story is recorded by human hand," The Mystic said. He shook his head from side to side as if it were a bell clapper. "So, we may never fully know the truth. In any case, Abraham's order came from the highest source, mine come from...well, certainly not the highest, that's for sure." He stepped toward Ayala and put an arm on her shoulder. "Besides, my dear, if what I ask were easy, it wouldn't be called a sacrifice, would it?"

"But—"

"Enough. The game has begun; moves have been planned; sacrifices must be made." He stormed out of the chambers.

****

It's a dark place, not haunted house dark, but so dim, objects are not easily defined; they have no form, no weight, no purpose, as if my mind is trying to recall what it needs in order to survive. A huge, empty void will not do.

I can't even begin to understand what happened to me. One minute, I'm eating a sugary glazed treat in The Mystic's chambers, and the next I'm here (wherever here is), face down on the ground.

I feel the area around me, trying to establish some bearings. A bumpy surface like cobblestones, uneven and rough, meets my touch. What I think is the leg of a chair gives me something to hold onto. I grip the leg with one hand, and use it to help me stand, then ease back and sit down before I fall. My head pounds, and I'm dizzy. It doesn't help having nothing to focus on. I'm lost in this vacant shadow world.

"Dixie." The word runs away from me in the form of an echo. Despite the constant throbbing in my head, I say her name again and again.

I thought I was alone, but a voice shouts back, spreading shivers over my skin. "It's no use. I'm so fucked, no one is coming to save me, are they? I thought you were here to rescue me…ha. It sounds like you can't even help yourself. Why are you yelling for Dixie? Do you mean Dixie Mulholland? You do, don't you?"

The darkness forces my mind to invent an image of the owner of this voice: an older man, cowering, lost and afraid. As a Giant Irish Wolfhound, I have keen eyesight, but as a human, my eyes are no better nor worse than this stranger. Still, I can now just make out his silhouette standing a few feet away. "Yes, Dixie Mulholland. How do you know her?"

"Her and I go way back," the man says. "And you?"

I don't want to answer his question until I get a handle on who he is and how he knows Dixie. So I ask some questions of my own. "Who are you? How did you get here?"

"I have no idea. One minute I was talking to The Mystic, and the next, I was in this cave. Uh, this is a cave, isn't it?"

I decide he's being honest, because the fear in his voice rings true to me. I find truth and fear go hand in hand more often than not, and so I relax my guard. "My name is Adam Steel."

"Peter Hudson."

"The news guy?"

The anxiety in his voice melts away at once. "That's right, you've heard of me, Channel Six news anchor. Dixie Mulholland used to work for me. That had to be, oh, at least three years ago."

Peter Hudson…the name sticks in my throat. Dixie told me what a jerk he was to her, to everyone at the station really. As a field reporter, she had to put up with his overbearing self-importance every time she filed an on-air story. Her description of him took only three words: rude, arrogant, and vain. "Dixie's told me so much about you."

"All good I hope." He pauses before he says anything else, as if he's not sure about my connection to Dixie. "Listen, The Mystic called me earlier. He often does, you know—calls me just to talk. Sometimes he wants to bounce ideas back and forth, just me and him. You know, I had an exclusive interview with him just a while ago. We're really good friends."

"That's why he threw you in this cave?" I didn't mean to sound malicious; well, after Dixie told me how he treated her, maybe I did. In any case, he's silent.

Enough time passes so my eyes adjust to the darkness as much as they ever will, which isn't much. It feels like I see this shadow world through an even darker veil, but at least I can make out shapes, forms, and outlines. Peter Hudson stands just a few feet away, quivering, his hands in his pockets. I almost feel sorry for him, almost.

There are no walls, as if the space is a vast expanse of nothingness. At first, I think we're in a cave, as Hudson suggested, but the temperature contradicts this theory. It's warmer than The Mystic's chambers, and I feel the presence of a natural heat source, like a hot wind blowing in an endless draft. For whatever reason, I have the distinct feeling we're in a kind of non-existent dimension; as if caught in a powerful spell, or curse.

But, if this is an earthly location, and not a curse, any potential windows have been painted over with black paint, or covered up so tightly no light seeps in at all. No sound of conditioned air blowing in from vents. And despite the constant gusts of heat, the temperature is moderate.

"Do you have any idea how we got here?" Hudson asks. His tone is candid, exposing the man's complete bewilderment.

I consider not answering his question, wanting to make him feel a bit more uneasy, but that kind of hard-hearted cruelty is just not me. "There must be a reasonable explanation." Although, to be fair, I can't think of one. "Have you explored?"

"Explored?" Hudson's voice quivers and cracks. "What do you mean by that? You want me to wander around an empty, dark cave? Are you nuts?"

"I don't think it's a cave," I say, trying to calm him down. "I think we're being held in some kind of secure holding area, like a safe house."

"A safe house? Safe from what?"

Just then a distant scream fills the air; a shriek growing louder, making me cover my ears. As fast as it started, it stops. Footsteps scrape along the cobblestones somewhere behind us, drawing closer step by step, *clip-clop*, *clip-clop*—whispers weave their way over and around the dark shadows.

Safe from what, indeed.

Chapter Thirteen

"Just to be clear, Miss Mulholland, why does The Mystic require a sacrifice?"

Dixie wrinkled her brow and groaned. "Wow, I must've really gotten bad at explaining things since I was a reporter." She took a moment, rubbing at her temples as she spoke. "Listen, The Mystic isn't the one who wants the sacrifice; he said his associate does."

Colonel Dayton took another sip of bottled water. "I have my reasons for asking, so please bear with me. Do you believe The Mystic's associate is The Devil?"

"Look," Dixie said as she stood and traipsed to the center of the room. Marco Ramirez, Charlie Nguyen, Adrian Gray, and Colonel Dayton watched her pace back and forth. "This will take way too long if you ask me the same questions over and over, and I don't think Adam has that kind of time. We have to concentrate on getting him back before something really bad happens to him. Instead of talking about it all night, what we need is some kind of strategy; a solid plan to get him back safely." She faced Marco. "Maybe it was a mistake calling in the colonel…no offense, Marco."

"No offense taken," Ramirez said. "But, I'm not in a position to call in SWAT for an assault on the Sterling; well, actually I am, but there'd be hell to pay and questions I couldn't answer." He turned to Dayton. "I'm glad you were able to join us on such short notice, but Dixie's right, the longer we delay, the more danger Adam's in."

"We could have handled it," Charlie Nguyen said, "Dixie and I have done this kind of thing before."

"Yes," Dixie said, "we killed a Daemon. But The Mystic is something more than that; much more powerful."

"She's right," Ramirez said.

Nguyen stood, looming over him, her hands on her hips. "What do you know about any of this, human?"

"All right," Dayton said to Nguyen. "That's enough."

"Or what?" She turned her attention to him, her eyes darkening. "What are you going to do about it? You're nothing more than a human as well."

"Ha," Adrian said, "you tell him, honey."

Dayton balled his right fist and slammed it into his left palm while shouting, *"Incantado disectum."*

Nguyen doubled over as if punched in the stomach by an invisible fist. Her words sputtered out, "Where…where'd that come from?"

"New Zealand, I believe," Dayton said. "Or was it Tasmania? In any case, I feel it's only fair to warn you, I've picked up quite a wealth of dark knowledge since returning to UNPAD."

"Wow," Adrian said, "that was cool. Can you teach me that one?"

"Ha," Nguyen said, recovering her breath and lifting her chin, "you were given a mutated Daemon's chant; a token spell, like a toy for humans to play with."

"Oh, I've made some good friends in the Daemon world over the past few months, and they've given me plenty of *toys* to play with. Would you like another demonstration?"

"No, no," Nguyen said, backing away and holding onto Adrian's hand, "we, uh, we don't have the time."

"Colonel, please," Dixie said, rushing to stand next to Nguyen, "she's right. Need I remind you, Charlie's my friend, and she's on our side? It won't help Adam if we quarrel among ourselves. Go easy on her; you know how she can get."

Nguyen gave Dixie a sideways glance and shook her head, but said nothing.

"Right then." Dayton took command of the situation as his training and personality dictated. "A few months ago, I met a Daemon in Italy; charming woman, as Daemons go—her name was Ariana. For whatever reason, perhaps loneliness, she opened up to me."

"I'll bet she did," Adrian said with a grin.

Dayton gave him a cold stare. "In any case, she told me about certain rumors making the rounds; rumors of a new order among the preternatural world. In a nutshell, as is commonly accepted, the River Styx forms a boundary between our world, and the next. No one is quite certain about the location of this toxic river, but many believe it to be located in the Peloponnese in the Middle East."

"Everyone knows this," Charlie Nguyen said.

Colonel Dayton focused on Nguyen as he spoke, "According to Ariana, Styx is the only way into, or out of Hell. As you can imagine, it's become quite congested of late; too many eyes capable of witnessing too many things."

Dixie nodded. "Of course, The Mystic spoke of it, but he called it a Gateway. He said now there's two."

"Ariana told me The Convergence was a mere diversion. Its purpose was to mask an enormous excavation project in Las Vegas."

"A diversion?" Charlie Nguyen said. "Gorgeous said nothing of this to me."

Dayton nodded at her. "I don't believe she knew. She was used, just as so many others were, covering up the construction of the secret Gateway."

"A gateway to what?" Nguyen asked.

"Hell."

Tears trickled down Dixie's cheeks. "So many lives lost; thousands of people killed, and for what, a diversion?"

Adrian Gray winked. "Ha. The ultimate construction project from Hell. Why, the cost of orange cones alone from here to Hades must be—"

"Fuck you," Dixie said. "We need to get Adam back and deal with The Mystic."

"That's the spirit," Dayton said. "What time is The Mystic's performance tonight?"

"Seven," Marco said, "but it's another sold out show—we can't get in without raising some eyebrows."

Dayton took his time answering. "Maybe we don't need to get in to see the show."

"What do you mean?"

A gleam came to the colonel's eyes. He smiled and stepped toward Dixie. "He's taken Adam hostage; let's see how he feels about being taken himself."

"But how? Like Marco said, the show's sold out."

"I've seen his show. As I recall, it finishes with him vanishing while on stage." Colonel Dayton beamed. "Might I suggest we arrange to meet the star of the show as he's leaving the theater…beneath the stage itself, and make it a *real* disappearing act?"

The Miscreant smiled. "I like magic."

****

The old woman squinted, focusing on a flicker of light in the distance, barely visible through the blackness, fog, and warm, sticky moisture. She'd been walking for days, longer than that, carrying a heavy burden in a rolled-up canvas bag. The bag had almost become a part of her, an appendage she lugged behind her over the slippery, uneven cobblestones. The weight of the bag slowed her down, but she'd rather die than forsake it.

"Look, my sweet, up ahead. The Gateway, it must be." She trudged on, hauling the heavy bag as she shuffled across the uneven stones. Distant sounds followed her: whispers, mutters, sighs. They'd been with her since the journey began; they'd always been there.

"Just a little farther, my darling, a little farther." She spoke to the contents of the canvas bag as if bringing along a companion, and, in fact, the bag had been her only travel companion since the journey began. "Just a few more steps."

The ground reflected more and more specks of light the farther she journeyed. Still no indication of walls or ceilings in the darkness around her, suggesting they did not exist, or the expanse was too great to return the shades of pale radiance. One hobbled step at a time brought her closer to her goal: the threshold of the fabled Gateway.

Sounds chased her, filling her ears, her mind, as they had since she started the journey so long ago. Cries, whimpers, screams, moans. Occasionally, in the guise of whispers, they wove their way through the darkness, "Stop, turn back."

But she would not stop, would not turn back no matter how the voices pleaded, begging for her return. This was her one chance, the only way out: forward—her and the precious canvas bag. "Closer, my darling, we're getting closer."

The light intensified, so much so, it forced her to squint. Her hand clenched the bag in a stranglehold. They would finish the journey together. What choice did she have? The voices grew louder as she reached the Gateway, screaming at her now, "Turn back."

She stumbled, almost falling, as her worn leather shoes faltered on the irregular grade of the cobblestones. A definite incline led to the light. Her heart pounded, legs ached, as she took the final few steps. Freedom was within reach.

"Behold," she said, as she stood in the muted rays of light touching her with warmth, the warmth of the sun, "Freedom."

A voice interrupted the moment, "Do you need any help?"

She turned, shielding her eyes from the glare. "Withdraw, doubt," she said, "retreat, defeat. We are free; you shall not block our path."

"I'm not trying to block anything. I just thought you might need some help, that's all."

She shivered at the sound of the voice. At once, another voice joined it, deeper, older. "Help us get out of here. Please, you've got to help us."

She scoffed at the older voice. "Help yourself. Are you not a man?"

"Forgive him, I have to apologize. He's a news

anchor. His name is Peter Hudson. I'm afraid he's a little out of his element here. My name is Adam Steel, and we—"

"Silence." The old woman waved her free arm in the air. Her command bounced off unseen walls, echoing in all directions. "The Gateway calls to me. Free yourselves if you must, as for me, my endless journey will soon bear the fruit of liberty."

"Just tell me," the older voice said, "where are we? How do we get out?"

She drew closer, scrutinizing him, a feeble and useless old man. She turned her attention to the one calling himself Adam Steel. This man was young, tall, with a kind face—rather handsome. She addressed him. "Do you not see the Gateway?"

He glanced about, his brow crunching together. "I can't see anything, it's too dark. You say it's a gateway?"

"Aye, the path from this world to the next." She opened her bag, her hands aching, weathered with age. "You and your companion are surely the Keepers of the way, sent to confuse me. Your deceptions are in vain. I know the tricks of the Keepers."

"Keepers of what?" The older man said. "We don't even know where we are."

"Surely, even as an ant knows its own hill, you know where you stand." She turned away from their nonsense, and busied herself pulling the precious objects from the bag. She lay them on the cobblestones, one by one, side by side, as she drew them from the canvas. "Behold, here lies the fee, my payment to pass."

The young man knelt down, scrutinizing the

objects. He shot up at once and turned away. "Good God, woman."

"What is it?" the older man cried.

"It's a body, cut into pieces." He backed away, joined by the older man. They cowered a few feet from her.

She cocked her head and grinned. "I know the old ways. This is measured payment: the severed limbs of a darkened soul; as Keepers, you must accept and allow passage."

"Pass then," said the older man. "But please, before you go, tell us how to get out of here. I can pay you."

She placed one foot on the threshold and cocked her head. After a few moments, she said, "Are you the canine?"

"No," the older man said.

"Yes," Adam Steel said. "I'm the canine."

She took another moment. "The way out is plain. Truly, you cannot see it?"

Both men shook their heads.

"Take my hands. Come now, time is short; the voices urge me back. Both of you; grasp my hands and I'll lead you out, for The Keeper must accept this payment in full for myself and those who travel with me. Quickly now."

The tall, young man reached out and took hold of her left hand. The older man hesitated, withdrew, and trembled.

"C'mon, Peter," the younger man said, "grab hold, it's our best chance to escape."

"Oh, God." The old man put forth his hand as if about to grab a cactus. She took hold, pulling him close as all three stepped into a dazzling twilight.

She felt a weight lift from her shoulders. The burden of the ages vanished. She'd released the canine, all was right with the underworld.

Rays of desert sunshine bathed her face. She let go of their hands and glanced at her new environment. Just to her left, surrounded by a crowd, a colorful sign heralded the Gateway of Hell: Welcome to Fabulous Las Vegas.

Chapter Fourteen

Shadows covered their movements as they took positions under the stage. Colonel Dayton kept one eye on his watch and the other on the trap door above his head. Dixie and Charlie Nguyen were stationed across from him, ready with the *imobili* curse. Adrian stood at exit stage left; Tina at exit stage right. Even though The Mystic ended his performance for the past two years via false bottom method, Tina convinced the crewmembers he had something new in mind tonight. As a result, the area under the stage, known in the business as "hell," was clear of all stagehands.

Applause thundered from the audience above as the show neared its conclusion. Colonel Dayton expected the next few moments, with any luck, to be something The Mystic would not anticipate. According to Dixie, The Mystic was a Sorcerer, a being with the ability to cross from one world to the next. He also held the gift of prescience. Dayton's hope was The Mystic would be focused on his performance above stage, not the trap awaiting him below.

Tina addressed his concern about The Mystic vanishing for real, without the use of a false bottom stage. She said he used the contraption to allay the fears of the stagehands. He carefully guarded his stage persona from his true essence. If they believed him a Sorcerer, that would merit unwanted attention to his affairs. And so, instead of actually dematerializing from the stage, The Mystic utilized an earthlier means of egress. He called it a win-win solution.

Final thundering applause filled the air. Dayton peered up at the weighted trap door. His heart sank as the platform remained in place. Another gush of clapping burst through the amphitheater and the trap door began its immediate descent. It took less than two seconds for The Mystic to drop twelve feet into "hell."

Colonel Dayton, Dixie, and Charlie Nguyen all shouted the *imobili* curse command toward the occupant of the small platform as it touched down. The movement of The Mystic did not halt at once, instead his gestures slowed to a crawl; syrupy and deliberate, as if underwater. The colonel threw a white cloth sack over The Mystic's head. The bag had been treated with agrimony, a fairly common herb used to deflect hostile magic. Charlie Nguyen supplied the flowering plant while Adrian provided the bag.

Tina rolled a black storage trunk toward the trap door platform and pulled it open. The Mystic, voicing hostile opposition to his treatment with a molasses-throated tone, did not go gently into the large container on wheels.

"Hurry now," Dixie said, "I don't know exactly how long we can hold him."

Colonel Dayton slammed the lid shut and turned the lock. He nodded at Adrian who pulled on a chain, which raised a metal roll top door. The chain squealed and clanged, torturing them all with its incessant noise. It banged against the frame when fully opened. Dixie ran outside where their black van awaited. She started the engine and backed in through the opening, stopping just a few inches from the trunk. Slow and steady thuds banged from the inside of the crate.

"Let's move," Colonel Dayton shouted.

"*Imobili. Imobili.*" Charlie Nguyen motioned toward two security guards racing at them from both sides. The spell caught them in mid stride, freezing them at once. Dixie touched each one and whispered "*dimentilora.*" When they were able to move again, in about ten minutes, they would not remember a thing moments prior to the invocation.

Colonel Dayton, the Miscreant, Tina, and Charlie Nguyen lifted the trunk into the back of the van, piled in after it, and pulled the doors shut. Dixie hit the gas and the van raced up a long driveway, turned onto The Strip, and sped away from The Sterling.

As Dixie negotiated the Friday night traffic on Las Vegas Boulevard, the others kept their left hands on the storage trunk in the back of the van. Those with knowledge of Daemonic spells shut their eyes and uttered "*Imobili,*" every few seconds. Tina, not having the gift, simply voiced her desire for a safe and speedy outcome.

"Can you go any faster?" Colonel Dayton shouted.

"I'm stuck behind rubber-necking tourists." She threw a few curses of her own out the window and sped around traffic as best she could. Despite her best efforts, it took nearly thirty minutes to travel the two miles from the Sterling International Resort to the Bellagio Hotel and Casino.

She pulled into the circular drive of the *porte cochère*. Dayton opened the back of the van and they pushed the trunk out. It came crashing down on the pavers, causing a muted groan from within to escape.

"Let me help you with that," a bellhop rushed forward, smiling at Charlie Nguyen.

She motioned him out of the way with a scowl. "Back off, asshole."

The bellhop froze, watching Dayton as he righted the trunk. After balancing it on its wheels, he maneuvered it toward the hotel.

"Sorry," Dixie said to the bellhop as she tossed the van keys to a valet. She grabbed her receipt and ran after Nguyen. "You have to learn to be nicer to humans."

"Why?"

"What do you mean, why?"

"Simple question. You tell me why I have to be nice to the humans and—"

"Ladies, please. Can that wait 'til later?" Dayton said to them. He grunted, rolling the trunk across the thick carpeting of the busy entrance.

They passed through the lobby, under the famed Chihuly glass sculptured ceiling. Hundreds of tourists, gamblers, and guests milled about, making the expedition to the elevators another time-consuming chore. Dayton weighed the consequences of stopping and laying the trunk down so they could continue the *imobili* curse. He chose against it, deciding time was not their friend, and raced toward the elevator lobby.

Once they secured an elevator to themselves, Dixie pressed the button for the twenty-second floor. Dayton lay the trunk down. They all crouched around it, evoking the spell, *"Imobili."* Even Adrian and Tina joined in the chant. When the bell rang, Dayton lifted the trunk, scooting it off the elevator. It took just a few minutes to wheel the awkward burden down the deserted hallway to Marco's suite.

Dixie banged on the door and Marco opened it. Dayton wheeled the storage trunk over the threshold, placing it in the middle of the suite as they all gathered around.

"What now?" the Miscreant asked.

After one last *imobili* chant, Dayton flipped open the lid. All eyes stared into the bottom of the empty trunk.

****

I take a quick glance back over my shoulder. Any sign of a secret threshold is gone; no visible door, no portal—nothing. The sounds of heavy traffic buzz in my ears. We seem to stand on an island between vehicles zipping by in both directions. I realize the old woman still holds my hand, her leathery clutch feels hot and sweaty; she's squeezing so tight, it's almost like a death grip. She still has hold of Hudson's hand as well.

Voices behind us shout out in gleeful tones; laughter, cooing, and snickers are accompanied by smirks, grins, and smiling faces. Dozens of people surround us on this traffic median. Even though they hardly seem to notice us, we must stand out in sharp contrast to their celebrations. The temperature is warm and moderate; shirtsleeves and shorts weather.

Despite the crowd's easy-going mood, it's nothing compared to the joy I experience. I feel so carefree and happy. I've never felt this way before. As I move about, wishing to explore this wonderful mood, my hand slips out of the old woman's grasp, which delivers an instant sense of dread. The mood swing is so pronounced, I reach for her touch at once, like a drowning man instinctively grabbing for a life vest. When I make contact with her, peaceful thoughts fill my mind once again. I'm certain the misery I experienced was a direct result of losing contact with her.

Hudson releases her hand and steps away, bumping into a man standing in the middle of a long line.

"Hey, wait your turn," the man says to him. "We been waiting for twenty minutes. We come a long way for this here picture, so back off."

Hudson's expression gives me the sense he's more afraid of being out of the darkness of the cave than being in it; it's hard to tell. He opens his mouth but nothing comes out. He trembles and weaves, rocking back and forth, seemingly looking for a place to crash. I want to explain the soothing comfort of the old woman's touch to him, but I don't understand it myself.

After a deep breath, I let go of her hand, knowing the euphoria I feel will soon evaporate. I convince myself, no matter how real it seems, it's just a false emotion manufactured by her touch. I put my hand on Peter's shoulder. He jerks back. "It's okay, Peter. Follow me, let's go to the crosswalk and wait for the light." Because of the giant obelisk across the street in front of the Sterling International Resort, I know exactly where we are, but Peter seems disoriented, as if in a trance. He keeps swiveling his head, glancing at people in line, at the traffic, and at the huge Welcome to Fabulous Las Vegas sign. His brow scrunches together; his mouth hangs open.

All at once, I notice the old woman has disappeared. I scan the crowd, trying to locate her, but she's nowhere in sight; as if she never existed.

"Come on, Peter. That's it, stay with me, you'll be okay."

He finally finds his voice. It's weak, and slow, but at least it functions, "Where…where the hell are we…how'd we get here?" He follows my lead, step by step, but they're frightened baby steps, as if being led away from safety to some kind of danger only he can anticipate.

"For whatever reason, we're at the Welcome to Vegas sign. C'mon, let's cross the street and go down the sidewalk to The Sterling. The Mystic should be able to tell us what happened. After all, we were both with him when we—"

"No." It's an emphatic declaration and he stops moving at once. "No."

I have to use a little psychology to get him off this man-made island in the middle of The Strip. After all, we can't stay here forever. "I thought you and The Mystic were good friends."

He turns to me at once, peering into my eyes. "We are," he assures me, "It's just that…well, maybe he's busy right now."

"Sure, maybe he is, but maybe we can get to the sidewalk and then decide what we're going to do, how does that sound?"

He nods, so I lead him past the long line of eager tourists waiting for a snapshot of the neon sign. We march to the short crosswalk heading east across Las Vegas Boulevard. Keeping my eyes open for the old woman who helped us escape, and anything else that seems out of place, I wait with Hudson as traffic zooms northbound toward Las Vegas proper. When the walk/don't-walk sign turns white, we join a large group of people dashing across the street. The mood of the tourists is carefree, a party-like atmosphere fueled by tall glasses of alcohol. Many of the visitors have the glasses secured around their necks by lanyards. I'm sure Peter and I, caught in the frame of cameras aimed willy-nilly at the sights, will ruin their vacation pictures. We're not exactly in celebration mode.

The sun settles in for the night behind the Spring Mountains, and the city comes alive with the promise of another spectacular weekend ahead. The casinos have already welcomed the coming desert darkness by firing up their massive and colorful marques.

The Mandalay Bay Hotel and Casino towers above the west side of The Strip, its golden façade gleaming in the fast-approaching sunset. It stands in sharp contrast to the enormous blue and white structure down the street known as The Sterling International Resort. The trademark obelisk of the Sterling changes colors at night, employing every shade of the spectrum.

Hudson stops in the middle of the sidewalk. I get the distinct feeling if he takes one more step toward The Sterling, he'll burst into flames. "What's the matter?"

"I'm gonna catch a cab."

"Don't you want to see The Mystic?"

"No." His arm flies into the air and within seconds a taxi pulls to the side of the road. Hudson jumps inside and slams the door. He doesn't even wave goodbye.

It's just as well, he would probably slow me down. I can't wait to see The Mystic and hear what he has to say about my kidnapping.

Chapter Fifteen

The Mystic held out his hand to Ayala.

She rushed to him and held his hand in both of hers. "I was so worried for you. I thought I'd never…" She kissed the back of his hand before he pulled it away and turned from her, facing the enormous glass wall of his chamber.

"You thought what?" He truly wanted to know.

She said nothing, waiting for him to face her again.

He eased into a recliner, kicked off his shoes, and sat yoga style. With eyes closed, he said, "I'm fine, my child. There's no need to worry about me."

She sat in the chair opposite him. A fire crackled in the chilly penthouse, sending reflections of yellow and orange over their faces. "After you couldn't be found, my heart cried for you."

"Your heart." A smile crawled across his lips. "Ayala, you know you have no heart."

She stared at the ground and sobbed. "How can you say such a thing? I have feelings for you—you've always known."

"Of course, I know how you feel. I wouldn't very well be The Mystic if I didn't know your thoughts, everyone's thoughts for that matter. But that doesn't change the fact that you're heartless. Not a judgement on my part, it's a simple matter of biology: Banshees have no heart."

She bowed her head, continuing to weep openly.

"There, there," The Mystic said, slipping a finger under her chin and lifting it so her eyes met his. "Why must you carry on so? Tell me, what is a heart anyway? A mere muscle, nothing more." He raised his hand in the air, balled his fist, and flexed it. "Pumping blood—inflating, deflating. Only humans attach so much syrupy gunk to the heart. After all, love doesn't come from the heart." He stopped flexing and opened his hand. "It's just a pump, and that's all it will ever be."

She grinned, wiping away tears. "You speak truth."

"Of course, I enjoy speaking to you in your true form, as you are now. If you prefer, I would be glad to alter the space between us that you may see the world as my human assistant once again."

"No, please."

"Good. I prefer you in Banshee form...your true self. And you needn't have worried about me, I was in good hands all along. He was there; part of their little merry band of do-gooders."

"Why would he associate with them? And why would he allow them to take you?"

The Mystic stood, clasped his hands behind his back and paced the floor. "Far be it from me to question his motives. Suffice to say, I'm back now and everything is as it should be."

"Yes but—"

"But nothing, Ayala. His ways are not ours; you'll do well to remember that. I'm sure if he wanted me to know why it was okay for me to be stuffed into a tiny storage trunk by a bunch of petulant, no-good, busy-bodies..." He stopped talking, took a deep breath, and exhaled slowly. Turning to face her, he smiled. "Do you see what I mean about the heart? It's fluttering in my chest like the wings of a butterfly—with anger, not love. Be glad you needn't worry about possessing such an anatomical anomaly."

She stood, sauntering toward him, folded her arms around his body, and rested her head on his chest. His hands wrapped around her. Ayala said, "Why do you think he asked you to make the arrangements, you know, for the sacrifice?"

In a moment, he released her and stepped away. She always ruined the mood, asking silly questions. "And why not me? Am I not unique—worthy of his trust?" He turned his back to her and walked away. "I will not have you tonight. You do not please me."

"But...why? Why would you say something so cruel?"

"Is it cruel to speak the truth? I'm afraid you've spent too much time among the humans. Remember what I told you: just as his ways are not mine, their ways are not yours. Humans can't be trusted—they're like animals. Go now. I want to be alone."

"But, sir—"

"Go. I'll call you when you're needed. Until then, I wish to be alone."

****

Marco Ramirez answers my knock. I peek over his shoulder, spying Dixie, Charlie Nguyen, Adrian Gray, Tina, and one more face that brings a smile to mine: Colonel Jon Dayton. Without the colonel's direct help a few short months ago, dozens of wolfhounds would have died. He's a welcomed sight.

I rush past Marco and give Dixie a tender kiss, but reserve the bear hug for the colonel.

"Whoa, big fella," he says, stepping back, his arms on my shoulders, keeping me at arm's length. "Let me have a proper look at you."

"Adam," Dixie says. "Where have you been? How'd you get away? We were all so worried."

"It's a long story, I don't even know where to begin; let's see: Peter and I were in a cave under The Strip—"

"Peter? Hudson?" Dixie says.

I nod. "I know, right? Anyway, we had no idea where we were until this old woman came along. She took hold of our hands and helped us get out. She said she was told to save the canine. That's me."

Colonel Dayton frowns and whispers, "Another player?"

"When we escaped, Peter jumped into a cab. I went to the Sterling to see The Mystic for some answers, but he was doing his show, so I decided to come back here." I spy a fridge across the room, but find a large trunk blocks my path to it. "Hey, what's with the luggage?"

"Talk about a long story," Tina says, "this one's gonna take a while."

"Sit down," Dixie says, "Let me get you something to drink—you look like you've been through hell."

I ease into a soft couch. "You have no idea."

She grabs a bottle of water from a small refrigerator, hands it to me, and sits on the arm of the couch. Sliding her arm over my neck, she says, "Believe it or not, we had The Mystic locked in that trunk; snatched him from underneath his theater at the Sterling. We were going to use him as a bargaining chip to get you back."

"Wow." Her revelation leaves me speechless. It must have taken tremendous courage for them to attempt something like that. "What happened?" I spin the top off the water bottle, downing its contents in one long chug. Dixie treks to the fridge and gets me another one.

"The Mystic pulled a disappearing trick," Adrian says. "He's good. He could be a headliner on The Strip."

Tina scoffs. "He *is* a headliner on The Strip."

Colonel Dayton looks at his watch. "You've been gone for almost twenty-four hours. Tell us again exactly what happened."

I take another sip of water. "Where should I begin? One minute, I was in The Mystic's chambers. He explained to Dixie he wanted her to make some kind of sacrifice in exchange for him removing her canine curse."

Dixie nods. "I already told them what The Devil wanted."

"No," I blurt out, "he never said it was The Devil. He kept using the term 'my associate.' I remember because he wanted to make that point very plain. I think if it was The Devil, he would have said The Devil, don't you?"

"You're right," Dixie says, her brow crumpled, as if trying to recall the conversation word for word. "He said my associate this, and my associate that. In fact, one time I used the term Devil, and he stopped me cold. He corrected me."

Charlie Nguyen chuckled. "He probably doesn't have the juice to rate The Devil."

"What do you mean by that?" Adrian says.

Colonel Dayton moves to the center of the room, a worried expression growing across his face. "Why do you suppose it's so important to him The Devil is not involved?"

Only one voice offers an opinion. "Maybe the answer's so simple it's staring us right in the face and we can't see it. Maybe The Devil isn't involved at all. Maybe The Mystic's associate has more balls than The Devil." Adrian Gray takes a quick breath and turns to me. "The more important question is how did you escape through the Gateway?"

My heart thumps hard. "I never said anything about a gateway."

Marco Ramirez turns to Adrian, an odd look on his face; is it concern, or anger? He approaches the Miscreant. Tina sidles up as well.

Marco uses a tone of voice I've only heard in movies; cops and robbers movies. "Where were you when we opened the trunk?"

"What?" Adrian says with a laugh. "What do you mean?"

"You heard him," Tina says in the same accusatory tone.

Colonel Dayton and Dixie move toward the Miscreant as well. I join them. In a moment, he's surrounded on all sides.

"Hey, wait a minute," Charlie Nguyen says. "You don't think—"

"Think what?" Adrian says as he stands. "Everybody calm down. I'm the one who saved your life, Ramirez, remember? I'm the one who got the white cloth bag for The Mystic's head. You're crazy if you think what I think you're thinking."

"Why?" Dixie says. "We don't even know you."

Adrian keeps rising, levitating a few inches off the carpet. His demeanor is deadpan sober. He stares at each of us in turn. In a bizarre voice, darker, deeper, he says, "You have no idea who you're dealing with." He raises his hand and touches the top of Tina's head. "*Exteritus.*" Tina falls to the ground. She's dead.

I peer into the Miscreant's eyes. They turn from blue to black in an instant. The others are in shock, glued in place where they stand. When I see his hand reach for Marco, my adrenaline kicks in. In less time than it takes to wink, I transform and lunge at him. I've never shifted into a Giant Irish Wolfhound so fast in all my life. It's a fight or flight reaction; I refuse to let this monster harm my Alpha.

A fraction of a second before he touches the top of Marco's head, my fangs wrap around his hand, chomping down hard onto his wrist. I shake my head back and forth, tasting blood, meat, and gristle. His scream fills the room. Somewhere behind me, I hear Dixie and Charlie Nguyen barking out curses and spells, anything to get him to stop in place. Their words seem to weaken him, or maybe it's the loss of blood. In any case, the hand that came so close to Marco, now hangs from his arm, attached by a few strands of muscle.

The Miscreant slaps my muzzle with his other hand, sending me through the air into a corner of the suite. Charlie and Dixie have him writhing in pain as they stretch out their arms, shouting, *"Carpe contorce."* I've never heard this chant before, but it seems to be an extremely powerful spell. The Miscreant thrashes and wriggles where he stands, brownish smoke rising from his face. The accompanying smell is disgusting.

In an instant, Adrian Gray holds out his one good hand and sends up some kind of shield against the curse as he yells out, "*Mors non est finis!*"

The room goes black. Shrieks bounce off the walls. When the lights come back on, the Miscreant is gone.

Chapter Sixteen

Mors non est finis. Death is not the end.

I dress myself in the tattered garments that tumbled to the ground when I transformed. They'll have to do until I can arrange a change of clothes. Eerie silence fills the room.

Dixie is beside herself, tears streaming down her cheeks. They form tiny rivers on her face. Charlie Nguyen stands in the corner, trembling. She stares at Tina's lifeless body lying on the thick carpet of Ramirez' luxury suite at the Bellagio.

Colonel Dayton and Marco Ramirez share the same comical look on their faces; a look that says, "this didn't just happen…it's some kind of illusion."

But it did happen. Someone we all thought to be a Miscreant, a safe and fun-loving entity just one-step above a human, murdered Tina. In reality, he was much darker; a creature bent on pure evil, and quite possibly The Mystic's unnamed associate.

Marco shuffles forward, wrapping his arms around me in a hug. "Thank you, Adam. If it weren't for you…" His words fade away. The room is dark as the sun completely sets. The only light entering the window is from The Strip properties surrounding the Bellagio.

I know what Marco's trying to say as I return his embrace. "I only wish I could have been faster." Tears blur my vision.

Without a word, Colonel Dayton, Marco, and I lift Tina's limp body and place it in the storage trunk. Marco shuts and locks the lid.

"What are you doing?" Dixie says, a nervous quiver in her voice. She strides to the trunk, reaching for the handle. "This isn't right. We can't just—"

"Stop," I say. I grab her hand, leading her away from the trunk. She glares at me, at us all, as if what we're doing is barbaric.

Marco speaks up, "Dixie, you know we can't explain what happened here. Even if we could, we can't explain *her*."

The reality sinks in: Tina, our friend, is dead and because she was born canine, no one could ever know her true identity. I shudder as the reality hits me harder than anyone else in the room. As a Giant Irish Wolfhound who chooses to live in the human world, this is my fate as well. In addition to a shared sense of destiny, tremendous guilt sweeps over me.

"It's all my fault," I say. "If I hadn't asked for her help—"

"It was Tina's choice," Dixie says, wiping at her tears. "She chose to help us; she chose to live her life as human. Don't belittle her decisions."

"What do you mean belittle..." I decide to stop before I say something I'll regret. Dixie's right. Nobody coerced Tina into helping us, just as nobody tells me what to do. If my fate is to live in anonymity, and someday die without the sound of trumpets heralding my existence, so be it; this is what I choose.

Dixie moans. "I knew there was something wrong with the Miscreant. I felt it as soon as I met him, but I didn't..."

A smile brings her lips to life. It's so out of place, I find myself frowning. "What is it, Dixie?"

"Death is not the end."

"I don't understand what—"

"You said that to me when Aunt Rose was killed, do you remember?"

I don't. Death is not the end, doesn't sound like something I'd say, but I'm not about to argue the point—not now. I sweep tears from my eyes and nod at her.

Colonel Dayton steadies the trunk and we march down the hallway in silence. We all understand this is as close to a funeral procession as Tina will ever have. The drive back to Claremont is solemn, each of us lost in our own thoughts.

After laying Tina to rest beside Cutty's grave, we each say a few words about her bravery, commitment, and friendship. They're heartfelt words, earned by Tina's fierce loyalty and determination to help all canines in need. She kept the packs together after The Convergence, gathering them at Claremont, and coordinating the relief effort. Without her dedication, dozens of wolfhounds would have died in the harsh desert environment surrounding Las Vegas.

Dixie and I walk hand in hand, up the hill to my old house. After changing clothes, I join the others around the kitchen table. Candlelight flickers on the walls, giving the room a dark, church-like atmosphere. My mood is somber; a sense of helplessness sweeps over me. Glancing at the others, I sense they feel the same.

The early morning sun sends rays through the window. Colonel Dayton breaks the silence, "What did the Miscreant mean by 'death is not the end'?"

Dixie shakes her head. "I don't know, but he wasn't a Miscreant, that's for sure."

Charlie Nguyen comes to life, speaking slowly, methodically, "He was a Fiend. It's in their nature to play with other souls, you know, mess with their minds. If anyone should have known, it was me. There was a dark aura about him, an aura I ignored."

Colonel Dayton barks, "Does messing with minds include killing them, or sleeping with them?" His obvious anger silences everyone.

Charlie Nguyen shoots out of her chair; she holds a hand over her mouth and rushes to the restroom. Although I've never thought of Nguyen as a friend, her and Dixie are close, and that's good enough for me. She didn't deserve the way the Miscreant, or whatever the hell it was, played with her for his own pleasure, while playing the rest of us for fools.

Dixie rushes down the hall to comfort Charlie.

Colonel Dayton rises to his feet, telling us what I know he'll say to Nguyen later, in private, "I'm sorry. I spoke out of turn; I apologize. This whole sacrifice ceremony has put me beside myself. I'm missing something here. For instance, what makes Dixie the Treasure?"

I grab a bottle of water from the counter and plop back down in my chair. Dixie's never held anything back from me; she's always been honest. "She once told me what Aunt Rose said about her. Aunt Rose said Dixie was meant for greatness. And the Daemons called her the Treasure at the Daemon house."

"Interesting. But what does it actually mean?"

"I don't know," I say. "I don't know what any of

this means." All at once, the absurdity of it smacks me right between the eyes. Have we all been used in some kind of good versus evil game? Sitting here at the kitchen table, surrounded by friends, I can't help but remember the good people I've known and lives cut short: Aunt Rose, Cutty, Major Jean Ransom, every one of my siblings, and now Tina—and for what? Anger wells inside of me. Too many people have died in their prime. And now Dixie's name is tossed about as some kind of "special one," and that scares me. It's time this sick and twisted game came to an end.

If Adrian Gray spoke the truth—if death is not the end—I'll do my best to make him the exception.

****

Fuck The Devil.

Adrian Gray stepped onto the outdoor terrace of his two-story lodge. Built into the side of a hill in the exclusive McKinley Ranch development in Henderson, the balcony afforded him a stunning view of Sin City.

Sunrays painted the blue skies over Las Vegas in broad strokes of pinks, yellows, and orange. A crisp freshness in the morning air chilled the basin. Just a temporary chill; triple digit weather lay in wait, like an assassin, preparing to attack the Silver State's largest city with a new record high for October. Adrian raised his glass of brandy and toasted the heat—the wonderful, glorious heat.

At night, he often built a raging fire in the chiminea, enjoying the neon glow of The Strip from this outdoor perch. Life was good, the brandy sweet, and his plan perfect. Well, almost perfect.

Fuck The Devil!

Three years ago, The Devil granted him full

authority over the entire Gateway project. Why? The project had stalled, and The Devil was afraid of losing face (that was Adrian's best guess, anyway). *Since I took over, the venture has been on time and under-budget.* Not that there was a time limit, or even a budget for that matter, but in his mind, he'd set, what he considered, a reasonable deadline. Besides, he couldn't wait to receive the reward he'd been promised by The Devil upon completion of the project: absolute rule over The Lake of Fire.

The construction required thousands of workers and, to Adrian's surprise, he discovered he was quite adept at negotiating complex treaties between various factions of the underworld to get the job done. The Jinn did the heavy lifting and underground excavation. They worked for anthrax, which they traded for basic necessities and human hearts, a Jinn delicacy. Vampires, Ghouls, and Goblins paid in blood, sweat, and souls acquired the hearts. Obtaining the anthrax, well that was another story altogether. The entire process was so complex, even Adrian had to admire his own project administration skills. It took time, careful planning, and shrewd collaboration, but the whole thing worked—by God it worked!

Three years ago, however, *El Diablo* began to meddle. Adrian poured another glass of brandy and toasted, "To your lowness…you prick."

First, The Devil insisted on the construction being kept secret. Fine. The Convergence took care of that. It served as a diversion, covering up the massive excavation necessary to tunnel down to Hades.

Next, The Devil stipulated The Convergence itself be covered-up. Okay. Adrian used The Mystic's relationship with President Walker to facilitate that little detail. A commission was appointed to "get to the bottom" of The Convergence. That commission was spoon fed gibberish to explain, in human terms, the possible causes of The Convergence. In fact, the commission was so successful the very name of the tragedy was reworked. Thus, The Las Vegas Disaster was born. Ha, another obstacle conquered.

Then, The Devil demanded test runs of the newly constructed Gateway. Sure, why not? What's another delay? So Adrian ran *Sangre di Real* in and out of the Gateway proving its viability. More time, more planning...more delay.

At this point, Adrian suspected The Devil of foul play. For whatever reason (jealousy, resentment, maybe even an inferiority complex), The Devil seemed to *want* the project to fail. Who knows, perhaps The Great Deceiver intended to renege on Adrian's reward.

And now, on the eve of the grand opening, The Devil meddled again. He claimed a sacrificial trinity was required to commemorate the event and consecrate the hallowed ground. That entailed more planning, which meant more delay. And since the Sacrificial Trinity was required to take place on All Hallows Eve, he had two days to arrange it—or postpone until next year, which he would not!

Adrian seethed, throwing his empty glass over the balcony to the golf course below. Obviously, The Devil wanted him to fail. Bah! That prick didn't know the first thing about building things. His forte was destruction.

After a moment of inner chaos, Adrian took a calming breath, found a new glass, and poured another drink to ease his thoughts. It didn't work.

Glancing at the wooden planks of the balcony, he pointed down, and spoke out loud. "You must be enjoying yourself, you bastard. But I'll show you. I'll jump through all your hoops, and prove my worth. The Gateway is ready, and if it's a grand opening you desire…then thy will be done."

Damn the rituals! He swallowed another glass of brandy, mulling over the qualifications of the Treasure. *Dixie Mulholland, indeed.* The bitch didn't even know she was a Daemon until quite recently. In fact, she'd been destined to end her pitiful life as an actual bitch. Ha.

But, thanks to The Mystic's powers, prompted by Adrian's not-so-gentle nudge, she was now a viable candidate to perform the sacrifice. After all, she couldn't very well hold a knife with doggie paws. He laughed at the image and guzzled more brandy, spilling a few drops down the front of his shirt. *Shit.*

With a fresh drink in hand, he swirled the brandy in the snifter. If any way existed to get around the damned sacrifice, he would be a much happier Fiend. He took a sip, feeling the liquid burn down his throat as he recalled his own plan to speed along the Treasure's decision. *I must have been drunk when I came up with that ridiculous idea.*

He'd taken the guise of a buffoon: a Miscreant. Using his guile to infiltrate the Treasure's little band of do-gooders, he'd intended to convince her the sacrifice was in everyone's best interest. He wanted her to stop thinking of herself, the father, and the baby, and start reflecting on the bigger picture: a brand new Gateway to the netherworld. He'd planned on using her best friend, Charlie Nguyen, to influence her decision, but even that simple scheme fell through, enjoyable as it was. Ah well, it was worth a shot.

Massaging the scars on his wrist, he cursed the mutt who'd nearly bitten his hand off. He'd have to remember to make Adam his very first guest of honor in The Lake of Fire. *After all, revenge* is *the best medicine.*

Adrian spent the afternoon examining the language of the sacrificial document for loopholes. Any ambiguity or obscurity in the wording would render the ceremony null and void, but, no doubt, The Devil and his legal team worked overtime on the document's phrasing:

> *Three now must die,*
> *By hand of the chosen,*
> *Not eye for an eye,*
> *So, ransomed not cozen.*
> *For loss to endure,*
> *All martyred, all pure.*
> *All Hallows Eve by day*
> *All Hallows Eve by night*
> *One true human,*
> *One true who is known.*
> *There be one True Love,*
> *As true to bemoan.*
> *True blood's final sin,*
> *True as one's own kin.*

Streaks of the new morning sun broke over Sunrise Mountain, washing away the colors in the sky. The temperature soared, shooting for the record. Adrian poured the remains of his glass into the chiminea, resurrecting the flames. He opened the sliding glass door and stepped inside, turning for a moment to view the miles of desert surrounding him. He used the time for a little quiet introspection:

Not to brag, but I possess all the true virtues: lust, pride, vanity, greed...uh...and so on and so forth. He couldn't quite remember them all; too much alcohol. *I've always done my best to upset the natural order and such. Wicked I am, thank you very much. The Gateway is built, and I deserve my reward: The Ruler of The Lake, its master and its lord.* Adrian emptied his glass with a toast to his rhymes, "To Lennon and McCartney and Gray; here comes the sun and a beautiful new day."

So, if The Devil wanted the old ways observed, that's what The Devil would get. Adrian would give him an unbelievable grand opening cultivating in a glanderous scarface...uh...culminating in a glorious sacrifice. He shook his head, cleared his throat, and brayed like a mule. Adrian mulled over one final thought before passing out: *Fuck The Devil.*

Chapter Seventeen

We wait 'til dark to return to the Welcome to Fabulous Las Vegas sign. Traffic is still heavy, even for a Sunday night, but not as congested as it might have been on a Friday or Saturday. A few older tourists mill about the base of the city's famous logo, while a group of young people, wearing identical t-shirts, catch my eye as they play about and laugh aloud, the way so many visitors to Vegas do. I smile at their exuberance.

"Doesn't this sign thing ever close?" Charlie Nguyen says, glancing at the tourists with her nose in the air.

"Nope," Marco answers, "like most everything else on The Strip—it's open twenty-four-seven."

"Okay, gather round." Colonel Dayton waves us into a tight huddle once we're all out of the van. "We obviously have no idea what we're looking for, but I suspect we'll recognize it; something out of place, something that doesn't look quite right. If we don't find anything suspicious here, we'll go across the street to the Sterling where we can have a little chat with our Mystic friend." He peers at his watch. "His performance ends in about thirty minutes, so let's get cracking and have a looksee."

"And be careful," Marco adds, "keep your eyes open for Adrian."

"You mean the Fiend," Dixie said, "I can't even

bring myself to say his name."

"Might I suggest," Colonel Dayton added, "Adam and Marco pair up, same with Dixie and Charlie Nguyen. Both teams advance on either side of the median in order to cover more ground."

"What about you?"

"I'll follow close behind, keeping the teams in sight. Remember, we don't know what we're dealing with yet, so be very careful." He lowered his voice. "If Adrian Gray appears, I'll give a shout, right?"

I acknowledge his warning with a nod and tilt my head toward Marco. "Shall we?" He gives me a thumbs-up and we're off, advancing toward the iconic sign from the right side of the median, traffic whizzing up behind us, heading toward downtown. Dixie and Charlie approach from the left side, vehicles racing past them, leaving Las Vegas. I glance behind at the colonel, about thirty yards away. He nods and waves me on.

I remember everything about the old woman leading Peter Hudson and I across an invisible threshold, except the most important detail: its location. Even though I know it's here, somewhere near the Vegas sign, I have no idea where to look.

Marco and I fall in behind a group of excited tourists wearing green and yellow t-shirts with the likeness of a kangaroo drawn on the back. "Excuse me, sir." A young blonde-haired girl turns to me and smiles. "Would you mind taking our photo?"

"Oh, that'd be bonza, mate…er, I mean that'd be excellent," a fair-haired boy says with a grin. He shouts to them all, "Oy, listen up; let's gather round the base of the sign. This man's gonna snap our photo."

"Good onya mate," one boy says as he hands me a

phone.

"Ta." A dark-skinned girl places her digital camera in Marco's hands.

They hand me four iPhones, each a different color. Marco helps me out and we shoot at least three dozen photos of the jovial group. They're not shy about posing and mugging for the cameras. Their enthusiasm is a welcome boost to my somber mood.

"Thank you, sir." The blonde girl gives me a dazzling smile. "Were you able to get us all in the pic? I want at least one shot with all of us together."

"Oy," the fair-haired boy laughs, taking back his phone, "he's a bloody yank, ain't he? He's the full bottle with an iPhone, yeah?" He turns to me. "Good onya, mate. Man, this arvo was blazing. Is it always like that?" He laughs. "We been going flat out like a lizard drinking, but I can't wait to hit the fruit machines later."

"Save the Pokies for me, Bob," an excited voice shouts out.

My mouth is ajar; I have no idea what they said.

The young girl gives me another stunning smile. "Sorry, sir. Don't bother with them," she gestures toward the others, "they're just prawns."

I shake my head, slack-jawed again.

She laughs. "What I mean is they're acting foolish. We just arrived this arvo—uh, afternoon—and I guess we're all a little loopy from the time change. We're here to support the Socceroos; they play this Wednesday."

"Socceroos?" I ask.

"Australia's national soccer team." She giggles again. "We must sound as strange to you as you do to us. Listen, can we return the favor? Take your picture at the sign?"

"Oh, no thank you. We're here just looking for something we lost."

"Do you need help?"

I shake my head.

"Honestly, I wouldn't mind. What'cha looking for?"

Her charm is downright disarming, so I answer her with a grin, trying to be just vague enough so as not to alarm her. "We're looking for something that's difficult to see. It might be hidden, like something imaginary."

"Oy," she turns and calls to her "mates." "These two are looking for something beyond the black stump."

They laugh. "Looking for the bunyip in the desert, mate?"

Once again, I'm as silent as a ghost.

"Oy," an older voice calls out from the parking area behind us. "C'mon, rattle your dags. We can't stay here all night."

"Sorry," the girl says, "we gotta run. Good luck with your search."

Marco glances at me, shrugs his shoulder, and says, "Miss, excuse me, but what do you mean by the black stump?"

"Oh," she giggles, "it's just a silly saying, more for the older folks like yourself. It's like, something that's on this side of the black stump is of this world, and then something *beyond* the black stump belongs to the next." She starts away, but glances back and points. "Something like that over there."

I turn to where she pointed. Marco does the same. Just past the welcome sign, to the right, is the blackened stump of a palm tree. Shivers crawl across my skin.

"In fact, it's exactly like that." She laughs. "So, don't forget: Socceroos, Wednesday at the Silver Bowl. Hope you can make it."

"Go Socceroos," some of them shout as they run back to the parking area.

Marco and I stare at each other as we act like "prawns," our mouths hanging open like fools. The burned stump of the palm tree surrounded by yellow caution tape is so obvious, and yet so out of place, I don't know why we didn't start our search there in the first place.

The Australian girl's observation is spooky. We are, indeed, hunting for something just beyond the black stump.

I can't help but wonder out loud, "What the hell's a bunyip?"

****

She hoped he would return, the one called Adam Steel, but didn't know why. She had no good reason for the hope, and yet here he was. Another accompanied him; not the older human as before, but one much younger, more pleasing to the eye. They ambled near the Gateway, crossing it, passing over it without care, as if blind to its very existence.

Adam drew closer, after speaking with the youngsters near the sign. He and his companion would soon cross her path.

She wrapped a dark shroud around herself and stepped out from behind the black stump, blocking their way. She took a chance. "You seek the Gateway."

They jerked to a stop, her presence apparently upsetting them.

"I know you," Adam said.

"Indeed. Earlier, I held your hand and brought you into the light."

"Is she the one who helped you and Peter escape?" Adam's companion asked. "Do you know her?"

"She says I do." Adam closed his eyes, as if trying to remember, then stared at her and spoke in a firm voice, "But this is impossible. The woman who helped me escape was much older. Here, give me your hand."

She offered her hand, her breath shallow. He reached out, held her hand in his, and closed his eyes once again.

A grin crawled across his face. "Yes. This is the woman. Marco, she's the one who helped me and Hudson out of...out of wherever we were held. I feel it in her touch."

With a half-smile, she spoke his name, "Adam Steel."

The one he called Marco nodded. He turned and raised an arm, calling others who raced to their side. "Adam says this is the old woman who helped him escape earlier."

A short blonde-haired woman spoke. "When's the last time you had your eyes checked? This is not an old woman."

"No, not now," Adam said. "Now she's beautiful and young and full of life...er, uh, I mean she was old before, the first time we met."

"Don't backtrack, sweetie. You're right, she's quite stunning." The wise woman held out her hand. "My name's Dixie, and yours?"

"My name is Jayed." When their hands touched, she felt the connection: this one, the one called Dixie, was the Treasure.

Jayed knew she must create separation between Dixie and this place, so she feigned light-headedness. "I'm sorry; I appear to have taken ill." Marco steadied her.

"Are you here with anyone?" Dixie asked.

She shook her head, closed her eyes and put her full weight into Marco's more than capable arms. "Alas, I travel alone."

"Let's put her in the van and go back to Claremont."

"What?" the other, dark-haired female shouted. "We're going to take this stranger back with us, just like that? Isn't that kidnapping?"

"Listen, Charlie," Adam said, "she knows my name. She knows all about the Gateway. I felt a connection to her when I touched her hand. We came here to find something, and I think we have."

Marco raised his voice over the traffic as he tightened his hold on her. "You're right, Adam. I'd say we got pretty lucky tonight."

"I'd say you did," the one called Charlie said with a wink. "Just don't forget about what happened with the last person who befriended our little group."

"Enough," Dixie said. "There's nothing but kindness in Jayed's touch—no sign of evil." The blonde girl rushed to help Marco and together they marched her past the Las Vegas sign to a vehicle. The others followed without comment.

She felt safe with them, enjoying the night breeze running across her face. They placed her in the back of their vehicle and the one who had yet to speak drove. After several minutes, the vehicle bounced on gravel as they climbed higher over a winding road. The tires crunched to a stop and they helped her out.

Soon they were in a cozy, dark house miles from the Gateway. She sat in a chair while the others sat around a large table in the middle of a kitchen.

"Excuse me, my name is Colonel Jon Dayton. Can I get you something—would you like some water?" He was tall, dark haired, and attractive. She nodded. Colonel Dayton grabbed a bottle of water from the countertop, placing it in front of her on the table. "Sorry it's not cold, we have no refrigeration here."

"Here. Where is here?"

"Claremont Hill," Adam said. "This is my home. I grew up here. I used to—"

"Enough," Charlie Nguyen said. She rose, ambling around the table until she stood inches from Jayed. "We don't tell her about us, until she tells us about her. Are we in agreement?"

The colonel nodded. "I think, under the circumstances, Charlie Nguyen is correct. Please, tell us how you happened to run into Adam tonight, and how you saved him from something we obviously could not see."

She drank from the bottle of water, took a deep breath, and eyed the faces around her. With a nod, she said, "I travelled many days, so very far, following the path to the light. I carried the customary payment for The Keepers. The journey was treacherous. I followed the prescribed route. All the while, voices shadowed my steps, at times begging me to stop, to turn around; still other voices urged me forward."

"What did this voice, the one who told you to go forward, tell you?"

"To find the threshold, to save the canine." All eyes turned to Adam.

"And where was it you were travelling from?" Marco asked.

Without a moment's hesitation, she said, "Hell."

They stiffened, holding a collective breath as candlelight painted their silhouettes on the cream-colored walls.

Adam Steel cleared his throat. "Who did the voice belong to?"

"The Devil."

Chapter Eighteen

Her talk of Hell and The Devil sends a constant buzz of anxious chatter, insults, and worry racing around the kitchen table. It's late and everyone seems on edge. Jayed gives the impression (at least to me, anyway) she's more than on edge. Her reaction to our response verges on the edge of a panic attack. I have to shout above the din to gain everyone's attention. "You're frightening her." My tone catches them off guard and the room falls into eerie silence.

"You're right," Dixie says, her voice even and steady, "we all need to calm down. What do you suggest?"

"Everybody leave the room." It's more of an order than a suggestion. "Dixie and I will talk to her alone and try to figure out what's going on. Okay?"

Charlie Nguyen shakes her head. In her sly and cynical tone, she says, "Oh, please, why do we have to leave the—"

"Charlie." Dixie cuts her off. Nguyen frowns, but stands up and exits the kitchen without a sound. Colonel Dayton and Marco follow her into the living room. I wait for the swinging door to stop.

Turning to Jayed, I allow myself an embarrassed grin. "Sorry about all the noise. We can relax now. Like I said, this is my house, and you're safe. Everybody's just a bit nervous right now. We lost a close friend earlier, and we're confused about what's going on—you know, the Gateway; The Devil. By the way, I never did thank you for saving my life; I'd like to make it official now. Thank you."

"Yes," Dixie says, taking a seat next to me. "Thank you so much." She puts an arm over my shoulder. "I don't know what I'd do without Adam."

Jayed smiles. "The canine belongs to you?"

Dixie and I give each other a furtive glance. I know we're both on the verge of laughing, so I speak quickly. "Dixie and I are in love. So yes, we belong to each other."

"Of course," Jayed says, "I didn't mean to imply otherwise. May I ask do you know where the friend you've lost might be?"

"She was killed yesterday," Dixie says, "by a Fiend. Do you know what that is?"

Jayed nods. "I understand all manner of things belonging to the netherworld."

Dixie waits a beat and then asks, "And why is that, sweetie?"

"I'm a Witch."

Dixie and I glance at each other. "Tell us your story."

Jayed stares at us, leaning back in her chair, and bows her head. "As you wish. I crossed over many, many years ago. For my kind…no star waits. My fate, like so many others, lay in the Lake of Fire; a fathomless pit, known as the eternal inferno." Her expression darkens, as if recalling horrific memories. She takes a deep breath and continues, "The voice came to me—of the billions in the lake, the voice spoke only to me. The Master's own words told me of another way." She smiles. "A second chance. I was given payment for travel, and told to leave, given instructions to save the canine at the Gateway."

I feel my face turn red. "Me? The Devil spoke of me?"

Jayed nods. "And the human. So, I started back from whence I came. The voice told me to stop, to turn around and follow a new course, an untrodden path to a new Gateway. The journey was difficult, treacherous and unstable. Many times, I considered quitting. Other voices spoke to me—not his strong and kind voice, but the lesser ones, the crying ones—telling me to stop. They told me to return to the lake. Their banter only hardened my resolve. I travelled for many days. Then I came upon you."

"You called me a Keeper."

"You sure are," Dixie says.

Jayed grins. "And so, it is what I believed. But you were the canine—I knew it in your touch. The voice told me to help you, and the human, to cross the Gateway to the land of the living—to this very world."

"Was I dead?"

"Perhaps, it's not for me to say."

Her worried expression convinces me into changing the course of the conversation. "You look so different from when we first met."

She chortles. "The Lake of Fire takes its toll; the cruel and injurious wear of death is unmerciful." She raises a hand to her face, feeling her cheeks, her lips, and running fingers over her shiny black hair. With a smile, she says, "When I crossed, that is, when I died, I appeared as you see me now. Or so I can only imagine." She raises her hands to her face and shrugs.

Dixie stands up, raising her palm like a traffic cop. "Hold that thought." She rushes out of the kitchen.

I shake my head. "I don't understand why the voice you spoke of—"

"The Devil."

Shivers crawl across my skin. "The Devil...wanted you to save me. Last year, I killed his son."

She scrunches her eyebrows together. "I know nothing of that. I performed the task as instructed, and now I'm here, safe and alive."

"And beautiful." Dixie runs back into the kitchen carrying a small hand mirror. She offers it to Jayed.

Jayed takes the glass, studying herself in its reflection. A slight upward twirl of her lips suggests she's pleased with what she sees. Soon, the grin matures, and explodes across her face, lighting up her lips, her soul. She turns her brilliant blue eyes to me. "I can't believe it. I'm beautiful again. How can I ever repay your kindness?"

"No need to thank me." I didn't do anything.

"Then tell me, the one with you tonight—Marco. Is he..."

"He's a deputy chief with Metro."

"No, I mean, does he belong to anyone?"

"He's with us."

"No," Dixie says, "he doesn't belong to anyone."

Jayed grins. "It isn't good to not belong; not good for the soul. Marco is a worthy man—I sense these things."

Colonel Dayton jerks the swinging kitchen door open, bursts in, and shouts, "C'mon, hurry, we've got company." He blows out the two candles on the countertop. The room turns black.

"What's wrong?" Dixie says, she jumps up and stares out the window. "Is it The Devil? *Sangre di Real?*"

"Worse than that," Marco says, entering the kitchen in a panic, "It looks like a demolition crew."

Marco seems more than a little flustered. He has his hand under his coat where I know his firearm gives him comfort. "Not the kind of crew that lights up old casinos. These guys are here for us, heading straight for the house. Move it." He approaches Jayed and reaches out his hand. She takes hold and gets up. The hand under his coat relaxes.

"I'll get the van." Colonel Dayton rushes out the backdoor, silent as a ghost.

"C'mon, Dixie," Charlie Nguyen says, "let's vanish." She disappears in a cloud of yellow mist. We all watch her fade away. In a moment, she's back, reappearing in the same golden mist "C'mon, girl. I said we gotta go."

"Have you forgotten?" Dixie says, "My transportation powers are on the fritz."

Charlie Nguyen frowns, shakes her head, and stays with us.

****

They escorted Jayed out of the kitchen and back to the van across rocky, hardpan soil. Marco Ramirez steadied her with a safe and reassuring hand. She squinted, staring down the unfamiliar hill through the darkness. Between pine branches, palm trees, and thick overgrown shrubs, she caught a glimpse of lights in the distance. No vehicles, just men racing up the hill holding hand held lamps.

You put them all at risk. You should have stayed in

the lake. A voice, one she's heard before, filled her mind. "It's me they want." She pushed against Marco's strength and stopped. "The voice wants me to go back to the Lake of Fire."

"You're not going anywhere," he said. He pulled her along toward the vehicle. Dixie opened the back door and they scampered inside.

The vehicle faced downhill. Colonel Dayton pulled a lever and stepped out. He strained to push the van forward. Without a sound, it rolled, swaying back and forth over potholes and small clumps of brush, picking up speed. The colonel maneuvered the vehicle, narrowly missing palm trees and boulders. The black van glides across rough terrain like a spirit in the night, down the far side of the hill, and away from the oncoming lights.

"Stop here," Jayed said. "Let me out and you'll be safe."

Marco whispered, "Be quiet, and all of us, including you, will be safe."

The windows fogged over. She rubbed her palm across the smooth glass. The lights were well behind them, surrounding the house at the top of the hill.

A sudden blast rocked the earth. Trees appeared, as if apparitions, in a burst of light accompanying the explosion. The van swayed from side to side. Another detonation tore through the house, leaving little in its wake. Orange and yellow flames licked at the remains of the structure. Flashlights carried by the demolition crew receded down the hill in an orderly retreat. No cry of victory, no shouts of triumph. This was not a battle— this was assassination. In a few moments, they were gone, and silence, once again, ruled the night.

"What now?" Dixie asked.

"It depends on who just attacked us," Marco said. "If it was the work of The Devil, I doubt there's much we can do."

"This was not The Devil," Jayed said. All eyes turned to her, the amber glow of flames illuminating her face. "The voice I heard was not that of The Devil, but the one who tried to stop my escape from the lake."

"I don't understand," Dixie said.

Adam was quiet, watching his home burn to the ground. He did not appear upset by the sight, in fact, there may even have been a happy gleam in his eyes.

Jayed put her arm over his shoulder. "Your reaction is odd. Your house has been destroyed, yet you don't seem to mind. In fact, you seem—"

"Relieved." Adam turned to her and beamed. "That house represented everything evil in my life."

Dixie turned to him. "Adam?"

"Well, not all evil—not lately. But it's where everything wicked started for me and my family; where the Alpha beat my siblings; where we were taught to kill. I'm glad the house is gone. I never want to come back here. Ever."

Colonel Dayton cleared his throat. "Jayed, you said a voice told you to go back to the lake. Do you know who that was; who might have done this?"

She closed her eyes, taking her time to answer. "Dixie mentioned your friend being killed by a Fiend. The voice in my head, urging me back to the lake while I traveled to the new Gateway, was not The Devil. The Devil himself helped me escape, showed me the way, and garnered my payment." She opened her eyes, staring at Adam. "The Devil told me to save the canine.

And I did. I performed everything he entrusted to me. No, the voice I heard tonight was not The Devil. The voice sounded like a Fiend…it could be your Fiend."

"That makes sense," Marco said.

Colonel Dayton stared at him. "Meaning?"

"Meaning," Dixie spoke up, her eyes bright with excitement, "it appears, for whatever reason, we've identified the true evil in all this: the Fiend. We've also seemed to have picked up an unusual ally: The Devil."

"It makes sense," Jayed said, "for reasons that are yet unclear; The Devil seems to want the new Gateway to remain closed."

"Well, there must be some rhyme, or story, or thousand-year-old curse that can explain it all," Adam said. "I just don't know if we have the time to figure it out right now. We should get going."

"You're right," Marco said, "We don't have the time. But, I'll bet there's someone who already knows; I'd stake my career on it."

"The Mystic?" Colonel Dayton said.

Marco winked. "Bingo."

"So," Charlie Nguyen said, "The Fiend wants this new Gateway from Hell to our world, and The Devil does not. But if the thing's already built—"

"Built yes." Jayed spoke up. "And tested—I am proof. But not opened; not with ceremony and celebration. That's what you're for." She turned to Adam. "And the human. You were sacrifices for the opening."

"Sacrificed by who?"

Jayed glanced at Dixie. "The Treasure."

Dixie sucked in a large scoop of air.

"What is it?" Adam said, his arms folding around

her.

She whimpered. "I wasn't listening. I heard what he said, but I just wasn't listening."

"Who?" Colonel Dayton said.

"The Mystic. When Adam and I went to see him, remember? He wanted something in return for lifting the canine curse from me. He mentioned something about a consecration, or veneration...some kind of cleansing."

Jayed stiffened. "The old traditions."

Adam shifted in his seat. "Would you please tell me what—"

Dixie wiggled free from Adam's embrace. "The Gateway can't be opened—can't be fully used—until the site is made clean. That requires a sacrifice."

"How do you know?" Adam asked.

"You know, as well as I do, my darling. You learned during The Sufferings. Think. Three sacrifices are needed to cleanse any unearthly site: one true human, one true love, and one true kin."

Adam recoiled, his face twisting. "We know Hudson was chosen as the human, and I can only hope I'm the love. What about the kin?"

Dixie took his hand, placing it on her belly. "And one true kin."

Colonel Dayton turned the key bringing the engine to life. He navigated the vehicle across the hill to the gravel road. They passed the fiery remains of Adam's house, and made their way down the steep grade to a paved road. The steady glow of Las Vegas burned ahead. He turned to Marco who sat in the passenger's seat. "Exactly what do you know about this Mystic fellow?"

"Perhaps, I can better answer that question, Colonel," Jayed said.

Chapter Nineteen

Colonel Dayton maneuvers the van down Claremont Drive for, what I can only hope is, the final time. I will miss nothing about my smoldering house. The rusted wire cages in the basement where my siblings and I were "disciplined;" the human body parts buried in the backyard, to be found later by police; a savage battle against the unholy *Sangre di Real* Daemons. All of it needs to stay here, behind me. But I hope to never forget the final resting place of Cutty and Tina who joined the fight against evil, found each other, and lost their lives. This is my home, my legacy, and I'm more than ready to be done with it forever.

Dayton guides the van around a sharp turn at the bottom of the hill. He's alert and wide eyed, scanning the area for anyone, or anything, blocking our path. We roll off the bumpy gravel and onto a paved road that's not much smoother. Traffic on the I-15 North moves fast and free this early in the morning. Dayton merges onto the highway, keeping a sharp lookout for any suspicious activity in the rearview mirror.

No one in the van expresses any regret about leaving Claremont, even though none of us knows exactly where we're going. I've found having no certain destination can sometimes be better than knowing what waits at the end of the line. And so, I lean back and enjoy the ride, hoping the colonel suppresses his race car driver instincts.

"Brilliant," he says over his shoulder to Jayed as he jumps into the fast lane and steps on the accelerator. "Tell me what you know about The Mystic."

Jayed straightens. She sits directly behind the colonel but still has to raise her voice above the roar of the engine. "As soon as I stepped from the Gateway, I was summoned to The Mystic's chambers. The moment I saw him, I knew it would be a very unpleasant meeting."

Colonel Dayton swerves around a slower vehicle, then back into the fast lane, an operation that leaves my stomach somewhere on the highway's soft shoulder. His high-speed antics only seem to whet his appetite for composed conversation. "Tell us what happened at that meeting."

"Apparently, he'd gone to quite some trouble binding the canine and the older man to the threshold of The Gateway. He was extremely upset at me for releasing them."

I don't like the way she keeps calling me "the canine." It reminds me of when Dayton used to call me "the mutt." I really like Jayed, but I have to put a stop to this right now. "My name is Adam; not the canine."

She bows her head. "And so it is. I apologize, Adam. I mean no disrespect. My point is to convey how *they* feel about you, not I."

Colonel Dayton says, "They?"

"Yes, the Mystic and his associate, the Fiend."

Dixie leaps into the conversation. "You actually met with them both?"

"As I said, the meeting was not pleasant, not in the least. The Fiend voiced his hatred of me for releasing the sacrificial subjects. He said he would kill me for this unforgiveable act. At that moment, he raised his hands. I can only assume his intention was to evoke the curse of death."

I close my eyes, not chancing a glance at the speedometer. The last time I looked, the desert was a blur whizzing by us on both sides. I don't do well with speed and vehicles, or vehicles and speed. A human saying flashes through my mind, something about being a live coward instead of a dead hero. That doesn't help.

Calm down, Adam. Everything's fine. The colonel knows how to handle himself behind the wheel of a car. Dixie's right, of course, the colonel is an expert driver. Her thoughts ease my fears. She slips her hand in mine—that helps as well.

"What happened next?" Dayton asks in a relaxed voice, as he keeps his foot jammed on the gas.

Jayed giggles. "My benefactor, The Devil, spoke in a voice I can only describe as towering. The Mystic trembled; in fact, I thought he would faint. The Fiend could not lower his hands fast enough."

"What did The Devil say?"

Jayed clears her throat, and lowers her voice, speaking with a smile painted across her lips, "You shall not harm this girl. All violators will be prosecuted to the fullest extent of the law."

"No," Charlie Nguyen shouts above the clamor. "He would never say that."

"'Tis true," Jayed says. "The Devil has a sense of humor; something not many know about the supreme ruler of the underworld."

Nguyen huffs as she glances out the window and gnaws on a fingernail. "Bah!" She vanishes in a cloud of golden mist.

Colonel Dayton doesn't miss a beat. "What happened next?"

"They had no choice; they ordered me to leave at once and never return." A wry smile grows on her full lips. "Now I can't wait to see them both."

"That's the girl," Colonel Dayton says. He takes the Tropicana exit and turns right on Las Vegas Boulevard.

Neon signs wage their final battle against the coming sunrise; tourists fill walkways and bridge-ways in search of the best breakfast deals; traffic gridlock clogs the artery known as The Strip, as it does every day of the week. It's a relief to be off the freeway and stuck behind rubber-necking tourists for a change. I'm about to ask the colonel where he's headed when he makes a sharp right onto the drive leading to the Mandalay Bay Resort and Casino.

"I can't wait to meet them myself," Dayton says, "but first, we need to regroup. How about a night off, courtesy of the United Nations?"

"Can you do that?" Marco asks.

"Definitely." He smiles as he turns into the shade of the parking garage. "As an investigator for UNPAD, I'm allowed carte blanch should I stumble across anything…unusual. And from what I've heard, The Mystic and his associate, the Fiend, certainly fit the bill. Agreed?"

Marco whistles. "You must have one hell of a budget."

"Absolutely. It's all off the books, of course; basically unlimited."

Marco shakes his head. "Unlimited? Shit, you think

you could toss a little of that unlimited budget my way? Metro sure could use it."

I feel a collective sigh of relief purge the tension in the vehicle as small talk fills the van. The mood is upbeat. I also notice Jayed's gaze resting on Marco Ramirez. If I didn't know better, I'd say she carried a torch for him (a human saying, but I believe it covers Witches, as well).

We have a powerful ally in Colonel Jon Dayton. He parks the van, kills the engine, and turns back to face Jayed, Dixie, and me. With a wink and a smile, he assures us everything's going to be okay.

How could he have known his words would soon be nothing but an empty promise?

****

Dixie rolled her head from side to side, her eyes opening in stages as she attempted to focus on anything. Her blurry vision felt like looking through soap-smeared glasses. A massive headache sending shooting pains through her temples and into the base of her neck brought waves of nausea. Her mouth was desert dry, her throat parched, as if filled with sand. Trying to lift her head from the cool comfort of the pillow was as likely as running a 5k—not happening.

"Ah, Miss Mulholland," a cold and uncaring voice crawled into her ears, "welcome back to the land of the living. You must have a few questions for me."

The voice was familiar, but the jackhammer of a headache took priority over everything else. A vise-like grip threatening to crush her brain like a grape terrified her. Even though the room felt quiet and calm, her level of panic grew with each passing moment. She ached to crawl back into the bliss of carefree sleep. Her trembling hands perched atop her abdomen as she thought of the baby.

"The baby's fine, Miss Mulholland, don't worry about that. After all, we can't have anything happen to the baby, can we? Now then, you're probably wondering why I brought you here. Go ahead, move your mouth and make the sounds…why am I here?"

How to answer: a nod would intensify the kettledrum banging, full force, in her brain; words were impossible as well. She formed a telepathic thought, pushing it through her conscious, but it collapsed into a jumbled heap of questions and panic: *Who are you? Where am I? What did you do to me? Where's Adam? Why?*

"Oh my, what a mess you are. Here, let me remove some of your pain…not too much; wouldn't want you to overpower me." He laughed. No, not quite a laugh, more of a bellow, like the braying of a mule.

Shock buzzed through her senses. *You're the Miscreant.*

Ha! His return thoughts penetrated her mind like creepy-crawly bugs. *Very good, Miss Mulholland, very good. You knew me as a Miscreant: friendly, fun loving, and quite frisky, especially with your friend, Miss Nguyen. Let me re-introduce myself. My friends, of which I have none, know me as Adrian Gray, the Fiend.*

Fiends were nearly incapable of being stopped, in either their thoughts, or their actions; they were said to be immortal. She tried recalling any weaknesses Fiends might have—there *were* a few, but not many, and not fatal.

Finding it impossible to block her thoughts, she decided to mask them by concentrating on him. *Fiends are just one step below The Devil himself, the most dominant force of evil in the entire universe.*

Ha! The Devil's a joke compared to the likes of me, and you're going to help me prove that fact, once and for all. He grew silent, then smirked. *Yes, Miss Mulholland, I'm not afraid to admit I do have a few basic weaknesses; nothing you're in any shape to tackle at the moment.*

Dixie calmed herself, making a conscious effort to sooth the pain from her body. She had to get him out of her mind, to establish verbal communication with this…thing. Another second of his thoughts running loose in her mind was unacceptable. She spoke in a halting, sorrowful voice, "Be careful what you say. Aren't you afraid The Devil will hear you?"

"Bravo…she speaks! No, Miss Mulholland, as a matter of fact, He can't hear us. He doesn't even know where we are. This is, after all, hallowed ground."

"Native land?"

"No, silly girl, even better. We're inside the Black Canyon—the Sauna Cave, to be exact. He has no way of eavesdropping on our conversation here. So, please, say what's on your mind." He snickered. "Don't be afraid."

"I'm not the one who should be afraid. What do you want from me, and where's Adam?"

"The dog," he shot back, "you and that damned dog."

"Wolfhound."

He took a breath. "Do you know I'm the one who instructed The Mystic to remove that horrible canine curse from you? No, I suppose you don't. And what thanks did I get? None. Instead, you've done your best

165

to meddle in my affairs. Well, the time for meddling has come to an end." He approached, paused, and bent over her, glaring into her eyes. "Pay attention, Miss Mulholland. This is where you ask what I want."

She forced the words out. "What do you want?"

"Very good. Oh, just a small sacrifice on your part." He clasped his hands behind his back and ambled away from her as he spoke. "Well, three small sacrifices, actually. A simple request for such a powerful Daemon." He turned and glared at her.

Dixie felt her stomach curdle. She returned his hard stare while concentrating on the volcanic ash of the Black Canyon, the crystalline walls of Sauna Cave…and Tina.

He snorted. "What's the matter, cat got your tongue?"

She wasted no time in sending her thoughts directly to Charlie Nguyen. According to The Sufferings, unlike native land, volcanic ash could only block evil eavesdropping. All others could send and receive thoughts at will. *Thank you, Sufferings.*

"What was that?" Adrian asked. "I said cat got your tongue?"

Dixie screamed into his mind, as loud as she could. *Meow.*

The word washed through his head with the power of a tsunami, confusing him for a split second—she hoped it was all the time they needed.

Charlie Nguyen stepped from a golden cloud, waving her hands in the air. "*Imobili.*" The Fiend spun around, his hands posed to block the curse. A puzzled expression played across his face

A red cloud shot up across from Nguyen. As it

dissipated, Adam materialized. He stood on the other side of The Fiend, hands in the air. "*Imobili.*"

Adrian whirled around, raising his hands against Adam's curse.

Dixie lifted an arm in the Fiend's direction. "*Imobili,*" she coughed out in a hoarse whisper, not knowing if the curse would have any effect. It did. Adrian spun to block her spell.

"*Imobili!*" Nguyen yelled, forcing the creature to spin again.

"*Imobili!*" Adam barked.

"*Imobili!*" Dixie said.

Adrian slowed, as if an image caught in a malfunctioning projector.

Charlie Nguyen edged forward and spit in the Fiend's face. "Fuck you, jerk shit." She turned to the others and smiled. "Serves the bastard right for taking advantage of my sweet nature and tender heart."

Adam rushed to Dixie's side. "Great directions, sweetie. Sorry we took so long."

She beamed. "You tele transported, I didn't think you—"

"Shhh. Save your strength. I'll get you out of here."

"That was fun," Nguyen said, "using this piece of shit like a ping pong ball. Did you see him twist and turn?" A moan echoed through the cave. "He's coming out of it." She turned back to him. "Oh, and by the way, just so you know Adrian, my dear, I've had much better than you." She disappeared in an explosion of golden mist.

Adam scooped Dixie off the bed, holding her close. Together, they burst into a red mist, vanishing as one.

Chapter Twenty

My heart pounds, breathing hurried, and blood pressure sky-high. I can almost feel the oil slick known as adrenalin coat every muscle in my body. I just helped rescue Dixie from the Fiend, and learned a few things about myself along the way. Materializing, tele transporting, and re-materializing is a flat-out rush, like a drug—the bad illegal kind I've only seen in movies. My Daemon color is red, which is cool, because it's my favorite color. My scent is rain, which is just cool all by itself. I also discover I have amazing telepathic skills, and my knowledge of all things unearthly is astonishing. But the best part is my personal skillset is something called a redirection spell. Wow…me. I have my own personal spell!

A redirection spell means I can broadcast my presence anywhere I want, sending possible predators on any number of wild goose chases. I can extend this skill, like an umbrella, over those I chose to conceal, as well. Perfect. I try explaining this to Dixie, but because I'm so excited, it comes out rushed, like I'm speaking nonsense.

"Whoa, calm down, Adam. You'll hyperventilate." Dixie's color returns to her face. She sits in the back of the van at the Mandalay Bay parking garage. The dark garage is filled with vehicles, but void of people. "I know exactly what you're going through. I felt the same way just last year. My powers came to me all at once, because I'm full Daemon. You're not only part Daemon, but also Wolfhound and human, so I guess it took a little while for your Daemon powers to manifest. That's my best guess, anyway."

I nod, as if what she just said makes any sense.

Charlie Nguyen sits in the front passenger's seat of the van, smiling to herself. I take a short walk through her thoughts and see her replay her confrontation with the Fiend, telling him off and spitting in his face. Revenge lights up her brain.

The colonel and Marco whisper to each other a few yards away. They're discussing whether we should stay here at the Mandalay Bay Hotel, or find another place to lie low.

Dixie tugs on my shirt to get my attention. "Hey, where are you?"

"I'm okay," I tell her. "I just can't believe what a buzz all this Daemon stuff is. It's over the top. It's, it's…bonza."

With a wince, she says, "You need to slow down a little; let everything soak in, and get used to it—learn how it works. You need time to think, do you know what I mean?"

"Sure." I close my eyes and think about Casablanca, which is in Morocco. I've always wanted to go there. After all, it's my favorite movie of all time. And just like that, I'm standing on Boulevard Lamartine. I know, because I see the street sign on the corner. Somebody's cooking meat and it smells wonderful. I'm certain this is where Rick's Café Américain would have been located…if the movie were real. In any case, the city itself is real, and I can't stop grinning as I breathe in the fresh bar-b-que aroma and marvel at the fact I got here in a nano-second. Life is good.

I bolt back to the Mandalay Bay parking garage and give Dixie a huge bear hug. "I just went to Casablanca. It's my favorite movie."

She puts her hands on my shoulders, closes her eyes, and invites me into her mind. I dive in, eyes wide open.

She sends me a glimpse of the netherworld. We stand on a hill. Below us, billions of lost souls scream and cry as they wade through the Lake of Fire. One man sits on a hill above them all. The souls belong to him. It's his job to make certain they suffer, and he does his job well. The man is the embodiment of evil; he was born to play this role. His face is hidden from me. Dixie takes me by the hand and we edge closer. I draw in a breath and step back when I recognize him: Adrian Gray.

"That's who you rescued me from," Dixie says, bringing me back to reality. "I know you; I know you love the new powers you have. But you have to focus. We have a job to do; a job all creation needs us to handle. I entered the Fiend's mind; I saw terrible things. If we fail to take him down, the Lake of Fire and its tenants will belong to him. As it is, the lake is no picnic, but imagine the extreme torture he'll inflict if he's ever allowed full rein."

I am distressed. More than that, panicked. She senses my emotions and wraps her arms around me. "Oh, sweetie, that's a lot to put on you, but you're not alone. We can handle it—together. Between us we can stop that jerk and destroy this new Gateway, I know we can."

I'm silent for a few moments. I don't have to think about what she's just said—I know she's right. Roaming the world by tele transporting will have to wait. I have to concentrate and formulate a plan of attack.

She snorts. "You don't have to do it all, sweetie. That's why each of us is here. We each have our own skillsets. Colonel Dayton is a master strategist. He'll formulate a solid plan of attack. We have to work as a team like we did today to take down the Fiend. You helped rescue me...you were great."

I lean in and kiss her cheek. "That was the first spell I've ever cast. Not bad, huh?" I can't help bragging; casting spells, tele transporting—all of it is intoxicating.

"Not bad at all." She sends me her thoughts. *Why don't you talk to the colonel?*

She's exhausted, probably too tired to speak. She needs rest. I stroke her hair, trying to make her feel at ease. "Will do. Be right back."

At first, the colonel is reluctant to stay at the same place where Adrian waylaid us. He insists on finding a new location.

Marco agrees, telling me he's seen too many protective details go south once a location's been made. "With over sixty-thousand rooms in Vegas, it won't be too hard to find someplace else to stay."

I raise my voice. "You have to trust me. Everything Dixie knows as a Daemon is inside me as well. I acquired the skills during The Suffering. I also have an extra skillset. I know where I fit in now. Listen, the only reason Dixie was taken off guard earlier was because she had no idea who was after us. Well, that's changed."

They're listening, a good sign. "What kind of extra skillset?"

"It's called redirection. Apparently, it's 'my thing.' I can easily set up a spell, masking our location from the Fiend so we can grab a few hours' sleep—Dixie really needs it. We all do."

The colonel takes his time, but finally nods at Marco and turns to me. "Okay. But tell me something first. You said you know where you fit in. What does that even mean?"

"Hard to explain. It's like something just clicked. We're fighting something now that's truly evil; more than a legion of *Sangre di Real*; more than Gorgeous and her Convergence cronies—this is end-of-the-world-type stuff. I know, if we keep our cool, and work this through logically, we'll come out on top. I truly believe good will conquer evil in the end—it has to, otherwise what's the point?"

The hospitality suite at the Mandalay Bay Hotel Casino and Resort is amazing, and all it costs the colonel is a few minutes on the telephone with his superior.

"Yes sir, something called a Fiend. I couldn't agree more. It's the craziest coincidence. I know. Will do, oh, and thanks for the suite. Yes, I can vouch for them personally; some law enforcement friends I met here during the Werewolf Killer business. No, not at this time, I think we have things pretty much under control. Will do."

Colonel Dayton hangs up, and turns to us. "On behalf of UNPAD, may I be the first to say thank you for your service," he says with a wry smile.

"What do you mean?" I ask.

"The admiral wants me to thank you for your help. Unbeknownst to him, he's really thanking two Daemons, a shape shifter, and a..." He turns to Jayed. "By the way, what exactly are you, my dear? Another Daemon, a Banshee—"

"I'm a Witch."

Charlie Nguyen seems mildly interested. "The human variety?"

"Certainly not," Jayed says, "you mistake me for Pagan. I am of the universe."

"I still don't understand the difference."

The colonel laughs out loud, a deep rumbling sound that grabs my attention. "A Witch, you say. I doubt Admiral Garrison would be keen to learn the United Nations Paranormal Activities Division is putting this lot up for the night. In any case, as I said, I'd like to thank each and every one of you for your service."

Marco turns to Jayed. "A Witch? There must be a story attached to that."

She winks at him and smiles. "Many, actually."

****

The moonless night, one day before Halloween, presented various opportunities for differing souls. The promise of a late season monsoon sweeping across the valley helped some enter restful slumber, while thundering gusts of desert wind banging against windows kept others awake.

Marco and Jayed lingered in the main living area, enjoying the warmth of a crackling fire. Colonel Dayton waved goodnight, ascending the stairs in search of a bed. Adam and Dixie disappeared, hand in hand, down a long hallway, her head resting on his shoulder. Charlie Nguyen simply vanished, dissolving in a cloud of golden mist.

"Alone at last," Marco said as he eased back into the comfort of a gray leather couch facing the fire.

"Is that what you wish? For us to be alone together?" Jayed sat next to him, less than an a few inches away.

"Just a little humor, a line from…well, I don't know what it's from actually." He turned to face her and scooted back, creating distance between them in the process.

"Are you uncomfortable with me?"

He shrugged. He'd felt her eyes on him earlier (how could he not), and was flattered. And now, with rain pelting the windows and the fireplace warming his bones, he relaxed. Her smile and inquiring eyes invited conversation. "It's funny, I'm not a very trusting soul—twelve years on the job can do that. Anyway, I barely know you but I have to admit, I really feel—what is the word—comfortable around you."

Jayed blushed, only a little, but enough.

He smiled. "Do you mind if we talk?"

"What shall we discuss?"

He stretched his legs out. "It's been a long time since I spoke to anyone without having to look over my shoulder."

"I don't understand."

"Well, what I mean is, everything I know about your world requires a certain degree of secrecy in mine."

With a wry smile, she said, "It's the same world, is

it not?"

"True. It is, but it's so different. For instance, in your world mind reading is commonplace. In mine, it's the exception to the rule."

"And why do you think that is?"

"I guess humans aren't as in tune as you are."

She reached for his hand. He withdrew. "Relax." She held his hand with a warm and gentle touch. "Now then, close your eyes and clear your mind."

He did as she asked. "I should warn you, I'm not a very good subject—"

I disagree. Your mind is highly receptive.

Her thoughts entered his mind as clear as if she whispered in his ear. "Wow, that's amazing. I never—"

She placed a finger to his lips. *Speak with your mind...project your thoughts.*

I don't know what to say...er, uh what to think...I mean, this is fantastic. What an amazing interrogation tool.

She smiled, a broad grin, the glow of the fire dancing in her eyes. *You see, our worlds aren't all that different, are they?*

He laughed. "I guess not, up to a point."

"How so?"

"Well, there's a whole world humans know nothing about, and for whatever reason, I'm lucky enough to be a part of it. It's incredible, but not without its dangers."

"Are you frightened?"

"Not in the least. I love it. Most of it, anyway. I don't like the part where a spoken word can end me, or an evil being can appear out of nowhere; but I do love the magic, and the spells, and your eyes—"

"What?"

"Uh, I mean, I really enjoy being with you and speaking openly."

"As do I. What else shall we discuss?"

He sighed. "I guess I want to know everything, I suppose. For instance, how did you become a Witch?"

She laughed, a deep, heart-felt sound filling the room with a joy he knew he'd never forget. "What's so funny?"

"Answer me this: how did you become a human?"

"I see your point. I guess I just want to know more about you."

She gave him a hurried, yet brilliant smile. "Very well, I'm an only child. My parents raised me in traditional spellcraft. They were quite spiritual and, naturally, passed along their beliefs. We lived just south of what you now call Red Rock Canyon. At that time, we knew it as Red Rock Coven. We believed we were far enough from civilization—a distance we thought safe."

"Safe from what?"

Her expression changed. "Humans." As she spoke, images filled his mind. Her words flowing through his head, as if watching a movie through her eyes.

"We enjoyed the isolation of the canyon. Seclusion was our security. If anyone wandered onto our land, we befuddled their minds with a simple disremember spell—a spell to make someone forget whatever we chose—and sent them on their way. I had an ideal childhood. We worshipped the seasons, and lived modestly. I practiced my craft and learned it well, so well, in fact, I became a teacher. At the age of twenty, I'd mastered most spells." Her voice faltered. "I'd also been promised to a young Warlock. We were in love…true love. Have you ever been?"

He opened his eyes. "Once, a lifetime ago."

"You may say what's on your mind. Don't worry, Marco, I'll never enter your thoughts without permission."

His heartbeat raced at hearing his name on her lips. He lowered his guard. "Dixie and I were once involved…in love." After a moment, he said, "Anyway that was a long time ago. I'm happy for her now—for what she and Adam have. Tell me more about your life."

Jayed nodded. Her eyes told him she understood. "As I say, my skills were first-rate. There were few spells I could not create, and fewer curses I could not unravel. I was soon to be married. Times were ideal."

He lay his hand on hers. "Sounds perfect."

"Truly—until, one night, the Huntsmen came."

"Huntsmen?"

"Human hunters bent on ridding the world of anything…beyond their understanding. They called it cleansing, but it was murder. Fire and brimstone, beheadings and torture. The Huntsmen used talismans and tokens, as shields against our spells. Many of my kind died horrible deaths that night. A lucky few—very few—ran, turning to the vast desert for refuge. I had not yet perfected my vanishing spell." A tear rolled down her cheek.

Marco wiped at it as he slipped his arm over her shoulder. She snuggled against him. He examined the tiny drop of liquid on his finger. "Your tears are turquoise. How is that possible?"

She swallowed hard, and kept her silence. A quick

flash of lightning brightened the room followed by a distant rumble of thunder.

Their closeness allowed him to ask, "How did you die?"

In a whisper, she said, "Burned alive at the stake."

He grimaced. "How barbaric."

"True." She attempted a grin. "Out in a blaze of glory." After a deep breath, she said, "The Lake of Fire became my home, as it is with most of my kind."

"But The Devil offered you a way out."

Another brilliant smile seemed to erase her pain. "And I met you."

"You know, my *abuelita* in Guatemala believed in witchcraft. She wrote to me on occasion, telling me tales of the shamans, particularly a tribe of descendants from the Mayan culture. Of course, I read her letters with a grain of salt; a natural born skeptic."

"The *Chamanes* of the Witches Cave."

Marco's eyes widened. "That's right, but how could you possible know about—"

"It's part of my culture; my history."

He breathed her in and ran his fingers across the top of her hand. He wanted more; he wanted to stay with her through the night. "It's late," he said, as he bent forward, "You're probably tired." She placed a hand on his shoulder, holding him back. "Jayed, I don't think we should get too—"

"If you ask me, I think you think too much."

He eased back into the comfort of the couch, gazing into her eyes. "They're not blue, are they?"

"No. Can you guess the color?"

Marco leaned in, fascinated. The nearer to her, the faster his heart beat.

Rain fell in a torrent. Her lips brushed against his as her thoughts entered his mind. *I love storms, don't you?*

I do now.

Chapter Twenty-One

The Mystic sat in silent yoga pose, his chambers cool and dark. His breathing came and went in a slow and steady rhythm; his eyes half closed, as if in a trance. He seemed in complete control; the final stage of meditation nearly achieved: evenness of mind, and balance of spirit. Equanimity. All was right with the world, except for his one little tell, sweat.

It coated his brow, dribbled down his cheeks, and fell to his lap like rain. He'd done everything Adrian Gray asked. It wasn't his fault The Devil interceded. Oh, he knew it would happen, as he'd divined, but that didn't make it his fault, did it?

Now Adrian promised retribution. For what? It wasn't his fault!

"Sir." Ayala's songbird voice brought him out of meditation.

Her beautiful face greeted him as he opened his eyes. He had to find a way to convince her of his plan. It went against everything a Banshee stood for, but he'd crunched the numbers, ran the data; it was his only way out. "Ayala, thank you for seeing me. I hope I didn't disturb you."

She cocked her head and scrunched her brow. "Sir, as you wish."

The Mystic levitated from the chair and frowned as his feet touched the floor. Reaching behind him, he massaged his back. "Ha, getting too old for yoga, I suppose. In any case, my dear, can I get you some tea? No? Something to eat, perhaps? Please, have a seat." He motioned to the chair facing his. They both sat. He exaggerated a moan.

"I'm told you may miss your performance tonight," she said.

He said nothing, instead reaching across and touching her shoulder.

She smiled. "Is there anything I can do to make you feel better?"

"Ayala, we must travel to the other side."

"Sir? I don't know what…"

In a moment, her expression changed from one of curiosity, to that of an assured, self-confident associate. This was the side of her only he could summon at will, the side of her that lay dormant in the human world: the Banshee.

"Ayala, there's something I must speak to you about."

"Is it about last night? Sir, I wish to explain, I just—"

"No, not last night. Far from it. I need you to listen very carefully to what I'm about to say."

She bowed her head. "I live to serve. Ask, and it shall be done."

"Scream."

"My lord?"

"Scream…the Banshee cry. Announce to all the worlds, above and below, that I'm dead. This is what I ask."

"Sir, you know, better than most, this, I cannot do."

"Of course you can. Open your mouth and scream.

It's a simple request."

Ayala bowed her head, examining the ground. "Sir, I simply cannot—"

"Listen to me." His tone marked the seriousness of the request. "I've gotten myself into a little…what's the term? Oh yes, I'm in a little jam; a tight spot; a difficult circumstance. You see, if you don't scream, proclaiming my death to the world, as is your duty when I actually do, you know, croak—"

"Croak?"

"You know, kick the bucket, bite the dust, give up the ghost…oh hell, when I die. You've got to scream when I die—it's your duty."

"But, sir—"

"Believe me, the false death I want you to announce with your scream will surely become a reality if you don't. Now which do you prefer, my dear: a fake scream, or a real death?"

"My lord," Ayala said, standing and clasping her hands together, "it simply does not work that way. The Banshee's Scream of Death is sacred. If I break my vow, the consequences are devastating. It's forbidden."

"Times are changing, sweet girl. Is it not forbidden for a Daemon to kill another Daemon? Yet, Dixie Mulholland did that very deed only a few months ago. The world is full of rules waiting to be broken."

"And look what happened to her as punishment."

"Yes, the canine curse—something I removed from her as easily as…well, no harm, no foul, yes?"

She spun away from him.

Obviously, from the trembling of her shoulders the poor girl was crying. The Mystic trundled forward, placing a hand on her back. He sent soothing relief through his fingers and into her being. She calmed at once. "My dear, I would never ask you to do anything that makes you uncomfortable, or gets you into any kind of trouble, you know that. But in this case, it truly is a matter of life and death—my life, my death."

She turned slowly, soon standing eye to eye with him. "In all of history, my kind have never issued a counterfeit scream. Never."

His lip quivered, he hated when that happened, so he rubbed a hand across his mouth in an effort to halt the nervous tick. "My love, you're my last hope. Adrian has me in his crosshairs; I know he's coming for me…I see it. He plans to kill me this very night. I've cancelled my performance—I've never done that, not in three years running." He took her hands in his and attempted a smile. "Let's look at this logically, shall we? If I leave Las Vegas and hide from him, he would find me. You know it's true."

She nodded.

"You also know if I offered him riches in place of a pound of flesh…" He shook his head and made a tsk-tsk sound. "Not an option. He cares not for gold or silver. He seeks revenge. He believes I defaulted on our pact, which I *have not,* and so vengeance is the only thing he pursues. The only act which will cancel his bloodlust is my death."

"Sir, what you ask is…difficult."

"Difficult. Difficult is good, it's not impossible, is it? I can work with difficult."

"What I mean is—"

"Shhh." The lights in the chamber flickered. The Mystic felt a dark presence shroud the once peaceful atmosphere. In a whisper, he said, "He's here. In five seconds, Adrian Gray will stand in this very room. My life is in your hands. Please, dear girl, I beg you…" He disappeared around a corner.

"My lord, where are you going?" She rushed after him.

"Please, all I ask is this one small favor." He stuffed himself into an opening in the wall. The dumb waiter held his weight. A cramped space, but a perfect escape hatch. "Lower me to the bottom floor. Hurry."

She shut the access door and touched the "down" button.

The Mystic sent his aura back to the chamber, keeping abreast of the situation as his physical body descended to the first floor.

The lights in the chamber flickered. Sudden heaviness filled the air, like the still before the storm.

Ayala paced back and forth, hands on her hips. She shouted out, "My lord, please don't do this to me. My lord?" Silence. Her pace quickened as she gasped for air. After a considerable inhale, she opened her mouth, balled her hands into fists, and released the Banshee's Scream.

The glass wall of water in the chamber shuddered, sending droplets cascading about the room. As was her sacred duty, Ayala's scream announced to the underworld the death of The Mystic.

Adrian appeared on a black cloud of billowing smoke. He rushed to Ayala's side, grasping her arms in a vise-like grip. "When?"

"Just now, my lord."

"How?"

"He took his own life. He…"

"Where's the coward's body?"

"Claimed by the Boatmen."

"So soon?" He stared into her eyes, then released his hold. He stood, as if frozen for more than a few seconds. Finally, with a "Bah!" he vanished.

Ayala dropped to her knees, head buried in her hands, shedding tears as if the world had ended.

Poor girl, The Mystic thought, knowing he dare not invade her thoughts.

My poor, sweet Ayala.

****

As we pick at the offerings from the room service tray, Dixie turns on the TV, changing the station to channel six. She glances at her watch and furrows her brow. "This isn't right; it's too late for the morning news."

Images crawl across the screen in a gruesome horror slideshow: a fire on the top floor of the Galaxy Hotel and Casino claiming dozens of lives; a collapsed pedestrian bridge over The Strip taking many more; a gas explosion just west of downtown Las Vegas destroying several city blocks; an incoming flight at McCarran Airport skidding out of control past the end of the runway; a tourist bus crash on the I-15; heavy rain and flash floods in North Las Vegas threatening hundreds.

The bad news keeps coming. I didn't think it could get any worse until I hear the announcement of the Silver Bowl collapse. I remember the Aussies, laughing and playing at the Welcome to Las Vegas sign and my heart drops.

On the screen, Peter Hudson sits behind his anchor desk, reading news copy in a halting tone, as if he can't quite grasp the words on the teleprompter. "As unbelievable as it may sound, all these incidents, seem to have begun simultaneously. We've also received reports of hundreds of traffic accidents on U.S. 95, and the 215. Many fatalities are confirmed. We have..." Hudson grabbed a piece of paper handed to him from off camera. "This just in: a reported fire on the campus of UNLV. At this time, we don't know exactly what buildings are involved or if there are any casualties. What we do know, however, is it's a six-alarm blaze. Eastern Avenue, from Flamingo to the Trop is closed. We're still awaiting official word from Metro regarding their response...uh, if this is a terrorist event, or...what have you. As you can imagine, resources are stretched to the limit by the magnitude of this catastrophe."

Marco is visibly shaken. He tosses his glass of orange juice into the sink and reaches for his cell phone.

"What are you doing?" Colonel Dayton asks.

"They need me."

"We need you."

Ramirez ignores the comment and continues to dial.

"Hang up," the colonel says. "It's obvious, at least to me, these events are all intended to get our attention. I have little doubt they're the work of Adrian Gray. There's nothing you can do in your official capacity with Metro to stop him."

"I need to try."

"The colonel's right," Dixie says. "Metro has enough hands onboard. They can take care of this without you—but we can't."

Ramirez lowers the phone and glances at Jayed. She nods. He slips the phone back into his pocket.

Jayed rushes to his side, folding her arms around him.

"Good choice, Marco." I put my hand on his shoulder. The expression on his face tells me the decision tears him apart. I know how much he cares about "his" city, and he'd do anything to protect it.

But from what? According to the colonel, the Fiend is behind the mayhem. He thinks Adrian's trying to get our attention. Well, he's got it. Now what?

The building shudders, accompanied by an awful crunching sound. I feel like I'm trying to keep my balance aboard a ship at sea. The others crouch down and stare at the walls. It's an earthquake. Cupboards pop open in the kitchen, sending glassware crashing to the floor. A window cracks behind me. The rumbling settles down after what seems like an eternity.

"I'll contact the admiral," Dayton says, "and arrange for some relief, some protection from whatever's happening out there. In the meantime, stay calm. We need to formulate a plan of action; something that'll get Adrian to stop terrorizing the city."

This seems to satisfy Marco. He rights two fallen chairs. Jayed takes a seat, with Marco standing behind her, hands on her shoulders.

Colonel Dayton's sharp words on his cell phone reverberate through the room. "Yes, sir. Something called a Fiend. I can't go into the details at this time; suffice to say events in Las Vegas are directly related to this creature; part of a plan to open a Gateway from this world to the next. I need you to request activation of the National Guard; troops are needed on the ground. Then put a curfew into effect to keep the population out of harm's way."

"The city needs to be evacuated," Marco says, "and

sealed—nobody else in."

The colonel's voice grows softer as he walks from the dining room and through the kitchen, away from us. Every once in a while, a loud word or two echoes through the suite: weapons...panic...Devil, but not enough to piece together the conversation. I sidle next to Dixie, placing my arm around her waist. She reciprocates at once.

More bad news spills from Peter Hudson on TV. I keep my gaze trained on Marco. His head shakes from side to side as he watches the newscast. Jayed, seated beside him, raises a finger and the television goes dark.

"What did you do?" he asks her. "Put it back on."

"I will not. It distresses you. We know who's behind the disorder, and the colonel's right, we need to remain calm and formulate a plan."

Golden mist fills the dining room as Charlie Nguyen materializes. Her breath is uneven. She stares at us through blank eyes, as if she's in a trance. All at once, she collapses to the ground. Dixie and I help her up and into the empty chair next to Jayed.

"What's wrong?" Dixie asks. "Are you okay?"

After a few moments, Nguyen speaks in a halting voce, "Adrian...caught me—grabbed my hand—I got away, just in time. It hurts so much." She leans forward and places her hand on the table.

Dixie screams. Charlie's hand looks like a piece of raw hamburger thrown on a hot grill, horribly burned and blistered.

Nguyen glares at it, as if for the first time, and jumps out of the chair. She races to the kitchen sink, holding her injured hand under a free-flowing stream of cold water.

Jayed approaches and touches her arm.

Charlie swivels around, fear covering her face. "Get away from me."

Without a sound, Jayed places two fingers on Charlie Nguyen's injured hand and whispers something. The blistering wounds close up and smooth over. I can't believe my eyes as her hand is completely healed.

Colonel Dayton enters the kitchen. "Are you okay, Nguyen?"

She nods, turns off the faucet, and gives Jayed a bear hug. "Thank you. Thank you so, so much."

"'Tis nothing. A simple healing spell."

"Right," Dayton says. "The admiral will activate The National Guard. They'll begin evacuations straight away."

Marco straightens up and nods. "Good."

"The admiral is in New York for his yearly budget talks at the UN. He's flying out here to have a looksee in person."

That straightens me up. I want to remind Dayton I'm still sought after by the UN, but I feel it's wrong to put my concerns above the needs of the city.

"I think it's about time we pay The Mystic a little visit," Dayton says. "What do you say?"

Marco is already at the door. "Let's roll."

Chapter Twenty-Two

"Do you have any idea how to get through security to see The Mystic?" I'm all for Colonel Dayton's idea, but I need specifics first. I recall how tight his protection was when Dixie and I saw him, when we'd been invited.

"Leave it to me," Marco says. "As far as I'm concerned, he's a person of interest in an ongoing investigation. That'll get us past his security team."

"And if that doesn't work," Jayed says with a gleam in her eyes, "I have a simple persuasion spell at my disposal."

"You two make a great team," Dixie says with a smile.

Marco glances at Jayed and nods. "We sure do." With a hand touching her shoulder, his expression is calm, his mannerism confident.

Evidence of the pandemonium playing out on the streets of Las Vegas are clear as Colonel Dayton makes a right out of the Mandalay Bay parking garage and merges onto Las Vegas Boulevard. Black clouds of smoke billow in the distance indicating the location of various fires and explosions. Traffic on The Strip is stop and go as dozens of accidents block our path. Sirens wail, creating a constant soundtrack to the turmoil around us. I glance through the rear window of the van and see a fire at the top of the Galaxy Hotel and

Casino. It appears out of control, flames and thick smoke rise from the upper floor windows. To our left is the billow of smoke from the doomed flight that crashed at McCarran. I feel sick.

Colonel Dayton avoids the wreckage obstructing the street. He turns left, across The Strip and into the public parking garage of the Sterling International Resort. Before we enter the garage, I glance back, searching for the top of the obelisk. It's gone.

We pile out of the van and race for the elevators.

"Stairs," Colonel Dayton orders. We're on the third level of the garage, one floor above the pedestrian bridge to the hotel. Feelings of doubt and guilt cram my head. Is this my fault? Did my deal with The Mystic to remove the canine curse from Dixie cause all this destruction?

Stop that at once. Dixie entered my mind like an incoming missile. *This is not on you. The Fiend made this happen, not you, got it?*

I nod at her as we race toward the walkway. She's right, of course. Self-doubt has always been one of my weaknesses.

At least you know it. That's the first step.

"What's the first step?"

"The first step," Marco shouts. "Watch that first step."

I skid to a stop as Colonel Dayton grabs my arm, pulling me back. The walkway has crumbled away from the hotel entrance. Nothing but air connects the parking garage to the hotel. It must have happened during the earthquake.

"Quick," Dixie shouts, "take my hand and transport me across. Charlie, do the same with the colonel."

"A levitation spell for us," Jayed says as she takes Marco by the hand and they float across the gap to the hotel.

Charlie Nguyen wraps her arm around the colonel's back and they disappear in golden mist, rematerializing across the gap inside the hotel, next to Marco and Jayed. I help Dixie cross the gap and in no time, we're all safely on the other side of the breach. I turn around and glance down at dozens of lifeless bodies lying on the ground. Rage replaces the guilt I felt earlier. I promise myself, whoever's responsible for this will pay, be it The Mystic, Adrian Gray, or The Devil himself.

"Watch your step," Dixie says, "we've got to make it back up to the third floor. Follow me." She grabs my hand and we take off toward the escalators. I glance back, making sure the others stay close.

People wander the casino floor, most with dazed expressions, some with gaping wounds. There's not enough security or police to tend to the needs of the victims. Panic has gripped Vegas by the throat, squeezing tight, threatening its existence.

Slot machines have toppled over, forcing us to weave around the debris. Brightly colored chips and cards litter the floor. The main lights are out, and only harsh emergency lighting shows the way to the escalators. Dixie and I take the unmoving metal steps two at a time, sprinting up to the third floor.

Chaos greet us as employees race about the hallway. Shouts and screams echo across the smooth marble tiles. People stream passed us, shoving and pushing each other in a mad dash to escape. The Mystic's chambers are just one floor above.

"Where to?" Colonel Dayton barks over the din.

Dixie and I had taken the elevator the last time we were here, but that's out of the question now. We race to a door next to the elevators marked Private. I pull it open and peer inside. "Here's the stairs." I hold the door open for them. We attack the steps two at a time.

"There's a small lobby at the top," Dixie says, "the door to The Mystic's chambers is on the right."

"Let me go first," Marco says. He pulls his badge and opens the door at the top of the stairs. Two beefy security guards come toward him. He flashes his badge at them, but they don't stop.

Jayed rushes to his side, raising her hand in the air. "*Dorma*." Both men fall to the ground, their eyes shut tight. Jayed turns to us with a grin. "A sleeping spell. They'll be fine."

"Right," Colonel Dayton says. He grabs hold of the door handle leading to The Mystic's chambers, and mouths a silent count. When he gets to three, he slams the handle down, shoving the door open with his shoulder.

Bright sunlight illuminates the lobby. Nothing remains of The Mystic's chambers; it's gone.

Colonel Dayton stumbles forward, into the nothingness.

****

Adrian Gray watched the chaos plaguing Las Vegas from the back deck of his home in Henderson. Smoke billowed into the sky, heralding the fires and explosions he'd created. He closed his eyes, rubbing hard at his temples. One of the little band of do-gooders had created some kind of redirection spell. As long as it remained unbroken, they were impossible to find.

He'd taken hold of Charlie Nguyen earlier, but she managed to slip out of his grasp. As she did, however, he'd left his mark on her hand; payback for the canine's reckless attack on his own. He rubbed his hand, running a finger over the scar.

Like a mule, he raised his head, opened his mouth, and brayed. He grinned at how easily his impersonation of a mere Miscreant had fooled them all; how he pleased himself with Charlie Nguyen's body, a body now marred for life.

Concentrating on his inner compass, he focused on each section of the city before him: Green Valley, Southern Highlands, Paradise, The Lakes, Summerlin. Each sector came up empty so he brought more pain to bear: a traffic accident here, a gas explosion there. He'd keep the pressure up knowing the do-gooders would soon cave to their one major flaw: selflessness. Innocent lives hanging in the balance was their weakness. With another bray, louder this time, he raised his hands over his head, and spoke the secret words, causing the earth to shake.

He jumped out of his chair, kicking it over. With his hands on the railing, he screamed down at the valley below, "Where are you?"

"For heaven's sake, who the hell are you shouting at?"

The familiar voice startled him. He released his hold of the rail and spun around. "Heaven...hell? Nice phrasing, my lord."

"Thank you, I knew you'd appreciate the yin and yang of it. I do hope you'll forgive my uninvited visit, even though, come to think of it, I've never actually been invited, have I? My, my, what a spectacular view.

Oh, and a bar-b-que. I'm quite fond of bar-b-que, as you might imagine. Tell me, do you often sit out here, shouting profanities at the valley, or have I caught you at a bad time?"

Adrian bit his tongue, knowing if he said what was on his mind, there'd be hell to pay. Instead, he composed his thoughts and spoke in a calm voice. "You gave me full control of the Gateway project. Why? You never wanted me to finish it, did you?"

"I'm sure I don't know what you mean."

"Naïveté does not suit you, my lord. I agreed to put aside all my other undertakings and finish this project. And now that it's complete—"

"No," The Devil's voice boomed, "it's not complete; far from it."

With heart racing, Adrian spoke. "What I meant was the construction is complete. The markings are finished and the path is clear. The Gateway is ready."

"That brings us to the little matter of the sacrifice. Sacred ground must be cleansed—sanctified. Or are you skipping that part because it's too difficult? Remember this: the clock is ticking. If the Gateway is not opened by All Hallows Eve, our deal is off. You return to your job at—what was it?—oh, yes, new arrivals."

Adrian's face flushed as his voice rose. "My lord, I have one more night to force the hand of the Treasure." *New arrivals, my ass.*

"Why do you scoff at new arrivals? You never hear St. Peter complain."

"My lord," he tried a smile, "you've given me a huge opportunity, and for that I'm grateful. I'm not ashamed to admit, I derive great satisfaction at the prospect of completing this extraordinary project."

"Do I detect pride in your voice?"

"Thank you, my lord. I'm so close to achieving the goal. All I need is to find the bitch—"

"Ah yes, and the Witch. The small group of good Samaritans opposing you have fared rather well." The Devil laughed, a booming sound that resonated down the hill, manifesting in a thunderclap overhead. "I hate to think of a powerful force, such as yourself, being bested by a dog, two Daemons, and a Witch. Can you imagine the talk around the water cooler if you should fail?"

Adrian cleared his throat. "Yes, I'm glad you brought up the Witch. Just where do you suppose she—"

"What's that, you say? You need my help against the Witch?"

"No." He couldn't say the word fast enough. If he asked for The Devil's help, it meant shame, ridicule, and failure, and The Devil knew it.

The Devil snorted. "Very well. Good luck, my friend."

Adrian longed to actually see The Devil. He wanted to put a face to the voice. But that's not how the underworld worked. Nobody ever saw The Devil, besides close friends, and family; he hadn't been seen for two thousand years, thanks to The God.

These names were legend: The Devil, The God.

And now, he was so close to joining their ranks, he could taste it. All he needed was this damnable grand opening to secure his place.

"It will be done. I'll make it happen."

No answer.

"My lord? Are you still there?"

No answer.

He turned back to face the valley. Two new billows of smoke rose in the distance as he focused on the evil he'd caused, and the wickedness still to do.

He would find the Treasure, of that he had no doubt. He'd find her, or raze the city trying.

Chapter Twenty-Three

I reach out and grab the colonel's arm, pulling him back from the abyss. Done without thinking, impulse.

He turns and gives me a wink. "Ta." Shuffling back a few paces, he addresses us. "Looks like a dead end. We need to get out of here and find safer ground. Once we're away, we can decide on our next move."

I just saved his life, but aside from the "ta" (which I can only imagine stands for: Thanks, Adam), Dayton's voice is calm and cool. He seems to take everything in stride, which says something about the man, always composed under pressure. I've heard people use the term "cool as a cucumber." I don't like it. There has to be a more popular vegetable to characterize the colonel's composure, a cold carrot, perhaps, or a chilly potato. In any case, his courage under fire is contagious.

"Right," Ramirez says, "follow me." He turns around and steps over the debris in the office, guided by the bright beam of emergency lights. "Watch your step everybody." Jayed held his hand with both of hers. Dixie, Charlie Nguyen, and I stay close on their heels, while Colonel Dayton has our back.

Before Ramirez reaches the hallway, a sound grabs my attention. A swivel chair behind the reception desk moved just a smidge. I'm certain there's someone, or something, hiding underneath it. I glance back at the colonel. From his expression, I see he also noticed the movement.

He points at the desk, then raises the same finger to his lips. In one sudden lunge, he jumps over the desk and crouches down. When he rises, he hauls a woman up from the floor with him. I recognize her.

"Let me go," she says, struggling against his grip. Her voice grows louder, as if she weren't heard the first time, "Let me go."

"Who are you?" Colonel Dayton says, twisting her arm behind her. The pain of his hold shows on her face. He towers above her—this is not a fair contest. Probably because of that, he relaxes his grip on her arm. "Who are you?"

Dixie and I step forward. "She's The Mystic's assistant. Her name's Ayala."

Colonel Dayton releases her. "Why were you hiding from us?"

"I was afraid. I thought you were…"

"Who?" Ramirez says. "We won't hurt you. Who did you think we were?"

Her lips are sealed. I see the fear in her eyes and feel sorry for her. When Dixie and I first met her a couple of nights ago, she seemed so in charge, confident and assured. Now, after the earthquake, or maybe because of it, she's scared to death.

Charlie Nguyen steps forward. "Tell us why you're hiding, or I'll freeze your blood."

"Enough of that." The colonel takes Ayala's hand, helping her out from behind the desk. She resists until he explains, "C'mon, we should get out of here before the rest of the building falls down on top of us."

Nguyen lowers her hand at once and rushes to the

door leading to the hallway. "Good idea; let's vamoose, then question her later. In fact, I'll lead the way and meet you in front." With that, Nguyen disappears in a puff of smoke.

Dayton pulls Ayala with him as he speaks. "I have some questions for you when we're clear of this mess; namely, where is The Mystic?"

We forego the route to the parking lot because of the chasm we'd encountered earlier. Instead, we race through the debris in the casino and use the exit leading to Las Vegas Boulevard. The Mystic's obelisk, his signature marquee has crumbled to the ground, lying in ruins at our feet. A sea of people pass over and around the bricks, blocks, glass, and steel that once comprised the world's largest obelisk.

Colonel Dayton escorts Ayala through the panicked crowd. Dixie and I follow in their footsteps. I stop in order to find Marco and Jayed. They've fallen far behind, so I stand my ground, Dixie beside me, waiting for them to catch up. As they near, I see the strangest thing: Jayed lays her hands on those sitting or kneeling in the remains of the fallen structure. Most of them are crying, some in shock. As she touches them, they rise, their faces serene, as if taking a walk in the park. Jayed heals them, both in body and spirit.

Dixie glances at me, smiles, and pulls my hand, urging me to keep going. Even though I let Dixie guide me forward, I can't tear my gaze off Jayed. The people she touches have been through something I can't even imagine. I assume they were inside the Sterling Resort as it disintegrated around them. Some of them probably lost family and friends. Yet, with Jayed's touch, they appear filled with a joy so profound, any loss or pain they may have experienced seems forgotten.

We finally reach the sidewalk. Charlie Nguyen waves at us. Sirens blast out as dozens of fire and rescue vehicles fight their way down the boulevard. Hundreds of survivors, some bleeding, some limping, spill out onto the street—traffic moves like thick pancake syrup in both directions.

"Right, then," Colonel Dayton says, letting go of Ayala's arm. He glares down at her. "Why were you hiding? Who did you think we were, and where's The Mystic?"

Charlie Nguyen joins in. "You better answer him or—"

"Stop threatening her," Dixie says. She turns to Ayala. "Please tell us what happened. We're trying to help."

Ayala glances at each of us in turn. Her eyes water. Dixie puts an arm around her shoulder, and Jayed does the same.

Nguyen cackles. "Oh please, what an act."

"It's okay," Dixie says. "You can speak freely to us. All the destruction, all the madness, we think has something to do with The Mystic. Won't you help us find him?"

Ayala swipes a hand across her eyes and sniffles. "He had nothing to do with this. He's not evil. Rather, he helps people. He loves everyone."

"Then why won't you tell us where he is?" Nguyen says. "We need his help."

"More importantly," Colonel Dayton says. "I think he needs our help."

Ayala shivers, a tear rolling down her cheek. She glances back to the destruction. "He's hiding," she says in a whisper. "He's afraid."

"Where?" Colonel Dayton uses a soft tone, but it still startles her.

"Please help us," Jayed says in a voice so sweet I think it comes from an angel. "Where is he hiding?"

Ayala glances around, leans close to me and whispers, "He once said, if we were ever separated, I could find him where evil is forbidden."

Dixie raises her eyebrows. "Sacred ground. The Paiute Colony—"

"Shhh," Ayala says. "He might be listening."

"Who?"

Tears form tiny rivulets down her cheeks, as she appears to lose control of her emotions. She glances around and whispers, "The Fiend, Adrian Gray."

The colonel stares at the parking structure, which seems on the verge of collapse. "Wait here," he says to us as he backpedals toward the garage, "I'll pop in and grab the van then pick you up. Got it?" Before any of us can say anything, he turns and races for the garage.

Another explosion lights up the mid-morning sky just west of The Strip. I have a feeling this night's just getting started.

****

"My radar's working overtime," Dixie says.

"What does that even mean?" I ask as the colonel drives us onto the tribal lands of the Moapa Paiutes officially known as the Las Vegas Indian Colony.

"This is a big place," she says, "and true evil can't penetrate its boundaries from the outside. But that won't stop us from using our powers *inside* the sacred grounds. If The Mystic is hiding here, we should be able to locate him by putting our special abilities to the task: Daemon radar."

I rummage through the knowledge I acquired during The Sufferings. Dixie's right. She, Charlie Nguyen, and I can use our telepathic skills to hunt for The Mystic, while Jayed employs her inner eye to take an astral walk around the grounds. Marco, Ayala, and the colonel will have to sit this one out as the rest of us search the property using our special skills.

"Right, Ayala come with us," Colonel Dayton says as he steps out of the van. He leaves the engine running and the a/c on full blast. Even though it's October 30, the temperature is a stifling ninety degrees. "C'mon, Marco, let's have a human look around." He shuts the door and the three of them saunter away toward the casino leaving us on our own to conduct the real search.

I watch as Dixie, Charlie Nguyen, and Jayed close their eyes. I do the same and focus on locating any echo of The Mystic's thoughts. I've never entered his mind before, so capturing trace readings of his brainwaves will be new territory for me. I wonder what kind of thoughts he might send into the universe, thoughts I can latch onto.

Fleeting images enter my mind as I scan the ether covering the modest casino, convenience store, and smoke shop located nearby. I encounter a plethora of thoughts rising into the atmosphere. From their banal ideas, and frivolous patterns, I know them to be of human origin. Not that humans are in any sense trivial. They just seem to have patterns that zig instead of zag, a difficult distinction to describe.

I zero in on one pattern that seems stronger than the others, but I sense no superiority in its form. So, I expand my search, taking in the few structures located farther from the casino. Once again, only human thoughts enter my psyche. I make a point of touching ever so softly on their patterns, as I want to leave no trace of ever having been in their minds. I remember how repulsed I was when someone entered my mind unannounced. I don't want to impose those feelings on anyone else.

Now, I'm floating across vast areas of desert as a faint whisper rises up. It's so weak I almost ignore it. I delve deeper into its shadowy images, trying my best to acquire a better signal.

Help me…help me, please. The pattern is faint, but clear.

"I've got something."

"The Mystic?" Nguyen says.

"I don't think so," I say. "No. It's too quiet; too soft—probably human. But the images show someone in trouble. They need help."

"Ignore it," Nguyen says. "Let's keep looking for The Mystic."

"Ignore it? Somebody out there needs help."

"Charlie's right," Dixie says. "Stay on task and find The Mystic."

"You're joking. I can't ignore—"

"It might be a spirit-mask left by The Mystic to throw someone off his trail," Dixie says. "Much like your redirection spell."

"But what if it's not?" I say. "What if somebody really needs help? What if—"

"I'll go," Jayed says. "Show me where this pattern occurs." She takes hold of my hand as she scans my mind. I'm filled with an awesome sense of well-being at her touch.

Her telepathy surprises me. "I thought you couldn't do this."

"Only through touch, and only briefly. Got it." With that, she vanishes.

Ayala, Marco, and Colonel Dayton jump into the van, surprising me and opening everyone's eyes. The colonel slams the door, starts the engine, and throws the transmission into drive. He turns around. "Where's Jayed?"

"She's tracking down someone who needs help in the desert."

"What? We're after The Mystic." Dayton points to the right. "And he's in that red Volvo just leaving the car park. Ayala spotted him and he ran."

Marco opens his door. "I'll stay here and wait for her."

"No," I yell over the sound of the revving engine, my confidence peaking thanks to Jayed. "I'll transport into the Volvo. All of you wait here."

I know the colonel will object, but I don't give him the chance. In a burst of red smoke, I transport out of the van and appear in the backseat of the Volvo. It races through the open desert heading for the I-15.

"What the hell?" The Mystic turns to me and loses control of the car. It bounces off the road, fishtailing across the sand as he fights with the steering wheel and jams on the brakes. The sound of metal twisting and bending screams out as the car plows into a Joshua tree and comes to an abrupt stop. I'm not wearing a seat belt, so I bang against the front seat.

Steam rises from the engine compartment. Silence follows. The Mystic frantically tries to open his door but it's stuck.

"Stop," I yell. "Would you stop?"

He gives up, rubs his face where the air bag punched him, and sits still. "I'm a dead man."

"What do you mean?"

"If Ayala can find me that means anyone can. I thought I'd be safe here, on sacred ground, hidden away."

"You are. At least, I had trouble finding you. All the thoughts I picked up were human. I never detected your supernatural aura."

"And you won't. Not anymore."

The Mystic seems broken. He huddles over the deflated air bag. I see a tear roll down his cheek.

I shout to gain his attention. "Would you tell me what's going on?"

"I broke the rules. I lost my powers." He snorts. "But at least I'm alive."

"What rule did you break?"

"My Banshee, Ayala. I forced her to scream, announcing my death to the world. The only problem: I wasn't dead. I wish I was now. In my realm, the penalty for breaking the rules is losing your power. I knew that." In a louder voice, with a rap on the steering wheel, he says, "I knew that."

I furrow my brow. "So, that's why I couldn't detect your thoughts. They're human thoughts now."

"Now and forever." He slouches over the wheel and sobs. "I gave up my powers to save my life, but what kind of a life is it without my powers? Ayala...poor Ayala. She adored me; worshipped me, and I made her break the rules to save my life. And now that I'm human, I'm sure she won't have anything to do with me. I'm alone now. So alone in the world—just like a human."

"Why did you want the world to think you're dead?"

"A Fiend named Adrian Gray thought I betrayed him. But I didn't." He pounds on the steering wheel. "I didn't betray him. I arranged for you and that human to be held at the Gateway for the sacrifice. I kept my word. It's not my fault some fool happened by and rescued you. Not my fault."

I put my hand on his shoulder to soothe his emotional pain. It seems to ease his worries as he sniffles and wipes his eyes. "Let me tell you a story," I say. He turns to me with an odd expression. "Peter Hudson and I were held at The Gateway. We were trapped with no idea how to escape. And somebody did come along to save us. But she didn't just happen by. The Devil sent her to rescue us. Do you have any idea why he would do that?"

The Mystic closes his eyes and shakes his head. "I don't know anything anymore. My powers are gone."

"Try to think. Please. Las Vegas is being destroyed as we speak. It's important we understand why, so we can stop it."

He speaks slowly, as if recapping the moves of a chess game. "The Devil tasked Adrian to open the Gateway with the ritual sacrifice. I agreed to help him with that—I had no choice, and that's the honest truth. But now, The Devil meddles with the plans. If I had to guess, I'd say The Devil wants Adrian to fail. His ways are mysterious, barely understood by Sorcerers. And now that I'm only human..." He wails, burying his head in his hands. "Why? Why?"

The crunching of tires grabs my attention. Colonel

Dayton parks the van next to the wreckage of the Volvo. Marco flings open the passenger's side door, unclasps The Mystic's seat belt, and helps him out. I have to climb over the front seat, then exit the vehicle with Marco's help.

"Are you all right?" he asks.

I nod. "The Mystic was just telling me why we couldn't detect his thoughts."

Dixie hugs me and stares at him. She's angry. "What are you doing out here? Why were you running from us? You could have killed Adam."

"I'm so sorry. It's just that—"

Ayala steps forward; she locks eyes with The Mystic. Her expression changes. But it's more than just her expression, it's her facial features. They become softer, more innocent, if that's even possible—like she's become a different person right before our eyes.

"Ayala," Dixie says, placing a hand to the girl's forehead and closing her eyes, "you're not human."

I lean over and whisper in Dixie's ear, "She's a Banshee."

Ayala says nothing. She takes tentative steps to The Mystic, stops in front of him, and smiles. "You're alive." In one sudden movement, she folds her arms around him, burying her face in his chest.

He holds his hands out to his side, avoiding contact with her, as if she were made of porcelain. With a soft, childlike voice he says, "I'm human."

Her hug tightens. "I love you." He wraps her in his arms and smiles.

I glance at the van. Jayed and Charlie Nguyen are in the back. They sit on either side of a stranger. I detect quiet moans rising into the ether. "Who's that?"

"You were right," Dixie says with a smile, "a human was lost in the desert. You saved his life."

"No, Jayed saved his life."

Chapter Twenty-Four

"When you get home," Jayed says to the person she rescued in the desert, "hydrate and rest. You'll be fine."

Marco squeezes her hand. He turns to me and says, "The poor guy was almost dead when we picked him up. He said he'd taken hikes like this many times before, but a sudden dust storm kicked up and he became disoriented. Jayed brought him back from the dead."

She smiles and nods, a kind of "yes, I do this all the time" type of nod.

The Mystic and Ayala cozy up in the back of the van while Marco and Jayed occupy the bench seat next to them. Dixie and I take the middle seat, leaving the passenger's seat to Charlie Nguyen. Colonel Dayton turns onto I-15 south, back toward Vegas when his cell phone rings.

"Yes, sir. You are? As you can see, events have escalated. No, sir. Can I give you a call back in an hour? Yes, sir." He slips the phone back into his pocket and shouts above the roar of the engine. "That was the admiral. He's in Vegas and wants to meet with me face to face."

The hair on the back of my neck stands on end. I'm certain the admiral would like nothing better than to lock me up. In fact, I'm sure he'd insist on imprisoning every non-human in this van. The colonel's eyes meet mine in the rear view mirror.

"I told him I'd meet him later. Don't worry, Adam. You know you can trust me."

Dixie rubs my shoulder. Even though her words ease my fears, thoughts of prison run through my mind like a horror movie. "You mentioned something about a 'looksee' before. Why exactly is that? Doesn't he trust you?"

"He comes to the states every year in late October; some kind of annual meeting at the UN. I can only imagine he decided to see what's going on first hand. Can't say I blame him, he is, after all, in charge of the department. Hello, what have we here?" He slows down and stops behind a long line of vehicles. The freeway is gridlocked and traffic at a standstill. Flashing blue and red lights indicate a roadblock about a mile ahead. Dayton pulls off to the side of the road and parks. "Looks like they're stopping all traffic into the city. We'll have to get out and walk from here."

"Excuse me," The Mystic says. "Where exactly *are* we going?"

The colonel doesn't hesitate. "Las Vegas, of course."

"Can you be more specific?"

"The Gateway."

"Count me out. In fact, let me out, and then count me out." The Mystic puts his hands on the seat back in front of him, waiting for Dixie and I to move so he can exit the vehicle. Ayala does her best to calm him down, but he acts as though he might suffocate if he doesn't jump ship at once.

Jayed reaches across Marco, placing her hand on

The Mystic's wrist. "You're doing fine; relax and breathe." Her voice sounds like a pleasing song or poem floating through the van. My own heartbeat lowers as The Mystic smiles. In fact, her words have a calming effect on all of us.

"What's the plan?" Marco asks.

Colonel Dayton swivels around. "To get to The Gateway and have our supernatural friends here send Adrian a psychic invitation to join us, provided the destruction of the city stops."

"Then what?" I ask. Silence is my answer, but thanks to The Sufferings, I already know the answer. Daemons and Witches cannot kill a Fiend—those are the rules. The Mystic is no longer mystical, and his Banshee has lost her powers as well. If Adrian Gray agrees to meet us at The Gateway, as Colonel Dayton suggests, we have no powers to use against him. "There must be a better plan than that."

The colonel glares at me. "It's the best I have. Look, you immobilized him before, maybe you can—"

"What?" Charlie Nguyen says. "What powers do we have against him? Yes, it's true we immobilized him—when we caught him off guard. Even then, we stopped him for only a few moments. You don't seem to understand: a Fiend is nothing to toy with. We'll probably all die."

"C'mon, Charlie," Dixie says, "try to be positive."

"Okay. I'm positive we'll all die. Look, we need serious help from someone with a score to settle against him. There must be dozens of Fiends around somewhere who hate this guy. If we can't do that, I think we should accept our losses and lay low; until, like I said, we can find our own Fiend who can take this shithead out."

"There are no acceptable losses," Marco says. He pats me on the shoulder, prompting me to open the side door. Dixie and I step out into the plummeting temperatures of the oncoming twilight.

Marco steps out followed by Jayed. The Mystic and Ayala crawl out of the van next. We all huddle together on the side of the road, confused, scared, and chilled.

"I don't see as we have any choice in the matter," Colonel Dayton says. "I'm not going to force you to do what you clearly perceive as a suicide mission. Let's vote by a show of hands. Who's with me?"

Marco's hand goes up at once. Obviously, he can't wait to get back to Vegas and do what he can to stop the destruction. Jayed votes in favor as well. I raise my hand in support of the colonel. I'm not going to let him face this alone. Dixie raises her hand with mine. Charlie Nguyen shakes her head. The Mystic and Ayala keep their hands down.

"Fine." Colonel Dayton hands the van keys to Charlie Nguyen. "You take the van and drive Ayala away from here."

"What about me?" The Mystic says.

"You're coming with us."

"But I didn't raise my hand."

The colonel smiles. "We need to give the Fiend added incentive to meet us at The Gateway. That is you."

The keys to the van clink to the ground. Charlie Nguyen vanishes in a yellow mist. I capture her final thoughts as she disappeared; *I'm no fucking limo driver.*

Ayala takes hold of The Mystic's hand. "I'll go

with you, my lord."

"Charlie," Dixie screams into the desert, "come back. You're not safe alone."

I try to comfort her, but for the moment, she's heartbroken. Her best friend just placed herself in danger and Dixie's helpless to do anything about it.

"Right," Dayton says. "It's about thirty miles back to Vegas, let's get moving."

The Mystic hesitates. "You suggest we walk thirty miles?"

"No. I suggest we walk up to the roadblock. Once we're past all this bloody traffic, we can commandeer a military vehicle."

"I vote Hummer," Dixie says under her breath. She tugs on my hand and gives me a quick smile. We turn around and start walking.

****

I trace the path of the falling sun as we march toward the roadblock. It'll get dark soon, bringing its own unique set of problems. Some motorists stuck on the highway have turned off their engines; several lean against vehicles or sit on the hoods. Most have their windows down as they listen to music or try to tune in to the latest news. A few cars appear empty, sitting idle, abandoned in the ever-growing column of vehicles behind them.

Some people wander off into the desert, seeking cover behind Joshua trees or shrubbery in order to relieve themselves. The sun starts to touch the top of the Spring Mountains. In a couple of hours, the temperature will fall over thirty degrees. If the wind picks up, it will make for quite a chilly night in the desert. I can only hope the authorities are prepared to offer comfort to the immigrants of I-15.

Marco and Jayed lead the way, walking hand in hand. I'm glad for Marco. He and Jayed seem happy together. Marco's my best friend and that makes me feel good. Of course, who wouldn't be happy with Jayed? She's beautiful, friendly, and with the touch of her hand, can make you feel—

Feel what? Where're you going with this? Dixie wanders around in my mind again. I glance down at her and grin, followed by an awkward chuckle. "Just happy for Marco," I whisper.

"Uh-huh," she says.

Colonel Dayton follows behind them, then comes The Mystic and Ayala. I feel sorry for Ayala; she seems to live and die on his every word, while The Mystic acts as if she means nothing to him. When I spoke to him earlier in the crashed Volvo, he acknowledged his feelings for her. Why isn't he more open with her about the way he feels? They're such an odd couple.

An odd couple, indeed. Then there's us.

"Yup. Then there's Adam and Dixie and little baby to be," I say, placing my hand on her tummy, "the happiest couple in the whole wide world."

God, you're so corny. She puts her hand on mine. *I love it.*

The colonel picks up the pace as we approach the roadblock. There's a crowd of people milling about and angry words racing through the air. Soldiers stand at the ready, holding their weapons angled at the ground. They form a line across the road stretching at least fifty yards on either side of it into the desert. Soldiers waving their arms in tight circles signal through northbound vehicles leaving the city.

Metro cruisers, lights flashing, sit just behind the Hummers, troop transports, and military police vehicles.

"Who's in charge here?" Colonel Dayton says.

The only response to his inquiry comes in the form of an order, "Get back, buddy. Behind the line. Now."

Marco slides up next to the colonel and produces his Metro credentials. He glances past the soldiers to a police cruiser parked a few yards away. "Schmidt," he says as he waves an arm in the air. "Hey, Smitty, over here."

An officer rushes up, acknowledging Marco with a hearty, "Chief, what are you doing here? And why are you on that side of the line?"

"Smitty, we need to get past this mess. I have Colonel Jon Dayton here with the…uh," Marco leans over and whispers to the colonel, "Who are you with?"

I'm close enough to hear the colonel say, "FBI. We need to get through this line." He produces his wallet, and raises his identification for all to see.

"C'mon, Smitty, talk to whoever you have to. We need to get through and we need to borrow a vehicle."

Schmidt disappears for a few moments and returns with a man wearing a crisp uniform. I don't know what branch of the service, or what rank he is, but he clearly seems to be the soldier in charge of the roadblock.

"Captain," Marco says, "it's vital we cross this line."

"No can do, sir. Orders are clear: nobody in."

Jayed touches the captain's arm. "I'm sure you can make an exception for us."

"Let them through," the captain shouts.

Soldiers stand aside and we walk past the

roadblock. Marco hugs Jayed. "Now, what about that vehicle?"

"We need a vehicle," Jayed says, "and comfort for those trapped on the road."

"At once, ma'am."

Marco raises his eyebrows at her and grins.

"A persuasion spell," she says with a shrug.

In less than ten minutes, after Jayed expresses her desire to have heated shelters and food provided for the people trapped in the desert, we're on our way, stuffed into a Hummer heading south on I-15. The road is vacant on our side of the highway heading into Las Vegas. The northbound lanes on the other side of the median are congested, however, they're travelling at a good clip. The evacuation of Las Vegas seems to be proceeding smoothly. I glance through the window and catch the glow of fires rising from downtown. Housing tracts and shopping centers pop up along the sides of the road. First a few, then a lot, growing more numerous the closer we get to Vegas.

I stare hard at the structures and notice some of them have crumbled to the ground, now just a pile of bricks. Billboards have toppled over as well. People walk through the desert, near the sides of the road, their heads hanging as they shuffle along in slow motion. They look like refugees fleeing a city ravaged by war; I can't believe this is my hometown.

Twilight brings an extreme chill to the air as the sun sinks behind the mountains. My heart goes out to the thousands wandering the valley in search of warmth and food. I can't penetrate Jayed's mind, but her expression leaves no doubt she feels the same.

Colonel Dayton's voice brings me out of my

dismal thoughts. "When we get to The Gateway, I want you to lift your redirection spell. Can you handle that?"

I nod. "Will do."

"Right. We'll let Adrian come to us. We need to do whatever we can to eliminate him. That means immobilizing him, confusing him—" He pats the Glock under his coat. "Whatever it takes."

"Colonel," Dixie says, "there's no way to kill a Fiend."

He presses harder on the accelerator. "We'll see about that, Miss Mulholland."

He's a determined man, but I think we need more than determination to battle Adrian Gray—we need something along the lines of a miracle.

Chapter Twenty-Five

The Strip is alive with blue and red lights, military personnel, and thousands of displaced tourists. A blanket of darkness shrouds the world-famous casinos, no streetlights, no enormous marquees to light the way. What was once known as "Glitter Gulch" is now desert darkness.

In order to avoid the collapsed pedestrian bridges, Colonel Dayton follows a free-flowing line of traffic on the backroads of the city (the Sammy Davis Jr. to the Dean Martin; we have to jog across the Jerry Lewis because of debris blocking our path. Then back on Dean Martin to Trop, and finally onto the Frank Sinatra, past the Mandalay Bay Resort, to Las Vegas Blvd). Thankfully, the I-15 overpasses are still intact; otherwise, we would have had to walk to our destination, taking hours. As the colonel turns onto Las Vegas Boulevard, I stare at our objective: the Welcome to Fabulous Las Vegas sign (of course, since we face south, the words on the sign read Drive Carefully Come Back Soon).

Hundreds of emergency vehicles line The Strip in front of the ruins of the Sterling International Resort. The main tower still stands, but the casino, entertainment floors, and parking garage look like war-torn targets of strategic bombing. My heart sinks when I think of the loss of life caused by the earthquake.

Dixie squeezes my hand. "You mean, caused by the Fiend. Hang in there, it'll soon be over." I'm not sure I like the sound of that.

Jayed glances back at me. She reaches over the seat, placing her hand on mine. All at once, I'm filled with optimism; a euphoric feeling that surges through every cell in my body. It supercharges my attitude, re-energizing my spirit. I no longer anticipate a suicide mission; instead, I look forward to the opportunity to stop the Fiend.

"No way through," Colonel Dayton barks out. "I'm going to park along the pavement."

He pops over the curb and stops the Hummer on the sidewalk. There's a moment of silence in the vehicle as the seriousness of the situation washes over us. I'm still filled with Jayed's magic, so I'm good to go. Ayala and The Mystic, however, look as though they're about to blackout. His face is ashen and she turns away. Dozens of black body bags, glimmering under harsh emergency lights, line the sidewalk.

I glance at Jayed. "Can you give us all a touch?"

"Not me," Colonel Dayton says, "I want to keep a clear head."

"It's not a drug," Jayed says, "but, suit yourself." She lays her hand on everyone but the colonel. In a moment, chatter erupts in the Hummer.

"Let's get out and sprint to the sign," The Mystic says.

Ayala nods. "I'm with you."

Marco, who's been holding Jayed's hand the entire time, says nothing. He doesn't have to; his expression says it all: confidence, enthusiasm, and certainty. His grin is contagious as he pops open the door and jumps out of the Hummer. Jayed exits the vehicle next, followed by Dixie and I.

The colonel steps out and motions us toward him for another huddle. "Listen up. Quiet." He has to shout over our enthusiastic prattle. "I know you all feel pretty confident right now, thanks to Jayed. Don't let that go to your head. When we get to the sign, Adam will release his redirection spell, and then it's on. When Adrian arrives, we have to use every weapon at our disposal to take him down. Marco, for you and I, that means firepower." He drew his Glock and checked the clip. "Dixie and Adam, you need to use every spell you know."

"We know them all," I said, my zeal getting the better of me. Dixie nods.

"Good. Mystic, what powers do you possess?"

"Alas, since breaking the supernatural rules, I have none."

Ayala turns to him. "That's not quite true, my love."

The Mystic furrows his brow. "Come again?"

"It's about time I tell *you* a story. You didn't break the rules. I did. You never lost your powers, they are still intact."

"But I can't feel them. It's as if—"

"Listen to me. Like the man who sees a bird, and is certain he cannot fly because he has no wings, you have fooled yourself into thinking your powers do not exist. But they are there, and have been all along. Try."

The Mystic looks down at his feet as he raises up off the ground a few inches. He lets out a loud chuckle. "I can levitate." He lowers to the ground and closes his eyes. I feel him walk through my mind. "I have telepathy; I have vision."

The red and blue flashing lights of emergency vehicles fade into the darkness. Military and police personnel are no longer visible along with the victims of the earthquake. The obelisk stands tall once again. "Ha," The Mystic laughs, "I have the ability to alter reality. Will that be useful, colonel?"

"Can you alter Adrian's reality?"

"We'll see."

Ayala hugs The Mystic. He looks down at her. "And you, my love?" he says to her, "Your powers?"

She hangs her head. "Gone."

"Then, please, for your own safety, remain behind," Colonel Dayton says, motioning to the Hummer.

Ayala gives The Mystic a kiss and turns toward the vehicle. She takes one more glance over her shoulder before entering the Hummer.

"Right. Let's go." Colonel Dayton leads the way.

I can tell we're all still filled with the confidence of Jayed's touch. I don't know how long it'll last, but while it does, I love the sensation. The Mystic's altered reality has faded and I see the world as it is: a mess. I trot along behind the colonel, still holding Dixie's hand in mine. Marco and Jayed follow us. Marco has his pistol in his hand and a smile on his face.

In a few minutes, we reach the Welcome to Fabulous Las Vegas sign. The small park like area is dark and deserted.

Colonel Dayton draws in a deep breath and stares at me. He checks the clip of his Glock one more time. With a nod, he says, "Right, everybody get ready; all hell is about to break loose. Adam, it's time. Drop the redirection spell."

****

The Mystic wondered how different everything would have turned out had he refused to help Adrian in the first place. Then again, it wasn't as if he had any choice. Adrian explained it in simple terms: help me secure the sacrifice, or perish. Well, there it was; his hands effectively tied. Still, wasn't there always a choice?

He had to make amends for the wrongs he'd caused. He'd tricked Tina into enticing Adam into a deal to secure Dixie's services (wow, had his deceit really been so duplicitous?). Disgust seemed too thin of a definition for his acts. Tina was dead. Ayala lost her powers. No, it wasn't disgust he felt…perhaps loathing. And now fear. Ha, fear and loathing in Sin City—how fitting.

He approached Dixie and Adam, unsure of the words to use. He'd never had to apologize before. "Excuse me."

They turned to him. "Yes?"

The words came slowly, in small measures, "I'm so…sorry…for using you." He touched Dixie's forehead. "When I removed the canine curse, I withheld powers from you." With head bowed, he closed his eyes. "*Completario*. Your powers are now restored." Like a painful boil being lanced, a warm rush of relief poured over him.

Dixie smiled. "I forgive you."

With those three simple words, he was absolved; at least by Dixie. Ayala and Tina were different matters altogether.

A swift breeze rushed across the median, howling

like a frightened child. The Mystic shielded his eyes from its force. In a heartbeat, however, the wind died.

A booming voice commanded their attention, "Welcome, my friends, so good to see you." Adrian Gray materialized in a rush of billowing smoke. He approached Colonel Dayton and touched his shoulder, sneering as the human collapsed.

"*Imobili*," Dixie and Adam shouted in unison, "*Imobili*."

Adrian turned to them, scowling. "Fool me once, shame on you." Waving his hands in the air, he brought Dixie and Adam to their knees. He then turned to face Ramirez and Jayed. "What have we here, a Witch and a human hand in hand? If memory serves, humans burn Witches, don't they?" Raising his hands high in the air, he sent a fireball at Jayed.

She extended both arms in defense. The fireball stopped in midflight, turned a dull shade of orange, and died out with a sputter. He threw another fireball, which met the same fate. He did it again, and again. Jayed extinguished each one in turn.

"Sweetheart," Adrian said, "let's face it, we can do this all night, but that's not why we're here, is it?" He opened his palm, invoking a spell, "*Incudo*." Jayed convulsed and fell to the ground.

Ramirez aimed his pistol. "Son of a bitch." He emptied the clip into Adrian.

"Sticks and stones, Chief, sticks and stones." Adrian made a flicking motion with his fingers and Ramirez crumbled to the ground.

With a sly glare, Adrian turned to The Mystic. "Ah, back from the dead? I was told you killed yourself. Oh well, you'll soon wish you had."

The Mystic huffed and raised his hands. Levitating thirty feet in the air, he altered the surrounding reality. The sky changed from clear black to milky pink. Emergency vehicles melted and all uniformed personnel froze in place while the victims of the earthquake vanished. Misty green and blue clouds swirled overhead, obstructing the night sky.

Adrian directed a balled fist at him, forcing him back to earth. "I'm just getting started with you, my friend." Reality came crashing back into focus.

The rage, which overcame The Mystic only moments ago, was replaced by terror.

A series of pops sounded behind Adrian. Large, gaping wounds appeared in his chest. He stared down and scowled. "What the hell?" He swung around to see Colonel Dayton on the ground behind him, a smoking pistol in his hands.

"Bah!" Adrian waved his hands, and the colonel's body flew several feet, coming to rest, motionless, at the base of the welcome sign.

An energy force sprang to life behind The Mystic. Charlie Nguyen materialized.

"Shhh," Nguyen said softly. She placed her hand on his forehead. Thoughts filled his mind.

Adrian turned his attention from Colonel Dayton. "Ah," he said, noticing the arrival of Nguyen. "If it isn't the whore of the Daemon world."

"*Exteritus*." Nguyen shouted, her hands extended, "*Exteritus*."

He smirked. "Looks like the good little witch lent you a hand. Oh well, enough about the good old days." He slammed her to the ground with the slightest gesture, as if tossing a feather into the trash. "Oh, and just so *you* know, bitch, I've had much better myself."

Adrian turned away from her, strolling to the blackened stump. "Now then, if there are no further objections...no additional acts of futility...no more temper tantrums?" He spun around. "No? Good. Let the ceremony begin." A rumble shook the ground, as the earth parted, leaving a large fissure behind the welcome sign. "Behold, the New Gateway."

The Mystic froze, unable to move. He glanced at Dixie and Adam as they stood. Ramirez knelt over a motionless Jayed, holding her in his arms.

"Miss Mulholland," Adrian said, his left hand waving in the air, "front and center, please." He waggled his fingers and she soared to his side, as if pulled to him by an invisible rope.

Adam tried to race after her, but rammed into an unseen force field. Ramirez helped Jayed to her feet, and together they joined Adam at the edge of the invisible barrier.

"What trickery is this?" Jayed reached into the veiled obstruction. Both hands withered at once, becoming useless things at the end of her arms. She screamed. Ramirez did his best to comfort her, but her hands, the delivery system of her healing powers, had been taken from her. Her cries of pain soared to the heavens. The Mystic winced at the sight of her pain.

"Red rover, red rover," Adrian yelled, "let Adam come over." He wiggled his fingers and Adam careened through the unseen barrier, coming to a standstill beside Dixie. They latched onto each other.

"How pathetic you both are," Adrian said. "Look at you. A once proud Wolfhound who actually wants to be human. Yuck. And you, Dixie Mulholland, a Daemon of royal blood—pregnant, no less, with the canine's baby. What is it, by the way? You can tell me. Is it a Daemon child? A Wolfhound? Perhaps you're having a litter?" He choked back a snicker. "Forgive me, but if you can't see the humor in this...yes, well, speaking of humor, we need a human for the sacrifice, one acquainted with the Daemon." He glanced back at the colonel lying motionless, and shook his head. "Out like a drunkard." Scanning the immediate area, Adrian grinned. "Ah, how about the deputy chief?" He gestured at Ramirez, pulling him through the barrier.

"There, the sacrificial trinity is now complete: a loved one, a human, and baby makes three."

"You bastard," Charlie Nguyen screamed as she stood and joined The Mystic outside the barrier, just a few feet away.

Adrian ignored her and checked his watch. "Just a few minutes until All Hallows Eve. I thank you for your patience, and you," he motioned toward Nguyen, Marco, and The Mystic, "have me to thank for your lives. You see, the ceremony requires witnesses, and I've chosen you."

"Mystic," Charlie Nguyen shouted for all to hear, "now."

The Mystic levitated, soaring to the eastern sky, behind the Fiend.

Adrian Gray peered up, following The Mystic's flight. A faint glow, unnoticed by most, shimmered in the night sky, just above The Mystic's head. Adrian raised his hands, shielding his eyes from the glow. He shrieked, and disappeared in a dark cloud. The invisible barrier vanished with him.

In a moment, The Mystic flew down and stood

near Jayed. "How may I help?"

"My hands," she said, a smile brightening her face. She lifted her arms and waggled her fingers. Back to normal. Ramirez took hold of them and drew her near. He escorted her to the base of the welcome sign. They knelt over Colonel Dayton. She touched his forehead, and he sat up.

The Mystic turned to Nguyen. "Will you tell me what just happened?"

She furrowed her brow. "If I can. When I took off, back at the roadblock, I went to Claremont. I wandered the hill for a bit, looking for answers—maybe sanity. Eventually, I found myself standing over Tina's grave. She spoke to me from the other side, giving me the answer. She explained a weakness shared by all Fiends."

Dixie and Adam approached. "And that was?"

"She told me about the power of flare stars, one star in particular: Wolf 359. Flare stars emit rays known to drain evil power. The Wolf star is the most potent of them all."

Ramirez, Jayed, and a limping Colonel Dayton joined the others.

"Tina said the star would be particularly active tonight. She implored me to dupe him into turning toward it, if even only for a moment—"

"That's when you told me to levitate into the eastern sky," The Mystic said with a smile. "Well played, my dear. It's over."

Charlie Nguyen shook her head. "It's not. The star will be faint tomorrow."

Colonel Dayton winced in pain. "What does that mean?"

"In a few minutes, it will be Halloween, for twenty-four hours. He *must* arrange the sacrifice on that day, or wait one more year for another opportunity. He'll try again tomorrow when Wolf 359 is no longer in play."

"Adam," the colonel said, "we need another redirection spell. Let's get out of here. There's a long day ahead of us."

The Mystic led the way back to the Hummer. He opened the door, a smile on his face. He couldn't wait to see Ayala.

The Hummer was empty. The Mystic closed his eyes. "Adrian's taken her."

Chapter Twenty-Six

For the first time in my life, I understand the human emotion called despair. And it couldn't come at a worse time. I'm in love with a beautiful girl, she loves me, and we're expecting a child. Things couldn't be better…except for the fact today might be the last day of our lives.

It's Halloween, what many around the world celebrate as *Dia de los Muertos,* Day of the Dead. Traditionally, it's a day set aside in remembrance of the departed. If that's the case, I can't think of a more appropriate day to die, October 31st.

For the typical Las Vegas tourist, Halloween means a visit to the Bellagio Conservatory decked out to celebrate autumn—pumpkins and scarecrows; a tour of the Mandalay Bay Shark Reef Aquarium re-purposed as the Haunted Reef; a day of fun inside the Fright Dome at Circus Circus, billed as the scariest haunted attraction in Las Vegas.

The locals usually dress their kids up in costumes and go trick-or-treating at night.

This year, however, is different than most. A heavy military presence covers the streets of Las Vegas. Systematic evacuation takes place during the day while at night a strict curfew is enforced.

We chose to get some rest at the Luxor Hotel and Casino, not that the hospitality suite at the Mandalay

Bay wasn't available; Colonel Dayton recommended we change it up for tonight, just in case. In a few hours, we'll confront the Fiend again.

After covering our location with a redirection spell, I ask the colonel why we have to challenge the Fiend at all. His answer (the Fiend would just try again next year on Halloween, or the next, or the next. Besides, we can't keep hiding while the city suffers) makes sense. It's up to us to end the threat here and now, once and for all.

We come upon one man stationed at the entrance of the evacuated hotel. His nametag reads Hunton. He raises his weapon as we approach. "Halt. You are ordered to turn around and leave the premises; otherwise, you will be in violation of—"

"Stand down, Corporal," Marco says as he produces his identification. "I'm Deputy Chief Marco Ramirez, Las Vegas Metro." He waves at us. "These are special envoys of the United Nations, and agents from the FBI."

Colonel Dayton opens his ID book, flashing it at the hapless corporal. "Special Agent in Charge Jon Dayton," he says in his best American accent.

"We need a quick look around the building," Marco says. "Your commander knows we're here."

Colonel Dayton stands over the corporal. "I assure you we are neither tourists nor terrorists. Stand aside."

The corporal seems confused, which is good.

"We're going inside," the colonel says. "If you have any questions, contact Admiral Reginald T. Garrison of the United Nations. He's in charge of this operation. Now stand down."

Hunton lowers his weapon and stands aside. We

march into the lobby, each one of us doing our best to look as official as possible. Charlie Nguyen is especially good at it, so much so, Dayton has to pry her from the face of the poor corporal.

All services at the hotel, including food and beverage, are suspended. No electricity or running water means the escalators and inclinators are out of service as well. Marco smashes into a vending machine and hands out several plastic bottles of water to each of us.

After hiking up a few stories, we discover an open door to a two-room suite. I'm ready to crash on the nearest couch. Colonel Dayton suggests we get some sleep while he takes the first watch. Charlie Nguyen and The Mystic need a gentle touch from Jayed in order to relax. Soon, they sleep like babes on the floor. Dixie tucks pillows under their heads and covers them with blankets from the bedroom, which is where Marco and Jayed decide to retire.

My eyes are heavy, but I can't sleep. I have no idea what Adrian Gray has in store for us. His powers are stronger than all of ours combined.

Relax, tomorrow will take care of itself. Dixie's thoughts enter my mind. She snuggles next to me on the couch. *Tell me again about what you want when this is over.*

"I can't even think past tonight," I whisper.

She persists. *You said you wanted a house in Summerlin—*

"In The Lakes, remember? A house on the water."

That's right, her thoughts soothe me, like lyrics to a song, *on the water. And you want a brand new car, and a garden with a lawn, and a job—*

"A decent job and some kids." I feel myself drifting off. I know what she's doing, of course, with her calm thoughts and soft words. She's trying to make me forget all about Adrian Gray and the Gateway and the earthquake and the...

I float over a two-story house with grass—real grass—in the front yard, and a lake in the back. The hedges need trimming, and the roses are in bloom. I throw the ball for our dog, a black-haired miniature schnauzer. His name is Bogie, named after Humphrey Bogart who plays Rick in Casablanca my favorite movie. He's wide eyed and so clever; we fell in love with him at first sight.

Dixie steps out of the house, carrying our child on her hip. Her name is Lucy, after my sister. Her middle name is Rose—we use both names because it sounds so damned cute.

Dixie leans forward so Lucy Rose can give her daddy some loves. Sheriff Ramirez drives up and waves. He steps out of his car, marching up the walkway in his crisp uniform. "You ready to go?" he says with a smile.

"Nope, spending the day with Dixie, Lucy Rose, and Bogie."

"C'mon, we got to go."

"No can do," I say, "Bogie needs to get his exercise."

"Say goodbye to the dog."

"Not gonna do it." I pat Bogie on the top of his head.

"Enough with the soft life; we got work to do. C'mon, wake up." I feel a hand on my shoulder.

"But the lawn, the dog..." I open my eyes and look

around. Adrian and The Gateway and the earthquake all come pouring back into my thoughts. Dixie stirs next to me and yawns.

"Our baby," I say, still walking the fine line between dreams and reality.

Dixie kisses my cheek and tousles my hair. "Wake up, dreamer."

I fight the urge to crawl back into my dream, and start to fret; are all the good things in my dreams always going to be only dreams? "So, I guess it's my turn to take the next watch?"

"No," Marco says, "the colonel took the first shift, I took the second. Everybody got a few hours' sleep. It's time to get up and get out of here."

"What's the hurry?"

"There's been some aftershocks in the last few minutes. I guess Adrian is tired of waiting. He's trying to get our attention."

I roll off the couch and help Dixie up. Jayed and The Mystic are already in the living room. Colonel Dayton sits in a recliner, a bottle of water in one hand, and his revolver in the other.

I feel the building shake—two sharp jolts, as if Adrian punched the dark pyramid with his bare hands.

"It's getting stronger," Marco says, "we need to go, now."

"And do what?" Charlie Nguyen says. "How are we going to stop him?"

"I don't know," Colonel Dayton answers. "But we can't hide in here. People are getting hurt."

"The colonel's right." The Mystic stands up and rubs at his eyes. "That bastard Adrian has Ayala. I need to do everything I can to rescue her."

"My point exactly," Nguyen says, "what the hell can we do? We got lucky earlier because of Tina's advice. Well, unless anybody else was contacted by someone on the other side..." She waits a beat. "That's what I thought. It's suicide to go back."

Colonel Dayton stands up. "Are you going to run away again?"

"I should," she says. "That's the smart money."

"Enough." Dixie shouts, glancing at each of us. "We have no choice but to confront the Fiend. Even if we lose, even if we know he's more powerful, like Colonel Dayton said, innocent people are getting hurt. We have to at least try to do what we can, no matter what."

Charlie Nguyen steps forward. "And what happens when it comes down to the sacrifice? Will you take Adam's life? Will you kill Ramirez? Your own child? Because that's where this is headed. He wants the sacrificial trinity to—"

"I know what he wants," Dixie says, her voice shaking. "But it doesn't matter what evil wants. It matters how good responds."

"Here, here." Colonel Dayton says. He's the first to exit the suite.

As they file out of the room, I hold Dixie back. "Good and evil, huh?" I lean forward and kiss her. "I want you to know how proud I am of you right now."

"Great." She smiles with quivering lips. "Just to be fair, you should know how terrified I am right now."

****

Colonel Dayton led them down the stairwell to the main lobby. The air was chilly, now. Later, however, when the sun rose, the colonel knew it would cover the desert like the top of a saucepan, throwing heat across the valley in a rolling boil.

As they ambled past the reception area, a dozen lights sprang to life. Soldiers appeared as if by magic, encircling them with weapons at the ready. Ramirez moved his hand to his pistol but did not draw. Jayed and Charlie Nguyen stood motionless, eyeing the sudden arrival of military firepower. The Mystic fixed his gaze on the soldiers, while Dixie and Adam lowered their heads and kept moving, albeit at a much slower pace.

"Stand down," a familiar voice shouted over the commotion, an order directed at the soldiers. "Lower your weapons. Colonel Dayton, front and center."

"Admiral Garrison." Dayton strode toward the rotund man in a black suit. "Where did you—"

"Colonel, I believe I'm entitled an explanation; at the very least, I expected my calls returned. Instead, I need to rely on the U.S. military to pinpoint your location. What's the meaning of your silence, and who are these people?"

"Admiral, how did you find—" The answer dawned in an instant. "Corporal Hunton."

"Precisely. Now please be kind enough to explain the situation."

"Sir, I don't have time to explain."

"Make time." Another order delivered through clenched lips.

Colonel Dayton approached the admiral, speaking in a hushed tone, "Sir, we're on our way to engage Adrian Gray."

"And just who is Adrian Gray?"

"He's the one I told you about—the creature, a

Fiend. He's proven himself quite an adversary. The longer we delay, the greater the consequences."

"You have the might of the U.S. military at your disposal. Once again, who are these people?"

"Sir, they're a very special group of individuals. They've proven their worth—"

"Yes, but who exactly *are* they?"

Dayton took a deep breath. The time had come to let the admiral in on everything...well, not quite everything. "Dixie, will you come here? I'd like to introduce you to Admiral Reginald T. Garrison, my immediate supervisor."

"Admiral," Dixie offered her hand, "pleased to meet you. Dixie Mulholland."

The admiral wrinkled his brow and huffed. "I recall the name. You're the news reporter."

"I'm flattered you remember."

Colonel Dayton turned and waved The Mystic forward. "And this is The Mystic."

"I've heard of you as well," Admiral Garrison said. "The mind reader. Colonel, I don't understand what—"

"Please," The Mystic said, "world-famous telepath, visionary leader, futurist, or even spiritual clairvoyant...but mind reader? Never."

Colonel Dayton cleared his throat. "And may I introduce Charlie Nguyen, Jayed, and Marco Ramirez."

"Marco Ramirez," the admiral said with a huff. "What's your area of expertise in the colonel's makeshift team? A magician, perhaps? Acrobat?"

Ramirez produced his identification. "Deputy Chief, Las Vegas Metro."

"What's going on, exactly?" The admiral's words echoed through the lobby. He turned to the colonel. "I called you several times. Why didn't you return my calls?"

"Sir, we confronted Adrian Gray last night. You might say the specialists here have unique insight into his powers. We're working as a team to ferret out his weaknesses."

"Yes, but you haven't answered my question. Why didn't you return—"

"I ignored your calls, sir."

"You what?"

"I felt it more important to assemble my team."

The admiral took a deep breath and wiped his brow. In a measured tone, he asked, "How did you meet them—these so-called specialists—what are their qualifications?"

"This lot have singular skills, perfectly suited for our specific type of work. I hired them as freelancers. That's my right—no, my duty—as lead investigator on this particular assignment."

"But there was no assignment."

"Sir, is it not our directive to ferret out the evil in the world? This may not be a case assigned by UNPAD, yet here we are. Look at the city. This is a crisis, and I consider myself fortunate to work with this group of talented individuals."

The admiral raised his head, glancing over Dayton's shoulder. "And who's that, over there?" He pointed toward Adam.

"Who, him? Nobody, sir, just a gopher helping with this and that."

"He looks familiar. What's his name?"

"Honestly, sir, he's not important."

"You there," the admiral shouted at Adam, "come

here. On the double."

Adam turned away, keeping his head down.

Admiral Garrison frowned. "He's rather sluggish, isn't he? A bit slow for this type of work. And you say you hired him?"

Colonel Dayton stepped in front of the admiral, shielding Adam from view. "Like I said, he does the heavy lifting, that's all. Now then, I'm glad to see you, sir, despite the circumstances, but we really must move along. Every second counts."

"Yes, but I can't see how a former news anchor and a Las Vegas performer can possibly help with your investigation. And what kind of a name is Jayed? Does she have a last name? What do I tell the council about your team?"

The building shook. Panes of glass fell to the floor and shattered, sending shards across the lobby. Soldiers crouched down, raised their weapons, and waited for orders.

"Sir, the earthquake—the aftershocks—they're the work of the Fiend. He's restless; his way of insisting we meet. We have to go."

Another shake produced a gaping crack in the marbled floor.

"Everybody, out of the hotel," Admiral Garrison bellowed. "On the double."

Soldiers scrambled toward the exit. Dayton guided the admiral, helping him navigate outside. Another jolt shook the structure. The enormous statue of an Egyptian sphinx standing guard in front of the pyramid crumbled, crashing to the ground in pieces.

"Over there," Dayton yelled, waving at the others while pointing to an open space near the street.

Everyone assembled around Dayton in the clearing. "Admiral, if we don't leave now, the tremors will get worse. Adrian Gray doesn't care how many people he harms. He insists on our presence immediately."

The admiral's face drained of color. "Very well," he said in a slow, almost confused voice, "go, but keep in mind I'll need a detailed report when this is finished."

"Will do." Dayton motioned to what the admiral called his team. "Let's go. We'll meet at the Hummer."

"Yes, sir," Adam yelled as he grabbed Dixie's hand and sprinted off.

"Wait," the admiral said, pointing to Adam. "I know that man. Isn't he—"

"I'll report as soon as I can," Dayton said, cutting off the admiral's question. He followed the others toward the Hummer, stepped in, and took the wheel.

"Right," he said to them as he revved the engine, "let's head for the Gateway."

Chapter Twenty-Seven

Adrian Gray stood with one foot on the median near the Welcome to Las Vegas sign, and the other on the threshold to The Gateway. He felt its power, dark and potent, rushing beneath him like a thundering river. Kept in check, unnoticed by anyone, until now.

He peered across the valley at the morning sky: a perfect Halloween sunrise. And more importantly, no worries about the damned flare stars. They could not harm him in the daylight, and he'd complete his task, the grand opening, well before dark.

"C'mon," he bellowed into the empty sky, shaking his fist at the rising sun. A strong breeze picked up, blowing bits of paper and pieces of trash across the street. The swirling wind collected sand and grew into a sizeable dust devil, racing across the desert toward the mountains in the west.

"C'mon, c'mon, I can't wait here forever." He stamped the ground, sending a rumble deep into the earth, making the tallest buildings on The Strip sway back and forth. "C'mon," he shouted, raising a hand in the air, causing a gas explosion near the airport. "C'mon." More billboards crashed to the ground.

He focused on the one remaining tower of the Sterling Resort. Even though the building had been ravaged by yesterday's series of earthquakes, its complete demolition would send yet another message to the Treasure: get here now. He squinted at the blue and white façade and waved his hands. The spire rocked, swaying in one direction, then the other; glass broke, iron girders strained.

An ear-splitting crash cut through the crisp morning air as the tower gave up its fight against gravity, collapsing to the ground bit by bit as if in stop action. Rubble flew in all directions, smaller structures behind the tower smashed and covered in debris. Black and white plumes of smoke rose into the sky.

He smiled. "C'mon, c'mon."

Ayala lay unconscious at his feet. He'd taken her as an afterthought the night before. Her company, as he awaited the sunrise, had been interesting to say the least. He now understood The Mystic's attraction to the young woman. Her passions had taken a decided turn for the taboo. Perhaps he'd awakened the temptress in her. He enjoyed her repeated screams of, "No."

The dust cloud from the felling of the Sterling's last tower spread across The Strip and covered them both in ash. She coughed, grabbing his full attention.

"Ah," Adrian said, "good morning sleepy head. When I kidnapped you, I thought your friends would try to rescue you." He smirked. "They must think less of you than I."

"Not true," a voice rose above the smoke and dust. As the residue settled, seven figures emerged. They stood in defiant poses, facing him no more than twenty feet away. The Wolfhound and the Treasure held hands—how sweet. The two humans aimed their pistols at him—how futile. Charlie Nguyen and the Witch scowled—how predictable. And The Mystic? He wore the most absurd expression of all, a sort of rage mixed with fear, downright pathetic.

"Good morning all," Adrian said. "I'm so glad you found the time in your busy schedule to join me. Welcome to the grand opening ceremonies of The Gateway. Today, we usher in a new era of—"

"Would you shut up for just one minute?" The Mystic stepped forward. "Blah, blah, blah."

"Silence. You have no right to talk to me like—"

"I'll talk to you any way I please. You have no power over me."

Adrian strode forward and waved his hands, grabbing The Mystic in his supernatural clutches. *"Bastando!"*

The Mystic clutched at his throat and turned white. After a few seconds, he turned red.

Adrian grinned at The Mystic. "I just love a good murder in the morning."

The sound of shots fired stole his attention. He felt pins and needles scratch at his face. Letting go of The Mystic, he whirled around, focusing on the two humans firing at him. He lifted his hands in defense.

"Imobili." The shifter, witch, and both daemons barked out the immobilization curse in unison, making his movements sluggish, as if covered in a thick syrup.

So, that was it, their big play—the plan they'd, no doubt, stayed up all night formulating. The Mystic would taunt him to attract his attention, while the others used feeble weapons and useless curses against him. Bah!

"Enough!" he shouted, sending shock waves through the atmosphere. His cheeks bulged as he blew gale force wind toward his hapless foes. They scattered and fell to the ground like so many paper dolls.

He turned back to The Mystic, all humor gone from his tone. "I trusted you. I allowed you to help me. And what do I get in return? Your loyalty was a sham, a deception. For that you must pay."

"Very well," The Mystic said, motioning toward Ayala, "do what you will to me, but spare her."

Adrian glanced down. "Oh yes, I almost forgot about her." He placed a hand over her head and spoke the higher curse, only he and his ilk could use, *"Esplorado!"*

The Mystic's eyes went wide. "No."

Ayala glanced at The Mystic. She exploded into a thousand pieces, bits of her splattering The Mystic's face.

Adrian shook his head and grinned. "Wow, who needs fireworks for the grand opening? That was spectacular."

The Mystic raised his hands and altered reality, the sky clouding over, and the ground becoming sticky. Sheets of red rain fell, obscuring his view of Adrian. Waves of hot sand blew across the median. The Welcome to Fabulous Las Vegas sign collapsed, splintering into a heap of shattered plastic, twisted metal, and broken glass.

****

The Mystic fell to his knees, wrapping his arms around himself. "This is not happening. Ayala can't be gone. What have I done?" Tears came easily, trickling down his cheeks, falling to the ground. He bowed his head. "I'm so sorry…so, so sorry."

Her soft voice crawled into his ears, "Don't cry, my love, I'm here."

Her voice carried above the din of the rain, filling

him with hope and expectation. "Ayala? You're alive."

"No," she said easily, without the slightest hint of malice or regret.

"Where are you? I can't see you."

"I'm here, standing by your side."

The Mystic stood and spun around as a faint glow materialized next to him. The light took form, becoming solid, opaque. Ayala appeared, smiling at him—a sweet, innocent face amidst the turmoil in his heart. He couldn't help but stare into her eyes, wanting to stop time itself. With careless abandon, he waved his hands over his head, evoking the enchantment spell, which allowed him the power to cross to the other side. In a frenzy, he wrapped his arms around her, pushing his cheek next to hers. He sobbed.

"Do not weep, my lord. As you've taught me, death is not a final destination, merely a continuation of the journey; an unavoidable part of life—a nuisance, really."

He sniffled and drew back, taking the time to memorize her face. A picture of her formed in his mind; the color of her eyes, the slight curvature of her nose, and the clever smile on her lips developed into a living photograph; a picture he vowed to carry in his heart forever. He'd never become attached to anyone—Ayala was the exception. She seemed to anticipate his every mood, his every whim. She always knew exactly what he was thinking (ha! the world-renowned psychic, having his thoughts read by his assistant).

But she was so much more than a mere assistant. Ayala became part of his world—his very reason for being. On so many occasions, she helped him escape the prison his fame produced. She traded places with him, allowing The Great and Powerful Mystic to mix and mingle with ordinary people. She had no idea how much her voice, her touch, would be missed. "I can only blame myself for what's happened," he whispered.

"What do you mean, my lord?"

"I blame myself for not holding you every day. And now…"

She snickered. "Death is not the end. You, of all people, know that. Every one of us cross over; even those who claim to live forever find the curtain at the end of their travels, only to begin a new journey, a new quest, a new destination."

The Mystic wiped away his tears and joined her laughter. "You sound so much like me right now." He turned away from her to hide a new wave of sadness. "If only I hadn't agreed to help Adrian with the Gateway, none of this would have ever happened. How I wish to go back and change everything."

"Turn around, my love, and listen carefully." She tugged on his elbow.

He faced her again, wiping away the tears. "Let me look at you," he said. He attempted a grin, but failed. His hands trembled as he placed them on either side of her face. "I need to examine you closely, to remember every detail of you."

"Please, for my sake. Close your eyes."

He did as she asked.

"Now, use your powers to see all, to be all. Think back to when Adrian came to you in your chambers for the very first time. Recall the heaviness of the air, the sound of your heart; the words he spoke, the threats he made. You thought by agreeing to sacrifice the few, you could save the many. So, you acquiesced to his demands in order to avoid conflict. Remember? Now, imagine a new scenario—this 'what-if' you wish for. What if you rejected his request? Picture your response." She paused for a beat. "What if you said no to his demands? Do you believe anything would have changed? Do you think I would still live? Look into the new future your negative answer would have created. Look at the world...look, and see..."

The Mystic opened his eyes, allowing her hypnotic suggestions free rein in his mind: what if he *had* rejected Adrian's bid to help with the Gateway's opening?

Adrian Gray stormed out of The Mystic's nest, anger echoing in his words, "I came to you for help and you dare say no? You'll rue the day." On his way out of the Sterling Resort, he directed his destructive powers against the obelisk. It collapsed to the ground in a heap of jagged blocks and twisted metal. Many people died as the marquee crumbled. An arm protruded from under a huge piece of granite. The hand, contorted and motionless, belonged to Ayala.

"And so, you see, it's my time," she said, her voice bringing him out of the *what if* scene. "What the humans say is true: everything happens for a reason."

His voice was low, almost a whisper. "What reason can your death have for me?"

"Not only for you, but for countless others. In life, I knew little of the monster, Adrian Gray. In death, however, I've learned a great deal."

The Mystic stood in silence. Her tranquil demeanor was contagious, calming him and restoring his dignity. He thought of Charlie Nguyen and what the Daemon had learned from Tina about the Fiend. A new emotion

247

took the place of his despair. An emotion he hadn't experienced for a long time: optimism. "What have you learned of Adrian Gray?"

Ayala broadened her smile. "The Devil wants him to fail in his effort to open The Gateway. The Devil will help you end him."

"How?"

"Merely ask."

"Where can I find The Devil?"

"I must go now. Be strong, my love. Be brave." Her form dissipated in a light fog.

"Wait, how do I summon The Devil? How do I—

The rain vanished, but the ground still trembled as The Mystic's altered reality came crashing to an end, revealing the true state of the world.

Las Vegas lay in ruins. Ayala was dead. Adrian Gray stood over her remains, wearing a grotesque sneer. The Mystic stared at him, gazing in silence at the true face of evil.

Chapter Twenty-Eight

It felt as though I'd been kicked in the stomach by a horse, or an elephant—*any* large beast will do. I'm lying on the ground, taking shallow breaths, trying to suck in air that just doesn't come. Panic sets in for two reasons: I can't breathe, and I don't know where Dixie is.

I think about sitting up, but that's not going to happen, not until I get some oxygen into my lungs. It's even a struggle to open my eyes, but somehow, I make it happen. I glance down at my chest; the elephant I feel is Charlie Nguyen. Her body is draped across me, not moving, not breathing.

I try to call her name, but can't find enough strength to get the word out.

Marco, who seems to move without pain, lifts her off me, and lays her by my side. He leans over me and shouts, "Are you okay?"

I nod. Without Charlie's weight on my stomach, I regain the ability to breath. I can only assume when Adrian blew us over, I fell on my back and Charlie Nguyen tumbled on top of me, knocking the air from my lungs.

I turn to the right and take in the sight of Marco pinching Charlie Nguyen's nose shut. He tilts her head back, puts his lips on hers, and breathes into her mouth. I see her chest rise. He waits for the air to escape her lungs, then breathes into her mouth again. He does this over and over without a sign of stopping.

Jayed rushes to Charlie, placing her hand on her forehead. Charlie coughs and opens her eyes. Marco nods at Jayed.

Colonel Dayton is on his hands and knees, not too far away from me, blood dripping from his mouth. He must have hit the ground face first. The Mystic reaches down and helps him to his feet.

Now that I can finally breathe, I glance around, looking for Dixie. She's nowhere in sight. "Dixie." My shout is unanswered. Colonel Dayton stumbles toward me and joins in the cry, "Dixie." Marco chimes in as well.

"I'm afraid Miss Mulholland is no longer with us." Adrian's voice cuts through the sound of emergency vehicle sirens wailing in the distance. My heart sinks. "She agreed to the terms of the sacrifice."

"Bullocks," Colonel Dayton shouts.

"No, it's true. She consented, if I promised not to harm you—any of you. I gave her my word."

"Your word is worthless," The Mystic says.

"Is it? You're still breathing, aren't you?"

I feel sick. "She'd never agree to—" I can't finish my thought. Consenting to his terms meant she'd have to kill our child. I gag at the idea, so I change tact. "She has to kill someone she loves. How can you promise not to harm me if she has to kill me?"

He cackles. "You think an awful lot of yourself, don't you? If I don't miss my guess, and I don't think I do, she also loves herself. It's an ego thing. We all love ourselves, don't we? I know I do. So, one thrust to her abdomen with the sacrificial blade and voila…"

"But that means—"

"Yes, the child dies with her. Two birds with one knife; brilliant, no?"

"What about the human?" I say.

"Ah, thanks so much for reminding me. I'd use one of the two available here, but that would break my word, and that, I don't do. I'll just pop out and pick up Peter what's-his-name. Clean as can be...one, two, three." He giggled, obviously pleased with himself. "Now, don't go anywhere. We'll get started as soon as I return." He vanished in a swirling dark cloud.

"Where the hell is Dixie?" Marco said.

"Exactly right," Jayed said. "She must be at the threshold to Hell. The Gateway."

I spin around, taking in the panorama of ruin. Plumes of smoke rise in the distance, the Sterling Resort lies in rubble across the street, the eerie sound of screams and sirens pierce the desert air. "But where exactly is The Gateway?" I turn to Jayed. "You pulled me out; you must know."

She steps toward the Welcome to Las Vegas sign. Turning back to me, she says, "Here. Just beyond the sign. The Gateway rests here, below the earth, visible only to those few in tune with the other side. I see the edge of The Gateway, even now as I focus through the veil."

The Mystic rushes forward and points at the burned palm tree stump. "I had the foresight to mark the entrance with this stump. It's right here."

"I see it," Charlie Nguyen says.

Try as I might, I can't see a damn thing. "How can we get in?"

No answer.

"Jayed," I turn to her, "you escaped the Gateway; you pulled me and Peter Hudson out. It seemed so easy for you then. Why can't you go back in now and pull out Dixie?"

She hesitates, avoiding eye contact. "If I go back...I won't be able to get out. Payment must be made to The Keepers."

Dread fills Marco's expression. "Wait, what does that even mean?"

She glances at him and speaks in a calm voice. "If I go back in, I'll die."

I watch for his reaction. He loves Jayed, that's obvious, but he's only known her for two days, and Dixie is...well, Dixie.

"Marco," I say, "she has to go in and pull Dixie out."

He remains silent. I need to say something to help him, to reassure him everything will be okay, but I can't because it won't. "Marco."

He gives me a wild-eyed stare and draws his pistol.

****

Dixie stooped and took slow steps, giving her eyes time to adjust to the overwhelming darkness. The sudden silence, however, was another matter entirely. The constant *hee-haw*, *hee-haw* of emergency vehicles she'd grown used to, no longer cut through the air.

"Adam?" The name, an affirmation when it crossed her lips, turned to uncertainty as it transformed into an echo and faded away.

She reached out to him with her mind. *Adam, can you hear me?* No answer. Telepathically ignored frightened her more than verbally disregarded. Never before had she been unable to catch Adam's thoughts, or send him hers. The image of something happening to Adam distressed her more than her dilemma. *What now?*

She pulled her phone from her pocket and checked for a signal, none. She turned on the flashlight app. Her immediate whereabouts, a small circle of just ten or twelve feet, grew brighter. She established the location of a few recognizable, although unexpected items. A well-worn wicker rocking chair, a coffee table, and a recliner seat, apparently staged intentionally in a small triangle, on an equally out of place cobblestone floor. The remainder of the cavernous expanse was beyond the illumination powers of her small smartphone, but she knew exactly where she was: the Gateway.

The flashlight flickered.

She rushed to the rocking chair, ala musical chairs, and sat down before the phone died. *Great, someday they will find my cold, dead body on the* Highway to Hell *sitting peacefully in a rocking chair.* The weight of that unpleasant thought made her scramble to her feet. She tucked the phone back in her pocket and concentrated on forcing her eyes to adjust to the available light. Faint whispers sounded in the cavernous enclosure.

"Who are you?" she shouted at the voices, trying her best to throw a bold and confident tone at them. No matter how brave her words started, they ended their short lives as cowards, bouncing off unseen walls and fading away.

The muffled whispers coming her way, on the other hand, continued their journey toward her. "Show yourself," she shouted at them, wishing, almost at once, she'd remained silent. The darkness, the whispers, and the unknown served as kindling, fueling the pyre of her fear. She'd never felt so alone in all her life. *Where are you, Adam? Where am I?*

"Don't be upset." A woman's voice, peaceful and reassuring, called out; distinct from the whispers, this voice seemed solid—a physical remark instead of an ethereal noise. Still, the voice sent shivers down Dixie's spine.

She pulled her phone from her pocket, hoping for just enough "juice" to use the flashlight again. She pressed her thumb on the home button, bringing the screen to life. After swiping her finger over the screen, she pushed hard on the flashlight icon.

A familiar face shone in the light. "Jayed? What are you doing here?" The phone died, sending them both into the black void.

"I came to get you out," Jayed said. "You don't belong here; I do." Her voice sounded tired, without emotion.

"Great. I'm not going to ask how you found me—I don't care. I just want to get out of here as fast as I can. Is Adam all right? What about Charlie?"

"They're fine, but we must leave at once. Take my hand."

Dixie reached out little by little, seeking Jayed's touch in the dark. "How did you get past the Fiend?"

"He's gone to steal a human—Peter Hudson. Apparently, you know him. He's intent on orchestrating the ritual sacrifice upon his return. Hurry, take my hand, we haven't much time."

Dixie waved her hand back and forth until she felt Jayed's warm touch.

"How do you know which way to go?" Dixie said.

"I just do."

"And we can leave, just like that?"

Jayed did not answer. Her grip tensed on Dixie's.

"We *can* leave, can't we?"

"You may leave when we come to the threshold."

"What about you?"

Another long pause as they took tentative steps over the uneven surface.

"What about you?" Dixie asked again. "You do know I won't leave without you, right?"

"Payment must be made. For every soul who passes through the veil into the world of the living, the Keepers must be compensated."

"The Keepers?" Dixie searched the recesses of her mind through the knowledge she obtained during The Sufferings. She found nothing. Payment for underworld travel was strictly Witches' wisdom.

"Those are the whispers you hear," Jayed said. "The Keepers demand payment."

Dixie hesitated before asking, not wanting to know the answer, but guessing at it just the same. "What exactly is the going rate of passage?"

"As it always has been since the beginning of time, the severed limbs of a darkened soul."

Dixie felt sick as she asked, once again, not wanting to know, "And you have the payment?"

"Yes," Jayed said in a slow and cadenced voice, "I am the payment."

Dixie's eyes finally adjusted to the darkness. She made out the shadowy figure of Jayed. Still holding her hand, she squeezed tight. "This is unacceptable. I can't allow you to—"

"It's not your choice."

In Jayed's other hand, Dixie saw a long shiny blade. The thought of what was about to happen caused her to clutch Jayed's hand in a death grip. "No. What about Marco? You can't do this to him."

"This is my decision. Tell Marco I love him."

"It has to be my decision as well. I forbid you."

"You forbid me?" Jayed cocked her head. "What an odd thing to say." She raised the knife high.

Dixie followed the path of the blade. "No."

But too late.

Chapter Twenty-Nine

Colonel Dayton knew Admiral Garrison as a man who could use tone to garner attention.

"Colonel." The voice cut through all the commotion on the median near the Welcome to Fabulous Las Vegas sign. Even in the midst of the tragedies on The Strip, his voice demanded top billing. "It's not easy keeping up with you and your...uh, er...team." As he advanced on the colonel, two military policemen behind him, weapons drawn, kept in line with his steps.

"Stand down," Admiral Garrison ordered as he marched toward Ramirez. "Holster your weapon, man."

Ramirez seemed to wake from a trance. He tucked his pistol into a shoulder holster. "Admiral Garrison? What are you doing—"

"Colonel." The admiral trudged toward Dayton and stood facing him, hands on hips. "Blasted, man. Tell me what the bloody hell is going on here. If I didn't know any better, I would swear I just saw a girl disappear right before my eyes. Then the magician vanished as well. What gives?"

"Sir," he said as he placed his hand on Ramirez' shoulder and took a deep breath. He turned around to face the admiral. "Sir, the deputy chief...my friend, Marco Ramirez, just lost someone very dear to him. She's gone in to save Dixie."

"Gone in? Gone where? I haven't the foggiest idea what you mean. It's about time I hear the truth. Who are these so-called specialists you've teamed up with; tell me more about this Fiend; and exactly what is a Gateway?"

"It's the Gateway to Hell; an invisible crossing just behind the Las Vegas sign. That's what this entire mess is all about. I told you about the Fiend earlier. He's an evil force by the name of Adrian Gray and he's attempting to open a Gateway to Hell, but he needs a sacrifice to do it."

"And where is this Fiend?"

"He's gone to kidnap a human for the sacrifice. It's all very complicated, sir, and we don't have much time. We need to grab Dixie when she re-appears and leave."

"You two," the admiral motioned to the soldiers behind him, "ready your weapons." He turned back to Dayton, a smile growing on his face. "A little welcoming party for this Fiend when he returns. God, how I miss field work."

Dayton had to shake his head at the admiral's naivety. "I'm afraid it's not that easy, sir. Bullets have no effect on him."

"If bullets have no effect on him, what in heaven's name does your team use against him?"

"Spells."

"What's that? Did you say—"

"That's right, sir. Spells, curses, incantations. My team uses supernatural weapons against the enemy."

"I knew it." The admiral spun around and pointed at Adam. "That's the Wolfhound who escaped from prison last year, isn't he?"

"Yes, sir." *Oh, hell with it.* "Not only that, I'm the

one who helped him escape."

"You what?"

"Sir, with all due respect, not all supernatural creatures are our enemy. Yes, Adam is a shape shifter. Dixie and Charlie Nguyen are Daemons. The Mystic is…well, a Sorcerer, actually. And Jayed, the girl with no last name, is a Witch. At this very moment, she's risking her life to help Dixie escape the Gateway."

The admiral's jaw fell open as if a hinge had given way.

"Look around you, sir. The city is in ruins. You've witnessed people levitating and disappearing. These individuals, my friends, risk their lives to—"

A low rumble shook the ground, as if heralding another earthquake. The admiral crouched down, keeping his head on a swivel. All at once, not more than two feet in front of him, a shimmering glow appeared. The light intensified, sending flickers across the ground. The air around the illumination raced in a circle, like a whirlwind, creating a loud *whoosh*. Out of nothing, Dixie materialized. The ground settled and the light faded.

"Colonel," the admiral shouted, "what in blazes is going on?"

Ramirez and Adam rushed toward her. They engaged in a three-way embrace. The Mystic, joined them. Charlie Nguyen grabbed his hand and smiled. "Jayed did it," Nguyen whispered.

Admiral Garrison bellowed, "Colonel, I demand to know exactly—"

"It's just as I told you, sir. Dixie was saved from the Gateway by Jayed."

"And where exactly is this Jayed?"

Ramirez backed up a few feet. "Jayed."

"She's not coming out," Dixie said. "She gave her life to save mine."

"Oh, this is all too much," the admiral said. "MPs, arrest these—"

The earth growled, and thunder roared, cutting off the admiral's orders.

"Look sharp," Dayton called out.

"Did you miss me?" Adrian Gray said, materializing just a few feet away.

"Step back, Admiral," Dixie said, standing in front of him. "This is the Fiend, and he's lethal."

Adrian smiled. "Sorry I took so long, but it appears Peter Hudson is already dead. He was squashed like a bug during the earthquake." He gazed at Dixie. "How the hell did you get out? Where's the Witch?" He grabbed Dixie by the collar, making her vanish by throwing her into the Gateway's invisible dimension. At the same time, Adam transformed into a Giant Irish Wolfhound. The Fiend extended his hand, palm up, in a kind of protective pose.

"What the hell is happening?" the admiral put his hands on his hips.

"Well, well, well," Adrian said, "what have we here? A human?" A smile grew across his face. "And from what I've just witnessed, the Treasure is familiar with him. How providential."

****

The Mystic held his ground as a supernatural battle unfolded before him. Was he ready for this? It made little difference; it was happening.

Adrian Gray seized the admiral by the scruff of the neck and, using both hands, swung the hefty man into the Gateway. He wiped at the sweat glistening across his brow. "Holy crap that was a handful."

The two soldiers raised their rifles and opened fire, hitting the Fiend several times. With a wave of Adrian's hand, the soldiers ruptured like water balloons, spilling gallons of blood onto the artificial grass. They both collapsed into piles of flesh and bone.

Colonel Dayton made it halfway to the Fiend before Charlie Nguyen stopped him in his tracks using an *imobili* curse. She wagged her head from side to side.

Adrian's eyes glowed red; his hands held stiff over his head, on the verge of throwing a spell in the colonel's direction. Instead, the Fiend snorted, spun around, and disappeared into the Gateway.

Nguyen rushed to the colonel and touched his head, releasing him from the immobilization spell.

"What the bloody hell did you do?" Colonel Dayton said.

"Saved your life, that's all. Didn't you see the way he looked at you when you ran for him? He would have lopped your head off like a weed." She crossed her arms and scowled at him.

Dayton took a deep breath and shuddered. "Thank you."

"What now?" Adam said as he picked up his torn clothes from the ground and slipped them on. "We have to find a way to get inside the Gateway."

Charlie Nguyen held her arms out to her side and shrugged. "Where do we even start? I can't see where the Gateway begins or ends."

Colonel Dayton rushed toward the blackened stump of the burned palm. He tore at the yellow caution tape and waved at the others. "Over here, we need to find a way inside."

"There's no way in," Charlie Nguyen said, "not until the ceremony is complete."

"But that means..." Adam kicked at the stump. He clawed and pulled and pushed until he fell to his knees in exhaustion. "Somebody help me." He dug at the dirt around the stump. The blackened base of the palm tree did not budge. He hit it until his fists bled.

"That does it then," Dayton said, "we can't enter."

The Mystic knew the words had to come. "But I can."

Colonel Dayton turned to face him. "What did you say?"

"*You* can't enter The Gateway...but I can." The Mystic closed his eyes and raised his hands, fingers stretched up in the air. "*Entra inferno.*"

Total darkness met him inside the Gateway, as black as if he'd closed his eyes. He tried a myriad of spells to illuminate the area—no success.

Dixie's voice rang out. "Admiral, are you okay?"

"Where...where the hell am I?"

"We're inside the Gateway."

"How...how did we get here?"

"The Fiend pitched me in. I can only imagine he did the same to you."

The Mystic yelled, "Hey. Can you hear me?"

A familiar voice boomed out, "I can't believe my ears. If it isn't The Mystic." Adrian Gray. He laughed. "I've heard it said all those who wander are not lost. But you sure are."

The Mystic ignored Adrian's taunt. "Dixie, follow my voice."

"What's going on?" the admiral bellowed.

The Fiend mocked the admiral's voice with a high-pitched whine, "What's going on; where am I; why am I here?" A beam as bright as a flash of lightning removed the darkness of the Gateway. "There, take a good look around. You're on the path to Hell. Now, let's get this damned ceremony started."

The Mystic held up a hand, shielding his eyes from the brilliance. He gazed across the enormous cavern of the Gateway. A vast expanse of cobblestones covered the ground. He could not determine the size of the area, as the walls were not discernable. Dixie and the admiral stood about ten yards away. He wasted no time rushing over to them. Dixie smiled as he approached. The admiral backed away.

"Dixie." He put his arms around her. "I'm so sorry about this; I won't let anything happen to you. Admiral, come close, I'll get you out of here."

"Oh, you will?" Adrian spun The Mystic around and pushed him to the ground. "Now, just how are you going to do that? Will you save her just as you saved the Witch?" He pointed to the ground where Jayed lay motionless, a jagged knife in her chest. "I wish you would, you pathetic excuse for a Sorcerer. Will you save her just as you saved your beloved Ayala? There's no way you—"

"Shut up!" The Mystic levitated and reached out, clasping his hands around Adrian's throat. He squeezed tight, crushing the Fiend's windpipe, feeling the life force drain from his being.

Adrian's laughter drifted across the Gateway, bouncing off the cobblestones and low hanging rock ceiling. The Mystic tightened his grip on the Fiend's throat. He stared at the object he clutched: a thick rattlesnake wiggled in his hands. The Mystic released the reptile and scampered back, bile rising in his throat.

"You have no power over me here," Adrian said. "This is my realm; my project. And once the Gateway is opened, my reign will be limitless. The plump human here will be the first to enter my Lake of Fire." He turned to the admiral. "Stop sniveling; didn't you hear? You'll be the very first—what an honor." He approached Dixie and waved a hand over her belly. "You and your dog baby will follow. Ha! What fun we'll have." He yelled, "Welcome one and all. Welcome to Fabulous Hell!"

Chapter Thirty

The Mystic faced Adrian, his head held high; eyes steady and true—no fear. "The Devil will never grant you rule over the Lake of Fire."

The Fiend paused, as a cat might, surprised by a foolish mouse scampering by. He stared at The Mystic for several seconds, his expression performing a measured transformation from curiosity to contempt. "How dare you speak to me in such a manner. Once this little ceremony is complete, your soul is mine. You've always been such a pain in my ass, you have no idea. For years, I coddled you, indulging your fondness for the humans." Adrian mimicked The Mystic's voice in a high-pitched whine, "Oh please, Adrian, why do we have to kill her? Why do we have to kill this one? Can't we spare that one?" He stuck his face inches from The Mystic's and roared in his normal voice, "You disgust me. Everything I've done has led to this moment, in spite of your constant whining. The Convergence, the *Sangre di Real*—all of it orchestrated by me. And now you dare tell me what The Devil will or will not grant? I've planned every detail, every deception, every death."

Adrian Gray turned away from The Mystic and approached Dixie. "And now, at last, it comes to this." He pulled the knife from Jayed's chest. It produced a wet, sucking sound as he drew it out. With a salacious smile, he turned to Dixie, and offered the blade. "All you have to do is stick this into the fat man's chest."

Admiral Garrison barked, "Why you insolent little—"

"Ha! It speaks," Adrian said with a laugh. "I'm confused. Are you upset I called you fat, or that I need you killed?" He spun back to face Dixie. "Oh, how I wish I could do it myself, but I can't. More's the pity. Go on then, kill him."

The knife clanged on the cobblestones as Dixie dropped it. "I will not."

"Yes," the Fiend said, "I suppose that is an option—your choice." He shrugged his shoulders. "In that case, give me a moment. I'll be right back."

"Where're you going?"

"Up top to slaughter your boyfriend, the Wolfhound. Then I'll torture that bitch, Charlie Nguyen, right after I rip Colonel Dayton to shreds. Then God help any human still alive in Las Vegas. Oh, and remember, their blood will be on your hands. Be back in a jiffy."

"Wait." Dixie picked up the knife with a trembling hand. "I'll do it."

The admiral backed up a few steps. "Are you mad, woman?"

Adrian Gray reached his hand out to the admiral. "*Imobili.*"

Garrison froze in place, unable to move, trapped by the immobilization curse. "You'll never get away with this. You'll be hunted down and brought to justice."

The Fiend smiled at Garrison. "Trick or treat, Captain."

"That's admiral, you petulant coward."

Dixie extended the knife, pointed it at the Fiend, and shouted, "*Exteritus.*"

Adrian closed his eyes and hung his head. "Really? Instead of gutting the pig, you try to kill me? I'm so disappointed. When are you going to get it through those thick blonde curls, you cannot harm me? I'm in charge down here. I call the shots."

"Not true," The Mystic said. "We must all answer for our actions. We must—"

"Shut up." Adrian waved a hand at The Mystic without turning away from the admiral. The Mystic fell over backward. He struggled to get up, leaning back on his elbows. A shadowy figure, hands on hips, appeared beside him. He scrunched his eyebrows together. "Rosalyn Chase?"

"Aunt Rose?" Dixie said.

The Fiend chortled. "Is that the best you got?" He attempted to turn around, but could not move. His feet were stuck, as if glued to the ground. "Mystic," he yelled, "I tire of your illusions. Release me at once, or—"

"Or what?" Rosalyn said as she stepped in front of the Fiend.

His grin melted. "What are you doing here?"

"Just stopped by for the grand opening. Oh, and I brought some friends with me, I hope you don't mind. We heard how you arranged everything. What was it you said? Ah yes…every detail, every deception, every death. That is what you claim, yes?"

"Ha! Yes, but I did it at all at the command of The Devil."

"Is that so?" The Mystic said, rising to his feet. "What better time to set the record straight then. Are you saying The Devil deserves the credit for the Gateway?"

"Yes…no…wait, you trick me, Mystic."

"Well, it is Halloween," The Mystic said with a smile. "No treat for you."

Rosalyn stepped closer to the Fiend. Another shadowy figure joined her, becoming visible from a flowing mist.

"Hello, dumb shit," Gorgeous said.

Rosalyn shook her head. "Language, please."

"Oh, I'm sorry, Miss Chase. My bad."

"Well, I suppose under the circumstances, you're forgiven. But dumb shit doesn't quite seem to cover it. How about dumb ass? Or ass hat? I don't know, something with 'ass' in it."

Gorgeous put a hand over her mouth and chuckled.

More figures stepped from the shadows, their forms becoming clear as they marched forward. Adrian shouted, his voice wavering. "Who are these assholes?"

"Every detail," The Mystic said, taking a step toward Adrian, "every deception," another step, "every death."

FBI Special Agent in Charge Ed Miller materialized, walking side by side with Sheriff Gale Hendrickson. Followed by Adam's siblings: Mikael, Flynn, Lucy, Ivan, Bane, and Nina. The Mystic nodded to each one as they appeared. He knew their names, knew each story—the advantage of being a Sorcerer.

"Lucy," Dixie said as she dropped the knife to the floor. Lucy smiled in her direction, continuing the march toward the Fiend.

Major Jean Ransom winked at Dixie, followed by Paul Cuthbert walking hand in hand with Tina. Other souls joined them, hundreds, perhaps thousands, all marching toward the Fiend.

"This is bullshit," Adrian Gray yelled.

"Oh, this is only the beginning," Aunt Rose said in a calm and measured tone. "So many more are on their way to bid you welcome."

Dixie glanced at Aunt Rose. She whispered, "Death is not the end."

"No. No, it's not. People make life so complicated. It isn't. It's always been as simple as good vs. evil. Do unto others, as you would have them do unto you. Those who miss that lesson in life, eventually, find it elsewhere."

"What are all these souls doing here?" Dixie said.

"They've come for Adrian Gray," The Mystic said. "There's a special place in Hell reserved just for him. They want to make sure he gets there."

"Jayed," Dixie said. She glanced at the girl's body on the ground in front of her, then turned to view her soul marching in line with the rest. Jayed smiled.

"The Fiend is responsible for them all," Aunt Rose said.

"Like hell I am." He shrank away from the hands reaching out to grab him.

"Ayala," The Mystic shouted as her soul passed by. He rushed toward her and reached out. His hands passed through her form.

"My lord," she said. "I'm sorry, my love, physical contact is not possible."

"I feared as much," he said with a laugh, "something even I did not know. Then what's the point of it all? I mean, where's the reward?"

She laughed. "We keep love in our heart.

Memories live forever—so make good ones, always." She trundled ahead to join the rest.

"And now, it's time for you to leave," Rosalyn said to Dixie.

"No, I won't. I can't. I couldn't bear to leave you here. This isn't fair."

The old woman smiled. "No, death isn't fair, is it? I'll always be with you, my dear, you know that. Besides, Adam needs you; the baby needs you."

Dixie burst into tears. The admiral put his arms around her. She sobbed and held tight to the big man. After a moment, she composed herself. "Love is a powerful force, isn't it?"

Rosalyn nodded. "Indeed, the most powerful."

Dixie sniffled. "In that case…what I mean to say, uh…"

"Out with it, my dear."

"Marco Ramirez is deeply in love with Jayed. I don't know what to tell him. He'll be devastated without her. Is there no way of making an exception? I mean, can we…uh, is it even possible to—"

"None," The Mystic said, "even I know that."

"Well, well, well," Gorgeous said, "what an altruistic request. You wish to take Jayed back with you?"

Dixie sobbed while nodding her head.

Rosalyn and Gorgeous sauntered away, whispering to each other. The Mystic longed to hear their discussion, but respected their need for privacy. They took their time. In a moment, they both grinned as if sharing a private joke, nodded, and returned. Rosalyn spoke for both of them. "If Jayed leaves, one must stay behind to take her place." Before Dixie could object,

Aunt Rose raised her palm. "I'm sorry, that's the rule."

"In that case," The Mystic chuckled, "let it be the Fiend. He can stay here forever, no problem."

Rosalyn smiled. "His reservation has already been arranged by you know who. No, I'm afraid if Jayed leaves, another must stay behind."

Jayed stepped out of the slow procession of souls and returned to face Aunt Rose. "I would not ask such a thing of anyone."

"Jayed, be quiet," Dixie blubbered. "Don't you love Marco?"

"More than anything. But the sacrifice is too great and what of the payment to The Keepers?"

"Don't you worry about The Keepers," Gorgeous said. "They're friends of mine; I'll take care of them."

Dixie brightened. "In that case, I volunteer to stay behind. I want to—"

"No," The Mystic shouted over her, "I'll stay behind. I've meddled enough in human affairs. Besides," he said as he glanced toward Ayala. "there's nothing for me to go back to. Everything I value is here."

"Are you certain?" Rosalyn said.

He nodded and marched to Ayala's side. "Positive." His voice carried across the vast expanse of The Gateway. "You know, Ayala, I have a story to tell you. It's about a Sorcerer, a foolish, selfish Sorcerer, and his beautiful assistant."

Squeals rose from the center of the circle of souls. Adrian Gray begged for mercy. "Don't touch me. Stay away." Another shriek, then a muffled cry, followed by a desperate scream.

The Mystic gazed at the mob, then turned back to

face Dixie. He smiled at the love he saw in their auras.

"Aunt Rose," Dixie said, "they call me the Treasure. What does that even mean?"

Rosalyn beamed. "Someday you'll know, perhaps. Today is not that day."

Dixie grimaced. "I miss you so much."

"And I, you." Rosalyn Chase raised her hands over her head. "Remember, my child, *Mors non est finis.*"

The Mystic turned to Ayala. They sauntered away from the procession of souls, and strolled toward a path leading…who cared? They would always be together.

****

The bright yellow, two-story Cape Cod style house overlooking the crystal blue waters of Lake Sahara was a little out of our budget, but Colonel Dayton helped with the down payment, and we found employment that pays really well. A small party boat cruises by, its occupants wave at me.

"How's the fishing?" I say.

"Not bad, Adam. Why don't you join us?" The Mortons live two houses down.

"Sorry." I hold up a spatula and wave it at them. "We have guests."

"Maybe next time." The boat sails away, and I watch it for a minute or two. It sure would be fun to own my own boat, but that's gonna have to wait. I laugh to myself as I consider the thought of "fun."

"Hey, how about that beer?" Colonel Dayton calls from the comfort of his chaise lounge on the porch. He wears a pair of swimming shorts, declaring himself officially on holiday—didn't even bring his cell phone. He laughs at the antics of Marco and Jayed splashing in the hot tub. It's early March, still a bit too chilly for the pool, but the steaming water of the tub has invited us all in at least once.

"Coming right up, sir," Dixie says as she steps out of the house holding two bottles. "Nice and cold." She gives one to the colonel and hands one to me. I also get a kiss on the cheek.

"What, no kiss for me?" Colonel Dayton says with a grin.

"Nope. You're not wearing the goofy apron," Dixie says. "How are the steaks coming?"

I lift the lid of the bar-b-que and smile. Smoke rises; the aroma is amazing. "They'll be ready in just a few minutes."

Laughter comes from the tub as Marco and Jayed toss a beach ball back and forth. He glances at me, smiles, and winks. "Great," Marco says, "I'm starving." He throws the ball to Jayed, but it's high and out of reach. It lands on the grass, coming to rest against the fence. Bogie barks and chases after it. He's a great dog; a schnauzer mix from the rescue shelter.

Dixie sits next to the colonel and picks up the same paperback she's been reading on and off for the past few days. She loves to read, when she gets the chance. The baby takes up most of her time, what with the feedings and changings. I help when I can, but I'm all thumbs when it comes to changing diapers. Dixie insists I say that to get out of doing it. A sly grin crawls across my face; we both know it's the truth.

Lucy Rose Steel was born at Sunrise Hospital just east of The Strip. She exhibits all the signs of being a normal, healthy, human baby girl. She came into the world three months after Marco and Jayed were married; six months after the Fiend met his demise.

Marco works as a consultant for the Las Vegas Metropolitan Police Department. He says his new job gives him more time to spend with Jayed. They bought a home in Summerlin, and he tells me they're working on starting a family.

Las Vegas has already cleared away most of the debris of what they termed "freak" earthquakes from The Strip. Small fortunes are offered to numerous companies in the business of earthquake proofing the hotels and resorts. New construction is in full swing, and casinos pop up everywhere: The Desert Moon Spa and Resort, The Spring Mountain Casino, and The Canyons Hotel and Casino are already open for business. Most of the pedestrian bridges have been rebuilt. I'd guess nobody will remember the earthquakes in a few years. The Welcome to Fabulous Las Vegas sign has been painstakingly restored, and tourists return in droves.

I spot a quick flash of yellow mist coming from the window of our living room, followed by Charlie Nguyen stepping outside. "Sorry I'm late." She wears a bright yellow sarong, an enormous straw hat, and platform shoes, turquoise to match her nails. In her arms is a huge stuffed bear. "This is for Lucy Rose. Hello everybody."

Dixie dashes over and gives her an air kiss on each cheek as she takes the bear. "We thought you were going to skip."

"Are you kidding, I wouldn't miss Lucy Rose's first birthday for the world." She glances around. "Where is she?"

"Out like a light," I say, "at last. I don't know where she gets all the energy, but when she's done, she's done."

Bogie jumps up on Charlie's leg and barks.

"Somebody get this mutt off me. Is it fixed? Whoops, no offense, Adam."

I put Bogie inside and crouch down to pet him. "Stay clear of that one," I whisper, "she's the world's biggest pain." He and Charlie Nguyen have never gotten along. I stand up and glance at my sketches of Dixie and Lucy Rose on the walls of the living room. They're all quite good, if I do say so myself.

Stepping outside, I give Charlie a hug. "You're just in time for steak. What do you want to drink?"

"A shot of tequila would be nice, or maybe Jägermeister. I need hair of the dog. Whoops, sorry again."

"One beer, coming up," Dixie says, turning back to the kitchen.

Colonel Dayton sidles up to Charlie and gives her what he calls, a proper welcome. "Right on the lips, like a civilized man. How have you been?"

"Can't complain," she says with a laugh, "nobody would listen if I did." She bends down by the pool and points to her neck. "Right here, if you wouldn't mind, Jayed. Bit of a nagging hangover." Jayed touches her neck. "Oh thanks, much better."

"My pleasure," Jayed says.

Dixie steps out of the house, phone in hand.

"Oh my, don't tell me you're out of alcohol?" Charlie says.

Dixie looks serious. "Colonel, it's for you."

Dayton takes the phone and saunters toward the lake. He speaks at length before hanging up and walking back to face us all. "That was the admiral. He says there's a situation in North Las Vegas; something about a den of Goblins gone wild. He wants us to look into it as soon as possible."

Life has been interesting since joining UNPAD. At first, Dixie and I were against the idea, but Admiral Garrison talked us into it—he talked *all* of us into it: Charlie Nguyen, Marco Ramirez, Jayed, Dixie, and I. And who's our leader?

"Let's wrap it up, team," Colonel Dayton barks. "We gotta go."

"Can we eat first?" Dixie lifts up the bar-b-que lid. A plume of smoke billows into the air. "Oh, Adam, the steaks are on fire."

"Then how about just cake?" Charlie Nguyen says. "Cake and tequila?"

Marco and Jayed are out of the tub. "Did that dog run off with our towels?"

Bogie barks in the living room.

Lucy Rose cries upstairs.

Me? I'm the luckiest man in Las Vegas.

A word about the author...

Richard Arthur Newberry lives in Las Vegas, Nevada. He considers himself a person who "cannot not write" and regards Las Vegas as a unique setting for his short stories and novels. He has been published in *The Writer's Block*, an anthology, and placed second in the 2014 Las Vegas Flash Fiction competition.

Mr. Newberry, his wife, Betty, and their son, Samuel, share their home with Zady and Daisy, two loving rescue dogs who provided a world of inspiration for his Sin City novels.

http://richardarthurnewberry.com

Thank you for purchasing
this publication of The Wild Rose Press, Inc.

If you enjoyed the story, we would appreciate your
letting others know by leaving a review.

For other wonderful stories,
please visit our on-line bookstore at
www.thewildrosepress.com.

For questions or more information
contact us at
info@thewildrosepress.com.

The Wild Rose Press, Inc.
www.thewildrosepress.com

Stay current with The Wild Rose Press, Inc.

Like us on Facebook

https://www.facebook.com/TheWildRosePress

And Follow us on Twitter
https://twitter.com/WildRosePress